Intoxicating Pursuit

Missy Bloom

Heuchera Publishing

Heuchera Publishing, 100 Springdale Rd., Ste. A3 #166, Cherry Hill, NJ 08003

This book contains explicit content and is only appropriate for mature audiences.

ISBNs: 979-8-9986013-0-9 (trade paperback); 979-8-9986013-1-6 (e-book)

Library of Congress Control Number: 2025909100

Content Guidance

Welcome to *Intoxicating Pursuit*. I'm delighted you're here.

Amidst the romance and beautiful scenery in this novel, you'll also encounter some drama and thrills. As a result, I want you to be aware of some potentially triggering themes, including stalking, drug use, limited instances of violence, a threat of sexual assault, and a character struggling with anxiety and grief. Books are supposed to be pleasurable, so please don't proceed if those elements might overwhelm you.

Likewise, this is a "sexy" romance. Turn back now if you don't want to occasionally blush.

Be well and happy reading,
Missy

To my hall of fame mom.

For a million reasons, big and small, this book would not exist without you. Your love, warmth, and boundless support empower the people around you.

1

THE PREDATOR

SAMMY

When I realized he was following me, my heart exploded in fear. Could one stupid decision to bike alone through the woods cost me everything?

"Hey!" His voice erupted—demanding and loud. . . and far too close.

I tightened my grip on the handlebars and risked a quick glance over my shoulder. The biker's hulking frame rocked back and forth as he pedaled up the muddy trail after me, devouring the distance between us.

Flames of panic spread into a firestorm.

Is it worth it, Sammy? To save ten minutes? I cursed myself and stood up on the pedals, pushing furiously.

Last night's thunderstorm had trashed the trail with forest debris, and my tires twisted and slipped in the unstable muck. The edges of the woods grew fuzzy as spasms rocked my heart.

Another hundred yards to safety? Maybe? A blur of sunlight shone at the end of the path, and I begged my body not to quit.

I pumped with all my strength around a bend in the trail—and smashed headlong into a fallen tree.

The impact jarred my bones, launching me over the handlebars. I smacked into the muddy ground with a blunt, paralyzing impact.

"Lady!. . .Hey! Your meds!"

Stunned and confused, I lifted my head. Pain bloomed along my ribs.

"Yo!" A loud whistle split the air, close enough to hurt my ears.

The biker careened around the corner, then everything happened at once.

His bike tangled with mine, crashing and vaulting him forward. He landed helmet first near my hip, his leg twisted behind him, and an Epi-Pen tumbled from his bike jersey.

"Unh. . ." He slithered closer.

I scrambled to all fours, staggered to stand. My aching body protested, but I had to get away.

"My God." He flopped to his back, panting. Sunglasses masked his expression, but he gritted his teeth in obvious pain. "Why didn't you *stop*?" His shoelace was snarled on the dead tree's sharp roots. Blood welled along an angry gash on his leg.

A fallen branch the size and shape of a baseball bat lay nearby, and I grabbed it—held it high. He lay between me and my bike. *Could I go around him? Or should I leave everything? Run away?* My brain felt thick, my legs wobbly.

He grunted to a seated position and worked to untangle his laces from the jutting, splintery wood. His ankle was swelling like a water balloon. "Oh, shit on a biscuit!" He lifted it tenderly. "Are you *kidding* me?" He pounded the ground with his fist and lay back in the mud again. "God, I'm a *flipping* moron!"

The last few minutes hovered at the edge of my mind, emerging through the mists of panic. *Did he say something about medicine?*

I glanced at the Epi-Pen and the tiny saddle bag where I kept valuables. It was sagging open, unzipped.

Oh my God.

The facts stacked up in odd shapes, and I fought for a logic that fit them together. "Is that my Epi?"

"Yeah." He pushed himself to a seated position again and adjusted his ankle, wincing. "It fell out of your pack. Thought I could catch up to you real quick, but you're a *beast* on that bike." He managed a pained grin, but it vanished when he looked up. His jaw slacked. "Good Lord. What are you *doing?*"

The stick shook in my hand. *What* was *I doing? Was he seriously bringing me my meds?* I realized I should probably drop the tree branch, but I just couldn't.

A messy emotional cocktail fizzed inside me, threatening to spill over: fear, embarrassment. . . the first hints of guilt.

I inched toward him, snatched the injector from the ground, and backed away quickly.

"Are you *okay?*" he asked, incredulous.

"You scared the *shit* out of me!" The words burst out. I wiped at the stupid tears that escaped my eyes.

What's real, Sammy? Come on. Breathe.

"Hey, I was only trying to help." He held up his hands. "And I'm sorry I scared you. Like, *really* I am, but would you mind putting down the weapon? I'm kinda vulnerable here."

Tributaries of blood ran down his leg. His ankle begged for ice and crutches.

My heart was slowing, and I sensed a mistake—another Sammy McCallum overreaction. He was badly injured, he was trying to do me a favor, and I was threatening him like a deranged cave woman.

I *knew* I'd made a mistake.

I fumbled the branch in my trembling grip another moment, then forced myself to drop it. "Sorry."

Sanity was returning with each gulp of oxygen, with each gusting breeze that shook rainwater from the treetops. "And thank you. . . I guess."

Sunlight broke through the canopy, casting dappled shadows in the rain-soaked woods. The skittering sounds of small animals clicked and scratched along the hillside. I took another breath—tried to drain the last of my panic. "I should call you an ambulance."

"Oh, *please* don't. That's like the *one* thing that could make this worse." He seemed to search the ground around him.

"I have to help somehow."

"Do you see my smart watch? That would help," he said. "I feel like I'm losing my mind."

Nothing visible lay on the trail, and three-leaved plants snaked through the surrounding undergrowth. "I don't, and you don't want to root around too much. There's a lot of poison ivy."

His shoulders slumped.

"So, now, I'm hurt, my smart watch is lost, and I've scared a woman." He paused to gape at me. "No. . . I've scared *the shit* out of a woman! God, what a *colossal* mess!"

He hesitated, as if giving the situation one last chance to fix itself. Then without another word, he pivoted to face down the trail, lifted his bad ankle up, and started scooting through the mud.

I gawked at his clumsy effort. "Where in the world are you going?"

"My ride's at the Valley Green. I'm gonna go find him." He slogged over the mucky ground, ruining a perfectly good pair of bike shorts, his swollen ankle bobbing along absurdly in the air.

"That's crazy." I scanned the wooded embankment. You couldn't even see the white pillars of the old inn's front porch from here. "The Valley Green's at least a mile away."

He continued undeterred, bumbling down a few more inches of the craggy trail.

I sighed. "Not that you'd get there before dark, anyway."

He persisted with his stubborn, futile endeavor, and I just couldn't watch it anymore.

"Oh, for heaven's sake, you'll never get down the hill like that, and you need medical care." It only took a few strides to catch up to him. "Plus, you'll tear up your hands."

He finally paused in the mud and examined his palms, dejected.

"Come on." I extended my hand to help him up. "My business is only a hundred yards away. Let's get you taken care of."

"But I scared you witless! I'm an ass!" He stared at me helplessly. "I mean your hands are still shaking for God's sake."

I planted them on my hips, forcing them to hold still. "It's just adrenaline. Look. . . even if you *were* a predator, I don't think you could do me any harm right now." I finally bent down, tucked my shoulder under his arm and wrapped a steadying hand around his back. He grabbed a tree branch, and we managed to get him upright. "And for the record, you're obviously not a predator."

***

The Wissahickon Valley forest had long been my place of solace, a lush, two-thousand-acre haven slicing through the Philadelphia suburbs. But this morning, the wooded gorge was a minefield. The slippery mud, sharp rocks, and low-hanging branches I'd struggled to navigate on my bike were even tougher to avoid with two hundred pounds of man hanging onto me.

All stretched out, he was even larger than he appeared on the bike. Despite my height, his arm wrapped easily over my shoulder, and his back was broad and firm with muscle. With only three working legs between us, I concentrated on nothing but keeping us upright and away from the steep edge of the trail as we attempted to navigate the path. We made progress, though, step by careful step, and fell into a slow pace.

His sweat-soaked jersey slid beneath my grip at times, and I tightened my hold on the wall of his chest. "Sorry," I said.

"S'okay." He huffed with effort. "We're okay."

Actually, though, it was something different than okay. His body pressed against parts of me I would normally never let a stranger near. While the contact was obligatory, not sensual, my nervous system did not get the memo. The feel of his ribs against my breasts and the weight of his arm across my shoulders stirred my cells awake. I couldn't deny the gentle buzz it sent across my skin.

Despite the unexpected pleasure, with each dubious step, his weight became increasingly untenable, and I strained to keep going as we approached the edge of the woods.

The front door of the brewery had just become visible when his bad ankle hit a stump jutting up from the path. He cursed, grabbed a nearby tree trunk, and collapsed forward in pain. The poor guy couldn't catch a break. His swearing continued, and I held him steady while he fought the worst of it.

Despite his suffering, I did need to tell him something. He still had his eyes closed and was starting to compose himself when I finally spoke up. "Um, I know you're in a lot of pain right now, but you know that whole 'not a predator' thing? One of your hands is kind of on my breast."

His hand was off me instantly. "Oh my God." He fought to steady himself on one leg. "Sweet Jesus, I would *never* do that on purpose. I'm so sorry." He looked around like a mortally embarrassed teenager. "Could today go any more wrong?"

"Let's just get you fixed up. We're almost there."

He set his hand back on my shoulder with exaggerated care, and we finally made it out of the woods.

***

I unlocked the front entrance of the Forbidden Craft Brewing Company, wedging the door with my body as we struggled out of the humid July air into the cavernous tasting room.

My patient took in the space with the same awe I felt every time I walked in. After all these years, it had not gotten old.

The ceiling soared high above us in the former warehouse, and sunshine streamed through several stories of windows along the back wall, washing golden light over the twenty-five-foot-long, live-edge bar; rows of gleaming taps, and antique wood tables scattered throughout the seating area. Midnight blue walls, towering steel fermentation tanks, and concrete floors provided a cool contrast to the deep honey-colored wood and patches of old, exposed brick that lent a coziness and sense of history to the space.

"Did I say today was going all wrong?" He eddied about as he gaped, holding tight to my shoulder. "Maybe I'm confused. Maybe I've died and landed in some kind of heaven. This is *gorgeous.*"

I flushed with pride. "Thanks."

We staggered a few feet further in, trailing a wide swath of mud in our wake. The dining room opened in ninety minutes. Marco was going to kill me when he saw this mess. He had always been a neat freak, but he'd been a groomzilla since his engagement. Lately, he'd been jumping down my throat over minor transgressions and chewing out team members when they made mistakes. But being nasty certainly didn't make him right. On this occasion, he was going to have to cope.

All the same, I did have an idea.

"I think I know where we should go." I tottered us to the bar and hit a button to raise the back wall. Engines cranked to life overhead, and a wide panel of windows rolled up on tracks toward the ceiling, revealing a path to the outdoors.

A befuddled face peeked out of the kitchen. "Sammy, is that you?" My chef, Erin, rounded the corner, butcher knife in hand. She took in the scene. "*Oh my gosh.* Do you need help?" She laid the knife on the bar and hurried our way.

"It's mostly under control. I'm gonna take him outside," I said. "But could you bring out a bag of ice and the first aid kit. Maybe something to eat?"

"Right away."

Erin disappeared, and we hobbled out to the patio. I found some cushioned seats at a table nestled between tall grasses and sheltered in the shade of a graceful birch tree. I settled my patient and got his ankle elevated.

"I'll be right back." I ran inside and grabbed clean washrags, warm soapy water, some ibuprofen, and ice water. Then on second thought, I poured a few samples of beer into flight glasses. I carried the whole mess back outside. Erin followed me out with a plate of cheesesteak sliders, a bag of ice, and the first aid kit. "Thanks, Erin. I know you're busy with prep."

"I feel like I should help." She looked torn. "But honestly, Ben didn't show up this morning, and I'm super behind."

"Run, run, run. I've got this." I shooed her away and she hustled off gratefully, leaving us to the first restful moment of the last hour.

***

A few minutes later, his ankle was on ice, the meds were down, and I'd washed the worst of the blood from his leg. He borrowed my cell phone, made a call for his ride, and we sat back to refuel a bit. I peeled off my helmet, set it on a cedar ledge behind us, and offered to take his.

He stiffened. "Can we not touch it?"

"Your head? Does it hurt?"

"Everything hurts." He had the good nature to laugh, but he was obviously struggling. "Hard to tell where the pain's coming from at this point."

"Uh-oh." I handed him a sample glass. "Here. World's oldest painkiller."

"Thanks. Hope it's stupid strong."

"Actually, it is." Being wounded sucked, but he seemed to seek levity, so I played along. "Cheers to not being a predator?" I raised my drink.

"*Oh.* Nice. All right." He grinned and raised his own glass. "Cheers to not beating a defenseless man with a tree limb."

We chuckled, clinked glasses, and sipped.

He let out a low whistle.

"Holy crow, this is good." He lifted up the small glass to get a better look at the dark liquid inside. "What is this?"

"That's our flagship brew. A porter aged in cognac barrels. Damn good, isn't it?"

"Damn good is right."

He drank appreciatively, put down a few sliders, and looked around the gardens with a patient and curious eye. The patio sprawled over a quarter-acre with a view downhill to the treetops of the Wissahickon Valley. Enormous, evergreen magnolias anchored the remaining sides of the property, blocking views of anything other than sky. Their dark green leaves offset the lighter river birches and

Japanese maples that offered shade and beauty through most seasons. Branching ferns and wispy grasses surrounded winding paths of flagstone. Fountains trickled the soothing sound of water, while oak leaf hydrangeas and colorful day lilies bloomed in the early July sun. Tables hid in little nooks, while Adirondack chairs clustered around fire pits and bocce courts. Large picnic tables awaited the biggest groups.

"This is truly very beautiful," he mused.

Color was already returning to his cheeks, a sense of calm settling in. Amazing what a little blood sugar and pain medicine could do.

He studied the gardens pensively. "You know, one of my businesses has an outdoor patio, too. We worked hard on it, but this puts it to shame. Really, just extraordinary."

"Thanks." I remembered the dirt and sweat that had covered my hands and brows as I'd worked to lay everything in. It brought me gratification to see it every day, but having someone else appreciate it was always special. "We worked hard on it."

"Wait, *you* did this?"

"Well, not by myself of course. It started as a parking lot years ago. We stripped it back to gravel. Built it out in stages. It was a long journey and a lot of sweat. Really, the whole business has been a labor of love. It's wonderful to be on this side of it now. See it flourish."

A smile of recognition crossed his face. "I know that feeling."

"Yeah?"

"Yeah."

"Well, I'd enjoy hearing about it," I said. "Do you mean your business? Or something else?"

"Oh, lots of things, I guess. I've racked up plenty of mistakes, but it's nice to see the good stuff come to fruition."

"Agree." He was a bit cagey, but I had a teenage daughter. Prying information out of the tight-lipped was my specialty. "You know, is your place a restaurant? Is it here in Philly? I'd love to see it. Maybe get some inspiration."

"No, it's kind of far away. Down near the Smokies."

So much for that. "Well, do you have pictures?" I asked.

He chortled. "On my phone. In the car. Back at the Valley Green."

"Of course."

A drop of dark blood fell into his lap.

I winced. "Oh my God."

"What?"

I scooted around the table to examine him more closely. A thin crimson trail trickled behind his ear.

"What is it?"

"You're bleeding. From your temple, I think. I didn't see it before. We've gotta get that helmet off you."

He stalled for a moment, then he reached up, clicked the latch, and pried the helmet gingerly away from his sweaty, light brown hair. "Can you see it now?" he asked.

I held his face lightly and turned it side to side.

"Ugh. No. It's under the hairline. I think it's where your sunglasses meet your scalp. They must have dug in you when you fell. Can you take them off?"

He hesitated. "Don't freak out, okay?"

"*Pff.* This is a lot less blood than was on your leg. No freak out here."

The ice bag slipped from his ankle, and I reached down to wrestle it back into place while he peeled off the sunglasses. Partially melted, the lopsided bag flopped like a jellyfish, refusing to balance. "I think we need to refresh this."

I glanced back up at him. . . and found eyes I already knew.

Golden.

From up close, it was the only imaginable reaction.

His lightly bronzed skin framed eyes as warm and rich as honey, reflecting all the shades of amber and earth—along with a hint of trepidation. I noticed the tiny, pale scar above his left eye I'd always wondered about. The barely-there crook in his nose. *How did I miss it?* His features were more rugged than classically handsome, but they had nevertheless been my daydream for years—an image to accompany the awe-inspiring melodies, and soulful lyrics that had been the soundtrack of my life. Even with streaks of mud on his cheeks, even under a sheen of sweat, there was no mistaking him.

Gabriel Walker, in the flesh and blood, sat right across from me.

Everything went very still. I realized my knee was touching his under the table, and I pulled back. I let go of his ankle. *I'm violating his space. Like, right now.*

His eyebrows furrowed, and he spoke in his deep gravelly voice. "Sammy? . . . That's your name, right?"

What do I say? If I only have a few minutes, how can I express it all? Words failed me. *Everything* failed me.

"Sammy. . . hey, it's okay." He squeezed my forearms gently and leaned closer. "Come on. Same guy you've been with for the last hour. Same idiot who scared you in the woods."

"It's just. I just." I shook my head. *What am I doing? Get your crap together, Sammy!* "Sorry. You're hurt."

I centered myself and turned to face him squarely. I picked up the washrag and dipped it in the cooling soapy water. Then I braced the side of his face with one hand and gently dabbed his bloodied temple and matted hair with the other, hoping it didn't sting. Clear water came next, and I rinsed the spot with care. I peeled one last butterfly from the first aid kit and cinched the cut closed.

My hands fell away from his jaw, his close-shorn beard tickling my fingertips. I held his slightly concerned gaze. "I. . . just want to say *thank you*. Your music's an absolute wonder to listen to. It's been a gift to me. Never thought I'd get to say that."

A smile played across his lips. "Well, your care today has been a gift, and you listening to my music is a gift, too." He laughed lightly, a smile deepening the crow's feet at the corners of his eyes. "And not suing me for accidentally feeling you up is another. So, thank you right back." He looked over my face again and shrugged. "Cheers to being even?"

He raised another of the flight's sample glasses, and I matched the gesture. I felt like I'd been shot through by lightning, but if he could keep it light, so could I.

"Cheers, it is," I managed.

***

My cell phone pinged:

This is Charlie. Here to pick up Gabe.

I held it up for him to see. "Is Charlie your guy? And do you actually go by Gabe?"

"Oh, yes. . . and yes. Gabriel's only for the stage." He huffed a sigh. "If Charlie's here, it's probably time for me to go."

Something occurred to me, and I glanced at my watch. "You know, the staff might show up soon. Can you get your glasses back on without it hurting?"

He slid them on gently, easing past the cut. "I don't think I can bear to put the helmet back on."

"It should be okay. Just give me a second."

I got up and checked the tasting room. Finding it empty, I searched for the best escape route, then returned to Gabe. "Let me text your driver real quick." I picked up my cell phone and messaged Charlie back, indicating the location of a side door the employees couldn't unlock. "Okay, I think we've got a plan."

I put my shoulder under Gabe's once more, braced a hand across his broad back, and stood him up to his full height.

Whatever chemical reaction I'd had to his proximity and warmth before was significantly stronger now. The feel of his solid back, the heaviness of his damp, muscled arm over my shoulders, and the closeness of his torso pressed against mine—it all set my body embarrassingly aflame.

He was still the same guy he'd been an hour ago, but, at least to me, he was no longer a stranger. He was someone who had relaxed me after countless long days. His songs had added energy and rhythm to my life and had created so much beauty that it sometimes brought tears to my eyes. I felt like I'd known him through his music for my whole adult life. But he hadn't known me. I was still a relative stranger to him, and I needed to respect that. I tried to keep cool.

We hobbled into the tasting room and slowly made our way to the far wall and a door marked "Staff Only." I nudged it open to reveal a narrow hallway of exposed brick leading to an exterior door. The tight space was a former means of accessing the warehouse cellar and was now the location of the brewery offices—and an unfortunate landing zone for clutter.

"I know this is a little snug, but it will keep you away from unwanted attention," I said.

The door closed behind us, and we tottered down the hallway, squeezing around boxes of delivered goods and a vacuum cleaner left in the middle of the floor by last night's closing crew. The dim, confined hall forced us to clasp together even closer, and the warm, powerful mass of his body was everywhere. I tried to focus on the task at hand, but a highly distracting, tingling heat crept across my skin everywhere he touched me. In the last few feet of the hall, a huge mop bucket was planted by the door, directly blocking our path. I braced myself against the wall and tried to shove it out of the way with my foot, but everything was sandwiched too tight. I could hear the staff arriving in the tasting room and knew there was no going back.

I sighed. "I'm really sorry about this." Seeing no other option, I turned my body fully against his, held him tight, and tried to scoot us around the bucket.

One faltering step later, my brain shut down. His strong chest was pressed against my breasts, and the rough stubble of his chin grazed my cheek. *Had I wanted to go somewhere? Why would I move from this spot?* I breathed in the woodsy scent of his soap—pine needles, fresh moss, and resin. His body was throwing off absolute waves of heat, and my knees all but melted.

But he didn't seem bothered in the least. In fact, he smiled, no trace of pain in his features for a moment. "Now, then. This doesn't feel like something to be sorry about at all." He leaned his back against the brick for support and let his rough hand fall from my shoulder to trace a slow trail down my arm. "This actually feels quite nice."

His deep voice was a quiet echo in my mind, and his fingers left warmth on my skin. My lips parted, and I tilted my face up to his. His lips were just inches from mine, and for the love of God, he moistened them and took a deep breath, the rise and fall of his chest moving against mine.

Then the terrible, shrieking sound of ancient, ill-fitted, metal-on-metal ripped through the silence, and a blinding streak of light crossed our faces as someone yanked open the side door from outside.

"Honey, I'm home," Marco sang out, his keys jangling. He stepped into the dark hallway, and his eyes adjusted. He stopped short. "What the hell is this?"

Marco was even taller than Gabe, and his smooth, dark hair and sculpted face were set in a mask of disbelief. He glared at our bodies pressed together, at our filthy biking gear, and at the trail of mud we left behind us.

He stared me down, fuming. "Seriously, Sammy, what the hell?"

"Look, I can explain." *The guy was injured, for heaven's sake, and Marco's worried about a little dirt? Give me a break.*

"I don't want an explanation. Just get out of here. Both of you. I can't believe this." Marco lifted the mop bucket out of the way and pushed the wrenching, squeaking door back open, his lips pinched tight, his cheeks set in a scowl. "Seriously, just get out."

I had more important things to do than clapping back at Marco, but I would catch up with him later. He had to quit treating people like this. After all, who did he think he was?

Gabe and I managed our way out the door and onto the pavement, where a black SUV sat idling. He put a hand on the exterior wall and shifted his weight off my shoulder.

A tank of a young man with buzz-cut, dark hair hopped out of the car and stared in shock. "Gabe, dude, what happened? You look like shit."

"Thanks, Charlie. Just come and help me, will you? I can't get around at all."

Charlie hustled over, replaced me as Gabe's crutch, and practically carried him the short distance to the SUV. He planted Gabe in the backseat, and they worked to lift his lame ankle into the car.

As Gabe reached to close the door, he looked back at me, his expression mixed. He seemed to think for a minute, maybe settling on something. "Thanks, Sammy," he finally said. "Not sure what I would have done without you today."

"Of course. Thanks to you, too."

He made a sort of half-smile, the door clicked shut, and the black car pulled away into the distance.

2

—·—

A Reminder

After another hour tromping through the soggy, overheated forest, I managed to retrieve both bikes. I secured Gabe's Trek Fuel EX inside my personal office at the brewery, but I knew it was likely a futile gesture. His band toured the nation every summer. They likely couldn't spare time to chase down a mountain bike on a day already upended by bloody injuries. But it was his, and it was too nice to simply lock to the rack outside.

Besides, was there even a remote chance Charlie would swing by to pick it up? Or for that matter Gabe?

I decided right then. As long as my daughter was cooling off after our disagreement last night, and given the mountain of work awaiting me, I may as well return to Forbidden Brews once I'd cleaned up and checked in at home. I could toil over tasks from my office and give Meghan her space while I was at it. A win-win for sure. Plus, on the sliver of a chance that Gabe stopped by, I might be able to connect with him again. The mere possibility sent a flush of blood to my cheeks.

First though, a shower, a solid meal, and a bit of rest were non-negotiable. My bike leaned against the brewery's brick façade, and I righted it before easing my stiff, weary legs over the frame and setting off in the direction of home.

Progress up the quiet, sloping road was slow, and my mind ran in loops, replaying the moments I'd been crushed against Gabe in the dark hallway. Impossibly, my skin still tingled where he'd stroked my arm. Heat lingered where his whiskers had brushed my face. *Gabriel Walker had leaned in for a kiss! Is that possible? Maybe I'd imagined it. No. It happened. He'd wet his lips!*

My bike nearly bucked me from my seat, rattling my teeth as it crashed through a pothole I'd been too spaced out to avoid.

Good grief. Can I not get a grip? If I didn't pay attention, I was going to hurt someone. Probably myself.

Evicting the senseless, obsessive thoughts from my brain, I forced my focus where it belonged—on the bustling main road ahead.

***

Germantown Avenue stretched all the way from downtown Philadelphia to the village of Chestnut Hill, where slow-moving cars bumped along its trolley tracks and Civil War-era cobblestones. I slowed to ride on the sidewalk, pedaling past the town's time-tested storefronts. I rolled by the shoe shop where my mom took me for my first Mary Janes so long ago, passed by banks and antique dealers, and inhaled the heavenly, sugary scent wafting from Brendenbeck's Bakery. Tempting as it might be to stop in, I knew a box of their pecan-covered sticky buns already graced my kitchen counter.

On that thought, I picked up pace and turned off Germantown Avenue into the West side of the suburb. Here, old-growth trees sheltered a patchwork of historic, single-family homes and rambling stone estates, all nestled snugly together along quiet residential roads. I waved to a few neighbors before pulling up to a pre-Depression-era house crafted from thick slabs of Wissahickon schist.

I half-climbed, half-melted off my bike and pushed it up the patchy, blacktop driveway toward the backyard, where Mom was trimming her azaleas. The shrubs added a cheerful touch to the home's former carriage house—which had been renovated into a guest cottage years before I bought the property. Mom had insisted on moving in after Dad died, and the azaleas were her addition. She always kept them tidy.

"Hey, Sammy." She stood as I approached, beaming her usual, sunny smile and wiping sweat from the wisps of her brunette pixy cut. "Looks like you've had a big morning."

"Yup. Can't even *begin* to explain." I looked around for the car that wasn't there. "Have you seen Meghan?"

"She drove off an hour ago. Some friend was having a boyfriend emergency. Said she might be back after dinner." She flashed a knowing look at me. "She'll be fine of course."

I returned her warm expression and leaned my bike against the back porch's iron handrail.

She tilted her head. "Actually, she did seem a little stormy this morning."

Stormy was a good word for it. I sighed, eager to find calmer weather in my relationship with my daughter soon. "Last night was a little rough. I'm hoping she'll come around."

"Hang in there, honey."

"Thanks, Mom. Love you. Gonna go clean up."

She laughed. "Yep. You need it. Love you, too, sweetheart."

She went back to her azaleas, and I headed up the steps to the back door, eager for the comforts of home.

***

A window over the kitchen sink looked out onto Mom's cottage, and I watched her fuss in the garden while I heated up leftovers from the brewery. The kitchen was our main gathering area, and I'd splurged a few years ago on white cabinets, quartz countertops, and a large butcher-block island where we could all sit, eat, and chat. I pulled out a cushioned barstool, dug into one of the restaurant's latest creations, and was blissing out in the cool air when a text arrived from Tina:

OMG. Gabriel Walker!! Are you so excited?

I stared at the phone, puzzled. I was indeed very excited. . . and still shocked. . . and suffering a little disbelief, to be honest. But she couldn't possibly know any of that. I was positive Marco hadn't recognized him and was pretty sure we'd evaded everyone else. *Could Erin have placed him?* She'd brought ice and food to the table, but if *I* couldn't tell who he was at first—even up close—it seemed doubtful she would have made him out quickly.

I hedged:

??

Little dots flashed across the screen as Tina responded:

Are you flaking on me? Sammy!!

She was still typing, and I waited until her message popped up:

I already hired a sitter, and the tickets were NOT cheap. I swear you're too busy for your own good these days. Please don't do this.

Oh, for Pete's sake. The pieces clicked together.

Tina usually splurged on good seats for us when Gabe's band came to town, but I didn't realize she'd done it this year. Or maybe she told me at some point, and I forgot. In the whirlwind of launching Forbidden Brews' newest locations, I think I'd forgotten nearly everything.

I texted back:

Not flaking on you. I promise.

Tina's response arrived quickly:

Good! That's my girl!

Dots danced as she continued to type:

Pick you up at 4? Don't wanna be stuck in the back of the pit like last year. You might be able to see, but I'm way too short.

I glanced at the clock. Any last hope I'd been harboring for a productive day evaporated. But people walked away. . . work didn't. I could pay invoices and review financial statements tomorrow. Disappointing Tina would not be an option.

Plus, if we arrived early enough, we had a chance of being on the rail. Of being close. How could I resist?

I typed a quick response:
Will be ready at 4. Can't wait to see you.
And I truly couldn't. She was never going to believe what just happened.

3

CRAVING

THE USER

The incessant noise, demanding patrons, and daily complaints of a busy staff drove him to refuge in his office. He closed the door behind him, muffling the sounds of the clanging dishes and the servers' constant clamoring. Finally, a moment of peace.

Unfortunately, there was no time to enjoy it.

Need drove him to double check the door lock, then snatch a tiny mirror from his desk drawer. He fished the baggy from his pocket.

Why was it almost gone? Were they shorting him? He'd weigh it himself next time.

He grabbed a business card and pushed the powder into thin white lines, trying to conserve it. Then he rolled a twenty-dollar-bill into a tight straw and bent over to take quick snorts.

The drug numbed his face, and the familiar taste of turpentine trickled down his throat as a wave of relief rolled through him. Fireworks of euphoria sizzled their way through his cells. Soon, he vibrated with energy—an iridescent, electric joy that obliviated his worries. His confidence skyrocketed, growing bigger than his body. Bigger than the room. He could do *anything*.

"Hey, are you in there?" A voice called through the door. "Table five's complaining, and a couple taps are frozen."

"Coming. Coming." He wiped his nose and tucked everything back in the drawer. He hesitated a moment to straighten his clothes

and square the papers on top of his desk. Then he opened the door
and reentered the fray.

4

***

THE CONCERT

SAMMY

"Hubba hubba!" Tina called approvingly when I stepped out the front door.

I had genuinely tried. My top, with its thin shoulder straps and layers of white, gauzy ruffles, fell past the waistline of cropped, faux-leather leggings that I had purchased at the insistence of my discerning teenage daughter. I had blown my red hair out smooth and kept my makeup light but sultry, with a touch of blush across my freckled cheeks and just enough smoke and definition for my brown eyes. It was all reasonably classy. . . with the exception of a last-minute decision to leave my bra at home. After seeing my red, blotchy face and ruined hair this morning, I needed to reclaim a little womanhood and sex appeal. I wasn't dead yet.

I was eager to tell Tina about my morning, but as she pulled away from the curb and headed toward the freeway, she grew unusually quiet. I scrutinized her more carefully. Her curly brown bob obscured her face somewhat, but her gaze seemed far away. She wore no makeup, and her eyes were puffy and pink.

"Are you okay?"

She spared a glance in my direction, before refocusing on the road.

"Tina, what's going on?"

She stared straight ahead as the blocks fell away, then eventually shook her head. "Andrew finally did it. The papers arrived an hour ago."

A chill swept over my skin.

"I never thought it would actually happen." A mottled red flush crept up her neck, her telltale sign of distress.

Andrew had walked out a million times, stormed away in anger, but he'd always come back quickly. I wasn't sure how to respond, but going out to celebrate definitely didn't feel right. "Should we stop the car? Go back home?"

"There's really no point." She wiped her eyes with the back of her hand. "I didn't say anything to the boys, and they're happy as clams right now, eating pizza with their favorite babysitter and starting a HeroBots marathon. It's probably best I'm not there, frankly."

My mind raced, trying to find the right thing to say. "Do you know what you're gonna do?"

She shrugged. "Tomorrow? Make breakfast. Help Noah use the potty. Take the kids to the park. I don't want to think farther than that yet."

We pulled up to a stoplight, and I grabbed her hand. "I love you, and I'm here for you. Whatever you need. I can help with the boys anytime."

She took this in. Nodded. "Let's just try to have some fun, okay? I need to forget this mess for a bit."

We drove the rest of the way in silence—my mind on nothing but my friend, her young sons, and the road ahead.

***

We found parking without trouble and walked to a local deli near the pavilion. Once our toasted Italian hoagies were warm and securely wrapped, we carried them to the venue, prepared to picnic while we waited for the gates to open.

"Same drill as always?" I asked.

Over the years, Tina and I hammered out a process for getting a decent spot in the pit. We showed up early, got in separate lines, and assigned whoever made it in first with running to claim our spot. The person in the slower line grabbed drinks for us both, then worked their way in. The culture of the concert pit accepted one friend joining another, but that was about it. Otherwise, everyone defended their turf.

Today, after a long wait outside the gates, our effort paid off. We were just a couple of rows back, to the left of center stage.

The summer air was still hot, and a noisy crowd packed the pit as we waited for the band. Tina remained off, so I tried to keep the conversation light as we sipped slowly on spiked lemonades, knowing one drink was all we'd be able to get our hands on for the next few hours. The dense throng of people in the pit grew, crunching us in more and more tightly. We chatted with our neighboring fans, bonding over shared excitement and speculating on which songs the band would play.

Eventually, a wall of violet light came to life from high above the stage, and musicians trickled out from the wings, prompting an escalating ripple of cheers and applause as everyone realized the show was about to begin.

Years ago, when the Gabriel Walker Group suffered losses and Smith Town Soul was on the verge of splitting up, the bands merged. Walker Smith Revival was born, yielding a legendary mix of blues, soul, and rock—as well as a juggernaut of talent. Two percussionists, a bassist and lead guitarist, backup singers, and a collection of musicians on brass, woodwinds, and keys slowly gathered on the stage. Sauntering toward their instruments, they waved to fans amidst a growing roar of excitement.

Gabe came out last, with his ankle in a bulky air cast and a crutch under one arm, spawning a subtle groundswell of reaction. Fans leaned into each other's ears, snapped photos, and scrolled on their phones. I imagined them typing quick Googles: "Why Gabriel Walker crutches," "Injury Gabriel Walker." If the Internet didn't yet know what happened to him today, the news would spread soon.

Tina leaned in. "Doesn't look good. Wonder if we'll get a full show."

"Yeah. I dunno." I winced. He had to be tired and hurting.

A stool awaited Gabe at center stage. He settled in and pulled the mic close. "How you doing tonight, Philly?"

An eruption of excitement rose in all directions.

He let it reverberate until it eventually died down, the crowd expectant. "I spent the afternoon getting my leg fixed up by your fine doctors today. So, we're gonna need a little extra love tonight to get this rocking for you."

The crowd exploded and definitely showed all the love a performer could want. Then the lights swooped down, smoke machines kicked on, and the band dove headlong into the night.

***

Walker Smith Revival usually played one long set, and tonight was no exception. In between powerful songs that blasted us with energy, the band sometimes dropped back to quieter numbers, highlighting intricate, heart-achingly beautiful melodies. From this close, we could see the physicality of the drumming, the sheer breath required to blast horns into the atmosphere, and the sweat-drenched effort each of these amazing musicians poured into their music. Gabe's focus stayed on his bandmates and his guitar, but during slower numbers, he would look through the blinding stage lights in the direction of the crowd, creating a sense of connection.

In the closing verse of Tina's favorite song, his gaze wandered our way and seemed to hesitate a few moments before Gabe closed his eyes and lifted his voice to hit the big final notes, the veins in his neck bulging with effort.

Tina took pictures and recorded videos, and we sang the lyrics we knew, wishing the troubles of the world away.

The band was deep into the set when Tina tiptoed to my ear. "Sammy, I don't think I can make it," she shouted above the music. "The cocktail was too big. I'm gonna burst."

"You'll never get back in." Concert pits collapsed forward as soon as an inch of space opened up. You could sometimes leave. . . but you couldn't return. "I'll come with you."

"No, it's fine. I'll listen from the steps and meet you after. Sing extra loud for me, okay?"

Tina forced her way through the crowd as the band went on full tilt, thrilling the gathered masses with several more songs and two encores. The whole pit vibrated with whooping cheers when the final notes landed, and the amphitheater exploded with applause as everyone used their last opportunity to show the band appreciation.

The love was offered right back. Gabe's lead guitarist tossed handfuls of monogrammed guitar picks into the pit and I pocketed a few. Drumsticks and set lists were gifted to folks closest to the stage. Gabe was helped to the ground so he could scoot to the rail, where he signed posters and snapped selfies with his admirers.

He practically glowed with charisma and talent, and I watched as fans reached to touch his arms, his hands. As enthralling as his company had been this morning, he so clearly lived in an entirely different world, and this was just a tiny fraction of it. More cities, more fans, more listeners awaited—eager to bask in the power and energy of his band and their music.

Eventually, the band left the stage, and the tidal wave of the departing crowd grew in strength. I gave in to it, thinking that at least I would have a good story to tell at parties. Plus, if no one came by the brewery to claim his bike, maybe I could donate it to charity.

The teeming mass of humanity poured out of the pit, spreading out on the wider blacktopped area, where concessions and merchandise awaited.

It was time to return to the joyful chaos of my undeniably full, very blessed life.

Tina had said she would watch from the steps, so I got refreshed then headed in that direction. I climbed to the first landing as hundreds of exhilarated, inebriated fans made their way down the steep stairs, bumbling in the afterglow of a great evening. I scanned the passing faces—too many to make sense of—but Tina was nowhere to be seen. I tried to be patient; I knew she could be hard to spot. Scarcely more than five feet tall, with short, dark hair that disappeared into the night, my best friend was not the easiest mark.

I finally realized calling would be far easier. I picked up my phone and saw her text:

The sitter called. Nathan is throwing up. I have to go. Can you take an Uber home? Hate leaving you. . . and I'm worried you'll worry. Call me.

My heart pumped.

I hated being alone in cities at night.

Look around, Sammy.

Plenty of people still poured from the lawn and milled about the pavilion, providing safety in numbers. I could easily catch an Uber before the crowd thinned, but I didn't have time to fool around.

Feeling a quiver of unease, I descended the stairs and hustled to the exit, cracking open the app as I walked.

My phone vibrated and a message popped, blocking the ride share screen:

Sammy, this is Charlie- the guy who picked up Gabe at the brewery. He thinks he might have seen you in the pit. He has something for you. If you're here, can you stick around a minute?

I stopped short and stared at my phone, bewildered. I opened the messaging app and scrolled up. The sender was the same as this morning.

Could Gabe actually have spotted me amidst those blazing stage lights? And had I really just received an invitation to spend a few more minutes with him?

The idea of enjoying Gabe's company was more than appealing, but I also knew with each passing minute, the safety of the crowd was dwindling.

Hi Charlie. Am here. Would love to see Gabe, but worried about catching an Uber. Lost track of my friend.

The reply buzzed in quickly:

Is that you by the front gate? White ruffly shirt, black pants?

I looked around, and sure enough, the young, brawny man who had rescued Gabe from the brewery this morning was heading my way.

He waved and hustled over. "Sammy?"

"Yeah. Charlie, right?"

"Yup." He smiled and handed me a security lanyard. "I saw your text, but I'm sure we can get you home safely. We've got more vehicles than you can believe. Wanna come with me?"

I considered my options, but it was so tempting to see Gabe, and with the promise of a ride, I couldn't resist. I followed Charlie back into the now empty pit. We stepped around discarded plastic cups and spilled puddles of beer left by overexcited fans, to the far edge of the stage. Charlie guided us past heavy metal barriers, flashed his credentials at the security team, and led me behind the scenes.

Backstage was a beehive of activity. Spotlights lit the black walls and floors, and a dozen plus people scurried about, breaking down equipment and unplugging amplifiers, hustling everything into huge rolling crates. Ropes and chains dangled from the rafters above, where fearless riggers lowered gargantuan, wobbling speakers and lights to the floor below.

Charlie guided me past the frantic workers, down a set of stairs, and through a door to an air-conditioned hallway with vinyl floors and plain gray walls. It eventually emptied into a similarly appointed open gathering space, adjoined by a network of branching hallways. Staff bustled about with tablets and food trays while band members lounged on couches, downed cool drinks, or simply ambled back to the peace of what I presumed were private rooms. I managed to suppress any fan-girl behavior, but inside, I was elated to see these extraordinary musicians up close.

We turned down a narrow hall, our footsteps falling quietly on the vinyl, and a tall figure hobbled out of a doorway. Gabe turned our way on his booted foot, dressed in a fresh shirt, his hair damp from what must have been a quick shower.

"That was an amazing show!" I gushed before he could get a word out. "Thank you so much!"

A quick smile spread across his lips, and he leaned on his crutch for support. "Thanks right back at you, Sammy. Show wouldn't have gone on without you today." He looked me over as we approached. "Boy, I can't believe it's you. This is great."

"And *I* can't believe you performed a full set after the day you had. That's some legendary endurance."

"Well, I'll definitely sleep well tonight."

I chuckled. "I bet."

He scanned the hallway. "I have something for you. I just need to find my tour manager. Give me a second?"

"Of course."

He swung his crutch in the opposite direction and poked his nose into a few rooms until a forty-something, pony-tailed, blonde stepped out of one, a tablet in her hand. They had a quick exchange, both looking a little miffed, and Gabe came tottering back my way.

"Well, I *do* have something, but evidently, it's back at the hotel," he said in his low timbre. "Wanna come? We all get drinks at the rooftop bar after the show. It's a good time."

Did Gabe Walker just ask me if I wanted to have drinks with him? At his hotel? The answer was yes. *Hell yes.* Heat flushed my skin, and I felt suddenly aware of his proximity, of the strong arms he'd wrapped around my shoulders that morning, of the powerful legs that had biked up the steep hill behind me.

"I'd love that."

I said it casually, but my mind raced a thousand miles an hour. *And poor Tina!* I couldn't believe she was going to miss this.

5

UP ON THE ROOF

The elevator at the Liberty Grand climbed quickly, flip-flopping my already nerve-filled belly. Would I ever get used to standing this close to him?

"It's actually doubly good that you've come." Gabe adjusted his crutch. "I do have a gift, but there's something I'd like your opinion on, too. It's up at the bar."

"Sure thing."

We made our way to the rooftop and stepped onto a modern, luxe patio surrounded by a half-wall of glass. The openness granted an unobstructed view across the Delaware River, the Ben Franklin Bridge, and the sparkling lights of downtown Philadelphia. Concrete pavers led to sleek, white-cushioned sofas surrounding enormous copper fire tables aglow with amber flames. Toward the far wall, rows of dining tables awaited guests who might prefer a meal, and a scattering of potted evergreens brought life into the space.

I gathered two generously poured glasses of Gran Reserva Rioja from the bar, so Gabe could focus on walking with his crutch, and we found our way to the sofas.

Gabe set his crutch aside and sank into the furniture with a grunt of satisfaction. "Boy, I do love putting on a show, but I'm whipped. And my ankle hurts like hell."

"No fun. But at least you're human. I was beginning to think you were invincible."

"Not quite." He stretched his gimpy leg out, elevating the air cast on the side of the fire table, then leaned back deeply into the cushions, spreading his long arms across the back of the couch.

I handed him his wine and sat down just at the edge of his reach, eager to be near this enticing man but mindful of his space until he invited me in. I raised my glass. "Cheers."

"Cheers, indeed." He clinked his glass to mine and took a hearty drink of the Spanish red wine. "*Mmm. . . That is dangerously good.*" Gabe smacked his lips and took another long swill. "Wow. What is this again?"

"It's a Gran Reserva Rioja. The bar is really well-stocked." I took a long sip. The silky flavor of cherries, plums, and smoke filled my mouth, and I laid my head back on the sofa appreciatively. My hair brushed Gabe's wrist, and he responded by lifting a strand with his finger, twirling it idly.

He looked my way, his gaze meandering over me. "You clean up beautifully, Sammy."

"Thanks." I blushed. "You look very handsome as well."

And he really did. Denim jeans hugged his thick legs, and I tried hard not to stare at the muscles running the length of his arm, exposed by the short sleeves of his black t-shirt. His wide, stubbled neck hinted at a powerful torso. I tore my eyes away from his body, trying not to ogle him any worse than I already had, and took a few more long drinks of wine. The Rioja rushed blood sugar into my system and spread warmth through my chest. *Wonderful.*

The ponytailed blonde who had sparred with Gabe backstage breezed past our table and handed him a gift bag.

"Oh! The present!" Gabe looked over his shoulder as she hurried away. "Thanks, Ellen!" he called.

She threw her hand in the air, too busy to even turn around, evidently.

He handed the small metallic gift bag to me, complete with glittered tissue paper peeking out. "Please, keep your expectations low."

I tugged away the tissue paper, uncovering a few little treasures: a guidebook about local Philadelphia parks, a hot pink t-shirt that declared "Nursing is my Superpower," and a pepper spray keychain with roses on it.

"I was sort of limited to the hospital gift shop, but I thought these were appropriate," he said. "And the pepper spray is in case anyone actually does bother you. I hate that I scared you."

I couldn't help smiling at this extravagantly wealthy man and the charming irony of such simple, humorous, thoughtful gifts. "These are perfect. Thanks so much, Gabe. Should I try the shirt on?" I held it up to my torso and grinned.

"Hmm. . . I dunno." He peeled it back down and grazed one of his long fingers across the length of exposed skin on my shoulder. "I think these collarbones are too pretty to be covered up, Miss Sammy."

He was such a flirt. I tried to keep my body in check, but the barely-there touch felt like magic. Tingles and heat followed the line his finger had drawn and lingered.

If I didn't cool off my body and mind, I was going to embarrass myself. I took a swig of wine, which already had me feeling rosy, then set my glass down on the copper firepit. I watched the flames and the lights on the bridge. The dark water in the Delaware River churned toward the bay, just barely visible under the blanket of night, its endless ebb and flow ruled by the tides.

I tried to remember what I knew about Gabe. "You know, I think I read somewhere that you have a son. Does he come with you on tour?"

"Mmmh. Trevor? He was my buddy on summer tour for years. From first grade until a few years ago." Gabe gazed into the dancing flames. "We did everything together, traveled all over, but then he got a driver's license, discovered girls. I think he wants to hang with people his own age, not a bunch of middle-aged musicians. Plus, he started college last year, so he rarely has time for it anymore." He looked over at me. "But I think that's how it's supposed to work. He needs to pursue his own adventures, right?"

My heart squeezed. "I guess. . . but boy, it's so hard. My daughter, Meghan, is seventeen, and I'm lucky if I get a few sentences out of her most days. Some of the ones I get aren't very nice, either, and that's despite being really tight for the first fifteen years of her life. I'm not adjusting to it well."

The firelight was golden on Gabe's face. "I feel like every time I get a phase of life figured out, another one starts. Guess that keeps us on our toes." His words were those of a kind soul, and my insides did another flip-flop.

The couch shook. Gabe's wine splashed over the edge of his glass. Giant hands gripped his shoulders, rattling him playfully. "Hey, bro! You surviving?" One of his drummer clapped him hard on the back as he rounded the corner of the sofa. "Can't believe you're awake. Thought you were headed straight to your room."

Gabe craned his neck up at the hovering man. "Hey, Dylan. I'm surviving. Got a second wind."

"Good." The man squeezed Gabe's shoulder and seemed to take notice of me. "A second wind, huh?" He looked back and forth between us. "Or maybe what you got is a pretty woman to talk to. Hey, I'm Dylan." He offered his hand to shake.

I reached for it. "Sammy. Nice to meet you. The concert was just incredible. I love your music."

Dylan's eyebrows shot up. "Wait!" He glanced Gabe's way. "*Sammy?* The *famous* Sammy?" Dylan rocked back on his heels, a devil's grin creeping across his face. He looked me over. "The long legs and pretty red braid that lured Gabe to his doom today, huh? I *heard* about you." Dylan chewed on his lower lip, all playful mischief.

"Dylan, knock it off." Gabe looked annoyed. "She's not legs and a braid. She's a businesswoman and one hell of a designer."

"Yeah, but you didn't know that when you went tearing after her today, did you?"

It was quiet for a beat.

"Um, I think he was just trying to help me," I offered. "I dropped something important."

"Uh-huh."

Gabe's eyes squinted shut. He covered his face with his free hand and massaged his forehead. "Dylan, don't you have somewhere to be?"

"Not really." The man kept rocking on his heels, enjoying the needling. Finally, he clapped Gabe on the back again. "I'm just messing with you, man. Glad you're feeling good enough to hang a while. But, hey, Sammy?"

"Yeah?"

"Don't take any shit from him, okay?"

My jaw slacked, and Dylan sauntered away.

Gabe's eyes were still shut, and he nodded to no one in particular, an embarrassed, tight-lipped smile on his face.

I laughed. "A little brotherly love from your bandmate, huh? Appropriate for Philly."

"Yeah. I'm really loving him at the moment." Gabe snuck a peak at me out of one eye. "Sorry about that."

"Gabe, I'm a forty-year-old woman. If you called me cute, I'd hardly be offended." In fact, the stupid grin on my face was going to get me in trouble. "Look, why don't I get us some more wine. Want another round?"

"Dear God, yes. Please." He took the last long swig from his glass, and I carried our empties away.

A few minutes later, my smile was back under control, and I returned with our drinks. The bartender had poured two larger-than-life servings of the pricey rioja for us. Obviously, he wasn't the one paying to restock the wine cellar.

Gabe took his glass gratefully, and we sat and watched the flames as we sipped. The wine had turned me warm, soft, and relaxed. The night took on an alluring, alcohol-induced glow.

"You know—" I leaned back against his arm, gently— "I don't think I properly thanked you this morning for bringing me my EpiPen. I'm really sorry you got hurt trying to help me."

"Not your fault. I'm just clumsy. What are you allergic to?"

"Oh. Bees. Isn't that silly? Such tiny creatures."

"No. Not silly at all. I'm glad you carry your meds. Trevor is allergic to peanuts. I'm always on him about that."

A freight train of a man in a security shirt headed our way, his eyes fixed on Gabe. He looked at least fifty, with fair skin, a bald head, and a grayish black beard. His barrel chest was enormous, and he crossed his tree-trunk-thick arms when he arrived at Gabe's side. His voice was a deep smoker's rumble. "Claudia Gravess is here."

Gabe looked up at him, obviously not happy with this news. "She got past the guys in the lobby?"

"Yeah. We need to either convince them she's a problem or find new help. Sit tight. We'll take care of it."

"Thanks, Oscar. Appreciate the heads up." He looked down at his lame ankle, grimacing. There would be no quick escape from anyone tonight. He seemed to make peace with it, though. Security presence at the bar was strong.

A few minutes later, a commotion broke out near the elevator. Raised voices and scuffling disrupted the otherwise peaceful night, and I swiveled to see what was causing the chaos. A woman with slick blonde hair, a perfectly made-up face, and a petite, Hollywood-groomed body flailed her wrists and shoulders in a useless fight against the security team. She must have seen me staring, because her wild, livid eyes latched onto me as uniformed men hustled her back into the elevator. I couldn't hear what she was shouting, but I doubted the words flying from her mouth were compliments. *Yikes.*

I looked at Gabe, a question undoubtedly on my face. He glanced over his shoulder, then returned his gaze to me. "Sorry about that. Sometimes, weird things—and weird people—come with a public life." He shrugged.

"I bet." I tried to sound casual, as though it were normal to have angry women following you around. "Who is she?"

"Someone trying to make it in the entertainment industry. She had a hit song, and now she has a role on one of those documentary shows, where they highlight the tourist stops in various towns." He sipped his drink and looked toward the river. "She dated our bassist,

T.J., earlier this year and was backstage a lot, but she started acting really inappropriate. Showing up in my dressing room sort of. . . undressed. Not wanting to take no for an answer. That crap can rip a band apart, so I didn't appreciate it, and T.J. definitely didn't. He broke up with her, banned her from backstage, the buses, the hotels. He was just done with her, but evidently, she's not quite done with us."

He tsked, clearly annoyed. "And for extra fun, her TV schedule means she can show up in any city, anytime. Plus, her erratic behavior attracts paparazzi, which is something we haven't really had to deal with much before. She's a bit of a problem, honestly."

I nodded my head softly, looking into the fire. *What a strange reality he lives in.* I glanced back his way. "It's wild that you have to deal with that."

"Eh. I'm ridiculously lucky in most every way." He laid his head back against the cushions. Closing his eyes, he seemed to just breathe the warm night air. Maybe the oversized glasses of wine were softening his evening, too. After a minute, he tilted his head lazily in my direction. "Actually, Sammy, can I ask you a favor?"

"Sure."

"Today in the woods. Tonight at the hotel. All of it. I'd appreciate your discretion. There's a lot of great things about my life, but there are challenges too, obviously." He took another swallow of wine, then looked me in the eye. "Like, sometimes, I can't do anything normal or talk to anyone outside the industry without it going viral. Makes it hard to have a life." He shifted around on the cushions again, resettling his air cast on the edge of the fire pit. "So, I guess I'm asking if our connection can remain private and not make its way online?" He absentmindedly stroked strands of my hair again, holding my gaze. "Wish I didn't have to ask you that."

But really, it was a tiny request. I used social media for the breweries but almost never in my personal life. "No, that's fine. It's good to know how important it is to you." After a moment, I added quietly, "And for the record, I haven't told a soul we crossed paths."

A wicked grin crept across his face, and his eyebrows arched skyward. "So, I could take you away and ravish you, and no one would know it was me?"

"Yeah, don't push it. I've got pepper spray, remember?"

Gabe laughed, and we continued to relax and sip. The firelight danced, glowing in the coals and reflecting in a million shapes and shades off the hammered copper table.

"You know, I've got another question for you." He looked around. "This rooftop bar. . . We come up here each night, and I never want to leave. Your patio? It's like heaven. I could have moved right in. I've got a business in North Carolina, though, a little farm-to-table place. It has a big wrap-around porch, and we tried to build a pretty outdoor space, but people don't seem to make the drive from town as often as we'd expected. Plus, they don't stick around for dessert and coffee and extra drinks. I can't figure out what the secret sauce is, design-wise. I mean, why do I want to curl up and move in at your place? Why do I want to sit under the stars at this one? And why, at mine, do folks leave before we expect them to?"

"Hmm. That's a complex question." I took a moment to gather my thoughts. "First, I think you have to reverse engineer the whole thing. Think about what you want people to feel, what their needs are, what you're trying to accomplish. For example, Forbidden Brews has always been about friends gathering in a beautiful setting for a great time—and of course, fantastic beer. So, we built it for that, with all the nooks and crannies for small groups to reconnect, the open spaces for large parties, and the games for people who want to be active or maybe meet someone new." I looked around critically, taking in the details of the rooftop. "This place, in contrast, seems like it's all about luxury, and it looks like it was designed to host travelers and business groups. It's wide open—so there's no sense of privacy, but that can be nice when folks don't know each other, don't have anyone to gather with. Think of the proverbial restaurant bar. You can be all by yourself but still feel like you're having dinner with people. It also can be good when you have an event where everyone's supposed to mingle. The finishes here are also very high-end. I think they want people to know their luxury room price comes with upscale amenities. I'd say the only real miss is having a walk-up bar instead of waitstaff. If people have to serve themselves, they won't consume as much."

He looked at me incredulously. "How do you see all that so quickly?"

I shrugged. "The same way you probably pick up new music as soon as you hear it. You've spent an entire career doing it. Plus, when I did my MBA, they talked about customer experience and business design. So, it's something I've always watched for. And of course, we've consulted with really smart people. No one figures out everything on their own."

He nodded. "You know, you're so good at this, Sammy. Is there any chance you'd be willing to come down and look at La Fermata with me sometime. . . the farm-to-table place? We were hoping to invest in the outdoor space this fall, and I think your perspective would be really valuable. We hired a design team, but after the first time, I'm not sure I trust them to get it right."

The wine spoke before I could think. "I would absolutely love to see it." I was drunk on the magic of the night, the scrumptious Rioja, and this exquisite man. How could I not want to see something he created? How could I not want to see *him* again?

"That would be great. You have Charlie's number, right? Can I have him reach out?"

"Of course." I laid my head back again, the muscle of his forearm my impromptu pillow.

He looked over at me, heat in his eyes. I couldn't help but return the smolder—it was so intoxicating to be near him.

His brows gathered in thought.

"Sammy, you know, I should have asked earlier. That man who burst in the side door today? He seemed pretty ticked off. What's your relationship to him?"

"Ugh." I shook my head, disgusted. "That was my partner, Marco. He was really rude, and the whole thing was my fault. I'm sorry about that."

"No need. I don't blame him." He scratched his jaw. "Have you been together long?"

"We started the business about eighteen years ago. He had a great product but no capital to expand, and I was sort of the opposite. Flush with cash from a Silicon Valley job right out of college and looking for an investment—a way to lay down roots in Philly again. By the time I figured out I was pregnant, it just seemed like the only thing to do."

I paused and watched the firelight flicker. The second glass of Rioja had me shimmering from head to toe, and the proximity of Gabe's warm body was almost more than I could stand.

A last ounce of wine swayed in the bottom of his glass, and he drained it. Then he stood up slowly, propping himself on his crutch. He found my gaze and held it with a long, sultry look. "I think it's time for bed. Come on, Sammy."

He extended his free hand to me, and my world stopped.

I stared at his outstretched palm, which was broad, strong, and rough from a lifetime of playing guitar. My heart stuttered. Every nerve in my body stood on end, and the wine-softened city lights filled the background with twinkling light.

If I took his hand, I'd be breaking every rule I ever had: No out-of-towners. Never leave with someone from the bar. Only serious relationships.

Adrenaline coursed through my body, and a light tremble worked its way through my muscles. I took the last swig of my wine, set down the glass, and reached for his hand.

Rules be damned.

He steadied me as I stood. The amber glow of the firelight danced on his skin and reflected in his enigmatic eyes, which drank me in. His deep husky voice swept over me. "Let's get you home," he breathed. "Charlie can take you anywhere."

He squeezed my hand, released it, and hobbled back toward the elevators alone.

What?

I stared as he made his exit.

Maybe I should have followed him, but I just couldn't. I looked around at the bar, taking in the fuzzy lights and the people still talking and mingling under the dark sky as though nothing were wrong.

Did I misread everything? Could I feel like a bigger fool? Shame burned hot in my cheeks.

Then a flash of anger rose in me. *Was this all just a game to him?* When he walked away from me at the brewery, it made sense. His ride had arrived, and he needed medical help. *But now? Was he just trying to prove he could sleep with me if he wanted to?*

Flustered, I grabbed the t-shirt and book, tossed them in the gift bag, and picked up the pepper spray. I wandered among the sea of strangers, before eventually finding Charlie. I explained where I needed to go, and he led me to the elevators.

Just before we stepped aboard, I threw the pepper spray deep into my purse, where it landed near a rip in the lining. Over the coming days, it would slowly lodge itself between the silky fabric and the leather exterior of the purse, becoming all but unreachable. I would never think about it again—until it was far too late.

6

— • —

An Unexpected Guest

THE STALKER

Claudia's spine stiffened when the woman stepped out of the Liberty Grand's front entrance. *Is that her? Finally?* Claudia's parking spot didn't afford the best viewing angle, but the woman looked about right. Cheap white blouse. Long red hair. *Is that Charlie walking behind her?* The beefy man jogged toward a waiting SUV and opened the back door. *Yup, that had to be Charlie—which meant she was surely the tramp who'd been sitting with Gabe.*

The redhead climbed into the SUV, toting a purse and some kind of glittering gift bag. *Had Gabe given her a present? Seriously? Who the hell* was *she, and why would he be fooling around with someone so. . . ordinary?*

Charlie's car slowly pulled away from the curb, and Claudia eased hers onto the dark pavement of the city street behind him. She glanced in the rearview mirror to see if the paparazzi had seen her pull out, but no one followed her. The idiots were too distracted by their smoke break.

City lights colored the night, and aside from the noise of the other cars and the occasional outburst from someone wandering the streets, downtown Philadelphia was relatively quiet. Claudia hung back a car or two as Charlie's SUV made its way through the city blocks. *Where were they going? Was she staying at a different hotel?*

Charlie didn't stop in the city at all, though, and instead pulled onto the highway. Claudia kept following. *What the hell?*

After several miles, the car pulled off the freeway and began winding its way up a four-lane road crammed between a narrow creek and a steep wooded hill. Claudia gripped the steering wheel tightly and trailed Charlie's car on the curving road until the woods finally faded and a neighborhood emerged.

Seriously? The suburbs? Was she a local?

Ridiculous!

Claudia followed at a short distance all the way to a little side street, where Charlie pulled up to a two-story stone house. The woman waved to him as she got out, then walked up the darkened driveway and ascended the steps to the front porch. She searched through her purse by the glow of the porch lights, finally granting Claudia a clear view of her.

She wasn't all that pretty—long legs, maybe, but small breasts. She looked fit, but not Hollywood fit. Not even close. Her fair-skinned face didn't seem remarkable, either. Kind of plain, frankly.

Claudia glanced in the rearview mirror. Her glossy blond hair fell elegantly past the high planes of her cheekbones. She admired her own full lips; dark, steeply arched eyebrows; and perfectly sun-kissed skin. Her wide-set eyes sparkled like blue topaz. Everything looked flawless. She *knew* she was flawless! How could he even be interested in this other woman?

It was so obvious how this was supposed to go. *Why was he so dense?* He was practically a dinosaur. His fans were getting gray hair, their bodies growing soft with age. She could help him be relevant again—could attract a whole new generation of listeners. He could so easily return the favor. He had connections in the entertainment industry she couldn't begin to imagine. Plus, they could collaborate, feature each other in hit songs and promotions.

Her latest singles would drop in two months. Publicity started sooner. She couldn't let this get away from her.

Annoyed and disgusted, Claudia texted herself the address. She had thought filming in Philadelphia would be a miserable drag, but it just might prove worthwhile if it let her sort this bitch out.

7

THE LIGHT OF DAY

SAMMY

Sunlight streamed through my bedroom's dormer windows, beaming directly into my wine-soaked brain. Burrowing under my blankets offered little relief. Evidently, getting up to close the blinds or simply starting my day were the only choices.

I stretched my arms over my head, trying to ease the kinks out of my back. My body ached with exhaustion and dehydration. *What on earth happened yesterday? Had that day even been real?*

I sat up in bed, squinting around dumbly at my blindingly white room, the fog of morning still heavy in my mind. My laundry hamper overflowed; the space was disheveled from a busy week, and a metallic gift bag shimmered on my desk.

I jolted awake.

If I'd harbored any doubts, here was evidence the events of yesterday had indeed taken place.

My first thoughts raced to Tina, all the others to Gabe. Powerful memories flushed my skin with heat—his hand stroking my hair, his warm fingertips grazing my shoulder, the heft of his body as I helped him to the brewery. However, the abrupt conclusion of the evening bit right on the heels of those pleasurable thoughts. Rejection and embarrassment stung painfully. *Why did I think he would ask me to his room? I'm such an idiot.*

Ugh. I rubbed my eyes and swung my legs over the side of the bed. My dad always used to say "Feet on the floor, girl. Move on."

It was still good advice.

I toddled downstairs and found Mom hovering over the coffee maker as it steamed and sputtered through the last few drips of a brew cycle.

"Oh, thank goodness." I stumbled over to grab two mugs.

"I don't suppose it's me you're excited to see, or do I really rate second to hot coffee?" She took a mug from me and filled it.

I rolled my eyes. "You don't rate second to hot coffee. I love you very much, and you know it." I gave her a quick kiss on the cheek, then filled my cup as high as possible without creating a hazard. "You're up early."

"And *you* were up late. Your lights didn't go off 'til after two. I thought I was gonna have to bail you and Tina out."

I rolled my eyes again. "We somehow managed to avoid arrest. What were you doing up at two, anyways?"

"Who knows. But did you know you can stream old episodes of QuizShow? I may never sleep again."

She was so silly.

"I'll have to check that out." A finch flitted past the window, to the bird feeder Mom always kept full. "I didn't get anything done yesterday, though, so I might be a little chained to my computer today."

"No worries. I've got a lot of planting to do, and I'm meeting my girlfriends for lunch. Maybe we can catch up over dinner?" She blew on the steaming mug of coffee, waiting patiently for it to cool down from its most scalding temperature.

"Sounds good. Is Meghan still asleep?"

"As far as I can tell, yes. Sleeping Beauty is still conked out."

***

I crept back up the stairs to my room, sat at my desk, and made a list. I'd lost all of yesterday, and we had a big week coming up. We were releasing a new seasonal beer on Friday—a scrumptious blueberry Hefeweizen—plus the new locations still needed a lot of extra care. I settled in, got organized, and sipped the coffee greedily.

The first item on my to-do list was IT, which I could practically do in my sleep. Until the coffee kicked in, that was fitting. I pushed out a required system update, confirmed the firewalls and anti-virus programs hadn't flagged any problems, and ran a data backup. All was well, thank goodness.

Marketing came next. Our chef, Erin, had taken gorgeous, summery photos of the Hefeweizen set against our blooming gardens, and our social media management's software helped me transform the pictures and key promotional information into veritable art. I fiddled too long with the details and font but eventually felt pleased with the result. I timed the posts to hit the sweet spot for the East Coast and Midwest crowds, then moved on.

I monitored reviews next, thanked folks for the nicest ones, and took note of some negative comments. One guest described Charlotte as filthy, and customers continued to express frustration over wait times in Cape May. Before I posted replies, I wanted more context. So, I emailed a few questions to Griffin Parker, our longtime leader in Cape May, and to Bobby Boone, the manager we'd hired to kick off Charlotte. I also added "negative reviews" to the agenda of my "New Leaders" meetings with Bobby and his peer in Madison, Jesse Voss.

Last was finance, which was at least a familiar task. June books were closed, and I started with the P&L. It wasn't quite where I'd hoped. Sales were down compared to forecast, and expenses were oddly high. I squinted and checked again, but I hadn't misread the numbers. Not good, but probably not an emergency either. With two new locations, we might experience variability while the new businesses stabilized. The budget misses were yet another item to discuss with Jesse and Bobby.

The sun had climbed higher in the sky, and the hallway floorboards creaked faintly. I turned in my chair and found Meghan leaning against the door frame. She was dressed in her favorite pajama shorts and tank, and she yawned as she tugged her sleep-tousled red hair into a messy bun. Like most normal people, she was a few inches shorter than me, but otherwise there was no mistaking her as my daughter. She was pure McCallum. She squinched her dark brown eyes and pale freckled cheeks as she looked me over. "You know, you're staring at that laptop like you're mad at it, Mom."

Her casual comment was a good sign. Hopefully, spending time with friends had softened her. "Morning, sweetie." I got up and gave her a hug. "How was your day yesterday? Don't think I saw you at all."

"Fine. Some big drama with Marnie and Jason, but I think it's handled." She ambled over to my desk. "Really though, what's wrong?"

I turned back to my computer. "Oh, nothing really. The new locations are throwing off the financials a bit. Or at least, I think that's what's happening. I'll have to figure it out later."

"Can I take a look? I loved my accounting class. I bet I could help."

I glanced at the complex jumble of numbers on my screen. "Honey, I appreciate the offer, and I promise if I think of a good task for you, I'll ask. For now, though, I'm not even sure where to start."

She turned away and walked downstairs without saying goodbye.

I sighed, went back to the last few tasks, and finally checked the almighty cash balance. It was down by more than I would like—the second unusual finding for the day. I normally had the cash forecast buttoned up tightly, but if sales and expenses were off, that might do it. Of course, new businesses were less predictable than established ones, too. It was another item I'd need to double check long-term. We did have a credit line, so I wasn't truly worried, but I'd rather not pay the interest rates. I transferred some funds into the account, added that worry to my to-do list, and closed the computer for the morning.

***

Downstairs, I found Meghan shuffling around the kitchen. She spread cream cheese on a bagel and helped herself to a coffee before coming over to the island to sit. Recent mail, along with other trappings of daily life, lay scattered about. Meghan was an excellent student—and an even better soccer player—and the college mail piled up if we didn't manage it. Just glancing in the stack, I saw big names: Georgetown, Emory, Duke, Rutgers. Any way you cut it, Meghan was a kid in demand.

The college mail was a nice complement, but risky territory, and I waded in cautiously. "Anything good today?"

She quit sifting through the glossy postcards. "Are you *seriously* asking me that?"

I shrugged. "I'm sure there could be a lot of great options."

"For *you*? Or for *me*?" Heat flushed her cheeks instantly.

I should have kept my mouth shut. "*Both* Meghan. I'm *sure* we can find both."

"Disagree." She glowered at me with hard eyes. "I see nothing good you'd let me look at." She finished sorting through the letters, stuffed several in the trash, and stacked the remainder beside her bagel. "But I like pointless endeavors, so maybe I'll read them anyway." She disappeared with her breakfast, leaving a wake of negativity behind her.

Sometimes I thought if my business didn't kill me, maybe my relationship with Meghan would. She was angry and frustrated a lot these days, and she let me know it. I put my head in my hands and waited for the moment to pass.

Then I remembered Tina. She had much worse problems, and I always found doing a kindness for someone else was the best way to quit fretting about my own troubles. I set down my coffee, crossed to the pantry, and started dragging out big bowls, beaters, flour, and sugar. Banana bread and cookies were in order, and I sent Tina a text:

Made it home safe and sound last night. Hope Nathan is feeling better. Hope you're feeling strong. Comfort food is coming your way.

She sent back a hug emoji, and I got busy worrying about something more important than teenage power struggles.

8

— · —

AN INVITATION

A few days later, I was revising Forbidden Brews' cash forecast and listening to morning rain patter my bedroom windows when the text arrived:

Hi Sammy. This is Charlie from Gabe Walker's team. He asked me to check with you about some dates. He said there's a break in the tour schedule, and he's planning to be in Creekside July 27-July 30. There are guest cabins on site. He wants to know if any of those dates could work. If not, he said he could send photos. Hopefully this all makes sense to you.

It didn't. . . at least, not completely. I took another sip of coffee and minimized my spreadsheet, opening a browser instead. A quick Google of "Gabriel Walker" and "Creekside" yielded abundant links and images: a North Carolina visitor's bureau article about La Fermata—Gabriel Walker's farm-to-table haven near the Smoky Mountains; photos of Gabe posing with cook staff and assisting laborers in the orchards; quaint images of an old white farmhouse with a broad sun porch; Instagram selfies of guests lounging under sprawling cedar pergolas surrounded by endless acres of crops.

Fragments of our conversation came back to me.

Had he been serious about me helping with a patio redesign? More importantly, why did I tell him I could travel that far away? Just the thought of venturing more than an hour's drive from Meghan and Mom made my stomach turn.

My trips two years ago to close real estate purchases in Madison and Charlotte had not gone well, and after my unexpected visit to the Columbus ER, my days of being separated from my family had ground to a halt. Marco had been left with the burden of the company's business travel, and I had hunkered down at home, defeated.

If I went, though, would I see Gabe again? I remembered his powerful build, his warm hands, and his wicked grin. Blood rushed to my face, and a low vibration spread through me.

Oh boy.

My mind was hesitant, but my body sure wasn't. For now, I stalled:

Hi Charlie. Please tell Gabe I'll check the dates. Will get back to you soon.

9

GETTING CLOSER

THE STALKER

Claudia parked near the edge of the athletic fields as the teenager sprinted to join her soccer team. Her red ponytail flapped in the breeze and her gym bag bounced off her hip with each stride.

Late to practice. Flaky little brat.

Claudia killed the engine. The photographers staking out the hotel had failed to monitor the parking garage, and she was grateful for a moment of solitude. She unwrapped a makeup remover from her purse and wiped the heavy foundation from her face. *How could the directors expect her to be pancaked all day, then show up zit-free at 5 a.m. for another shellacking? Such assholes.*

When her skin could breathe, Claudia took a long sip of her lemon juice cleanse and picked up the stack of mail she'd managed to swipe.

Leafing through it, she found evidence of a tedious existence. College mail for Meghan McCallum. An AARP postcard and a parade of charitable beggars hounding Kate McCallum. Sammy McCallum was the lucky recipient of everything else— credit card and utility bills, insurance documents, restaurant supply catalogues— all the crap with financial burdens attached. Online property records listed Samantha McCallum as the homeowner. Everything tracked.

But what did it mean? Was there no man living in the house at all? And if they all shared the same last name. . . had this Sammy chick never been married? Couldn't even convince the girl's baby daddy to recognize his own kid? *Pitiful.*

And problematic, too.

After all, if the woman lived a shitty existence, would she treasure *anything* more highly than a chance for fame? For public envy? Trading mundane responsibilities for wealth and attention would be the ultimate temptation. If the woman could truly screw up her plans, Claudia would *have* to find the leverage to back her the hell off.

But, really, how hard could it be? One old woman, a middle-aged mom, and a skinny teenager made for nice, soft targets. Vulnerable. Weak. Spooking them back to the safety of their lame, suburban existence shouldn't take much.

Claudia was getting ahead of herself, though.

Risking exposure only made sense if the woman was truly a problem. And she still couldn't quite fathom that Gabe would turn her down for some plain-ass, single-mom loser.

A flurry of motion distorted Claudia's line of sight. Two sweaty teenagers toting mud-streaked shoulder pads were waving at her, pointing from the fence line. They jogged toward the gate, heading her way.

Shit.

One viral sex tape and suddenly every pubescent boy with a hard-on thinks she's fair game.

Claudia chucked the mail on the passenger seat, backed up without glancing behind her, and gunned it out of the lot.

10

THINKING IT OVER

SAMMY

Mom shared dinner with me that night, and Meghan even joined us after practice, which made it a rare event.

As was often the case, we tucked into food prepared by the brewery's chefs: homemade fried chicken and waffles and a cranberry apple crisp dessert. Both were potential specials for the fall menu. The long hours required to run a restaurant and bar didn't always make for the best lifestyle, especially these days when we struggled to get staff to show up, but the food sure was great.

Mom chattered about her gardens and the upcoming tennis tournament she was helping organize. Meghan complained about the soccer drills the coach was putting them through despite the summer heat. Finally, I mentioned the possibility of the North Carolina trip, as unlikely as it was.

Sneaking time away from my tasks today, I had researched a bit more about Creekside. The picturesque location was home to a small liberal arts college, decent Smokey Mountain tourist traffic, and a fairly robust population. It was the kind of town we liked to build in, and the trip really could be a good scouting opportunity for the business.

The real unknown was whether I could manage the journey. I stewed over the thought for a minute before noticing that the table had gone oddly quiet.

I looked up into a death stare from Meghan. Her lips were working, obviously getting missiles ready to fire, her teenage temper on full display. "So let me get this right. *You're* allowed to go away, but *I'm* not?" She looked to my mom for support. "Does anyone else see how *wrong* this is?"

"Honey, I don't even know if I'm going, and if I did, it would only be for a few days, not a whole year. It's just for business."

"Oh, I know. If *you* want to go someplace, it's okay. If *I* want to, it's the end of the world. You are *so* unfair," she spat. "I don't even want to *look* at you." She grabbed her plate and stomped up the stairs to her room.

Mom regarded me, her expression warm but even. The silence stretched out, and I massaged my forehead.

Why did everything with Meghan have to be so hard? Why couldn't we go back to spending time together, enjoying a safe, warm home with enough of everything?

Mom finally spoke. "You'll figure this out, honey. I know you will."

The words hung in the air, and the kitchen remained quiet except for the sound of the faucet dripping.

Mom looked at me patiently. "You know, she's worked really hard, and those schools she wants to go to are excellent. Plus, I think I remember a young lady who *also* wanted to go far away at that age."

She wasn't wrong—about any of it. But I felt stuck.

We finished dinner quietly, and I retreated to the front porch swing to read the last few chapters of my Ariel Lawhon book before turning in. I stopped outside Meghan's room on my way to bed.

"Still don't want to talk to you," she called through the closed door.

I took a deep breath. "Love you, Meghan. I'm sorry about this."

It was painfully true. She would be eighteen before long, and sometimes I felt the harder I tried to hold on, the more determined she became to get away.

***

As the day's distractions faded and the quiet reflection of night seeped in, I lay in bed and tried to find rest. Unfortunately, the realities of a trip to Creekside invaded my thoughts, keeping sleep at bay.

Nine hours. Creekside, North Carolina was *nine hours* away. Far too distant for me to get home quickly if anything went awry.

Who would be saddled with the responsibility of helping Mom in the worst scenarios? My daughter? My friends? What if Meghan had an emergency? And who would be here to support Tina? What if any of them failed to protect each other? The consequences were inconceivable, and I couldn't bear to burden them with crushing guilt.

My chest tightened around my heart. Three long years had passed, but my body still waited on edge, physiologically unable to dismiss the possibility of imminent crisis.

I remembered lush, white Casablanca lilies; wreaths of spicy carnations; elegant, drooping blooms of freesia sent by well-meaning friends and business associates. Dad had deep roots in the community, and an explosion of floral arrangements blanketed the church altar, overwhelming the sanctuary with their heady perfume as I sat helpless in the pew, freezing in the air conditioning, staring at his coffin in shock.

Damn it. Stop, stop, stop!

I sat up, clicked my bedside lamp on, and shuffled the images in my brain, refusing to let them imprint, muddying my mind's eye with thoughts of literally anything else.

Fighting the tension constricting my ribs, I struggled to take a deep breath.

I couldn't go down this road. Not again.

Tossing the comforter back, I got up and washed my face, then headed downstairs. My to-be-read stash was ample, and I plucked a romantic comedy from the bookshelf—something funny and heartfelt to distract me. I sought solace in chocolate, sipped on herbal tea, and laughed my way through the first couple chapters until my eyes grew heavy again.

Finally, I gave in and returned to my bedroom, staring down the enemy of my pillow.

My therapist had suggested a weighted blanket for these nights, and I fetched the heaviest one from my closet. I laid back down, turned off the lamp, and settled myself beneath its twenty-five pounds of heft. She'd also recommended turning onto my other side if I awoke from a bad dream, as if flipping like a pancake could somehow reset my brain. Absurd as it seemed, I tried anyway.

Tonight, it seemed to work.

I closed my eyes beneath the calming, ponderous pressure of the blanket and focused on the physicality of my day, on plans for tomorrow. I thought of soccer games, of groceries and laundry, of nothing. I thought of my daughter, of her need for freedom, of my desire to see her unfurl her talents and fly on the currents of her own choosing. Images of Meghan's toothless kindergarten smile filled my mind, her enormous brown eyes sparkling with youthful mischief as she climbed in my lap and squished my cheeks in her palms. I recalled the feel of her silky hair in my fingers as I braided it before school. The glint of sunlight on her skin as we sampled our way through the gelato and salt water taffy shops lining the Ocean City boardwalk before riding Ferris wheels high above the seaside. Driving, always driving to our next adventure—through the pinelands and blueberry fields of southern New Jersey, weaving through the Poconos. Images of rolling hills and weathered farmhouses. Verdant mountains in springtime.

My breathing slowed, my thoughts wandered, and my conscience finally. . . slowly. . . disintegrated.

11

NIGHTMARE

Clouds boil ahead—ominous, churning, and nearly black. Lightning cleaves the sky as the car motors through a blur of murderous thunder and rain, its windshield wipers flashing back and forth. Darkness encroaches, swallows almost everything except a tunnel-like view over the shoulder of a soft-bodied, silver-haired driver.

His voice breaks through the hammering downpour, disembodied, echoing from all corners of the car. "Sammy, I need you to come get me! I don't feel good!"

The car moves faster. The massive, seething storm rages.

"Dad, you know I'm in Nashville. . . can't come. . ." My voice cuts in and out, static in the darkness.

"Please. This can't wait. Something's wrong. Come pick me up." His voice booms. Rain thrashes the car.

"Dad, I can't. You're fine. . . sick after your card game." Broken, scratching words.

"Sammy, I can't hear you! Stop talking and come get me. I feel awful. I need your help!"

The car shakes, reverberates, a cavern of violent noise.

"Dad, you're not being reasonable. . . I'm not in town." My voice drowns in static.

"But my head is splitting. I'm gonna throw up." The car rocks amidst blackness. His blaring voice fights against the screaming gusts of wind.

"Dad . . . pull over. . . There are plenty of people. . ."

An abrupt, deafening explosion obliterates the conversation, and the front end of the car rips horrifically in two. Thick tree branches smash through the windshield. The view goes black.

"Dad?"

The wind shrieks.

"Dad?. . . Dad, answer me! Answer me!*"*

But his voice is gone.

All that remains is thunder, rain, and the terrifying sound of someone trying to draw breath through blood.

***

I sat up screaming, a white-hot panic burning everywhere around me—an inferno that scorched the air from my lungs. I covered my ears, tried to block out the gurgling death rattle, the savage sound of wind. Tears flew everywhere. I couldn't stop the screaming.

"Mom! *Mom!* There's nothing bad happening to you. Wake up!"

Meghan's voice from far away.

"Mom, come on, *wake up!*"

More distant sounds. Feet scrambling down stairs.

Terror pressed against my chest and mind, filled the space with blinding light. Grief and fear bore down with crushing force. The endless scream shrieked in my ears.

Then pressure on my shoulders.

"Shh. . . Shh. . ."

The sound of Mom's voice. So close. A warm arm wrapped around me. A gentle squeeze.

"Shhh." My mom again. "Samantha Louise. You're okay. Shh. . . You've got to calm down. Nothing bad is happening."

My breath caught briefly, and I finally managed a gulp of air.

Two.

My tears slowed as oxygen flowed into my lungs. A few more breaths. Shallow, stuttering efforts.

I opened my eyes. Meghan stared at me wide-eyed. Mom sat by my side.

The reality of what was happening. . . again. . . crashed down on me. I smashed my fists into the comforter, sobbed in sheer frustration and embarrassment. "Oh, God. Why won't this stop?" I grabbed a tissue off the nightstand, blew my nose, and wiped my eyes, trying to get my breathing back to normal.

"I'm glad you're okay, Mom." Meghan handed me another tissue. "I'll get you some water." She hustled down the stairs.

Mom continued to stroke my back. I wiped my eyes and looked around, fully aware of my room again, of my mom next to me. "This is so ridiculous. I'd do anything to make it stop."

"It hasn't happened in a long time. It's getting much better."

We sat in silence until Meghan delivered the water, saw things returning to normal, and retreated back to her room, gently closing the door on her way out.

Mom continued to rub my back, up and down, in long languid strokes.

"Samantha Louise," she finally said, "you're going to have to forgive yourself for this. You have to let it go."

We sat for another minute or two as my body finally settled.

"We've all been through a trauma, and yours was easily the worst. But Sammy. . . that aneurysm was going to take him, whether you were there for him or not. Car wreck or no car wreck. You have to let it go, honey. I know you can."

I hoped she was right. I really did. It was long past time to exorcize this demon.

12

THE DECISION

Something had to change. I couldn't keep allowing anxiety to govern the boundaries of Meghan's life. Or mine. I couldn't bind us all so tightly to home.

Maybe this trip was my chance to break the shell of safety I had built around us the last few years. That carefully constructed protective layer was meant to keep us together, but it clearly wasn't working.

I decided to pretend I'd made the choice, to trick my body into showing me its true colors. I told myself I was going to North Carolina and figured I'd tell a couple others, too. If I could make it a few days without panic, maybe I could pull this off.

***

The next day, I caught Marco at the brewery. He was dressed impeccably, as usual. His dark brown hair was swept back. His olive skin, high cheekbones, and full lips were a sight for anyone to behold. I buffed the bar with a wood conditioner, tested and wiped down the taps, laid out fresh napkins, and otherwise got the front of house ready, hoping it would settle him enough to talk. He still moved around manically, though, setting out new table toppers, checking on the cook staff. I kept talking, simply following him as he overworked the prep.

"It looks like a pretty cool town, Marco. It checks a lot of boxes. I know I haven't scouted out a new place in a while, but this could be good for us."

Business development used to be entirely my job, but that had stopped after the accident—then my own fears—had completely shut it down. The new Madison and Charlotte locations had been in the works for some time, but Marco had been forced to manage their construction once they got under way. We had nothing in the pipeline.

"Sammy, why are you telling me this? We open in a half hour. I've got a million things to do." His voice peevish, he brushed past me and hustled out of the kitchen.

I followed him anyway. "I thought you'd want to know. I thought you were interested in my life—and the business. What's going on with you, Marco?"

"I have more to do than I can get done here, Sammy. Staff that constantly no-shows. A wedding to plan. I can't think about anything else." After a minute, his irritation suddenly softened. "Actually, I've been meaning to ask. We need a down payment for one of the venues. Do you care if I take my next dividend early?"

It had been several years since I'd seen him hunting down cash. I looked at him more closely. The whites of his eyes were clear, but were his cheeks a bit more gaunt? Were his pupils dilated? With his face in partial shadow, I couldn't tell. "Marco, are you in trouble?"

"What?" He looked startled. "No. *God,* no!"

He plunked down at a table.

"Crap. . . I'm sorry. I've been a piece of work lately, and I know it." He huffed a sigh and rubbed his neck. "The wedding has me really stressed out, and Ian's not helping. His work's been slow, so his paychecks have been too, but he still wants everything to be a perfect—a huge surprise. Which somehow *I'm* supposed to orchestrate." He clawed his hair back from his forehead. "Listen, let me take the early dividend, get this payment made, and hopefully that will get the wedding off my mind for now, okay?"

He stopped fidgeting and looked up at me as though noticing my presence for the first time. "Actually, what's wrong with me? I feel like I haven't even been listening. Did you say you were going out of town? By yourself?"

Okay, this was more the Marco I knew. I sat down opposite him, leaning forward to rest my elbows on the table, propping my chin in my hands. "Yup. North Carolina. Miles and miles away. All alone."

He stared at me for a while. I knew what he wanted to say. I'm sure he didn't want to hurt my feelings or insult me, but history was what it was.

"Are you really ready, Sammy? The last time you tried, it didn't go well. What if you're driving when it happens?"

"It's never happened when I'm driving, and if it happens at all, I'll simply *have* to pull myself together." We both sat with that idea for a moment, and I quieted my voice. "I think I need to do this, Marco. I know I'm telling you because it might be good for business, but that's not the real reason for the trip. I think it's important for Meghan's sake. If I can't get more comfortable with a little distance, with being separated from my family, I think it's gonna backfire. She could ultimately just run off and never come back. She's almost an adult."

Marco sat up straighter, cracked his back. "I hear you, I guess." He squirmed another moment. "But I don't know if I can keep doing this. You start these projects, and then I have to step in and finish them. I'm worn thin, Sammy. The business is big enough already."

"I know. I know. Look, let's call it an exploratory trip for now, okay? No contracts. No purchases. Nothing like that. I just want to look around."

That seemed to calm him down. "Fine. If you promise we're not buying anything, I'll support you. I mean, I get the whole Meghan angle, but I can't tell you that I love the idea of you being so far away, doing the very thing that kicks off these attacks, with no one nearby. It leaves me in a bad spot."

"I'll be all right," I promised, my resolve growing. I was already glad I'd decided to tell Marco. Maybe committing to this was what I needed.

But why am I only thinking about myself? I wasn't the only one at the table with problems. Didn't Marco deserve my support? He wasn't asking for more than he was owed, just a little in advance. After all, it was his company, too. I thought about it for a moment, but I knew it was right. "Marco, if you need to take the dividend early, it's okay. I'll transfer the cash to you when I get home."

He gave me a quick hug of thanks and got back to bustling around the tasting room. He watched me from the bar as I walked out to my bike, a look of concern on his face. I waved at him one final time for the morning and pedaled home.

***

Work consumed the next few days, but I made time to do economic research on Creekside, checking on incomes, population, regulations, and taxes. I even sketched out a preliminary financial model. It felt good to think like this again.

The budget issues deserved a deeper dive too, so I sifted through the financial statements as well.

The new locations, Madison and Charlotte, were indeed driving the sales miss. The expense surge, on the other hand, was caused solely by the cost of goods sold in Charlotte. I quickly scanned the transactions but found no accidental charges—mostly hops, flavoring, and barley. I compared production and input quantities, but no one seemed to be wasting product. Finally, I dug into price, and that's when it popped. A single vendor, HopNBrew, was charging us an outrageous unit cost. *Had I agreed to that?*

I pushed aside my laptop and called my high school classmate, Debbie. She had grown into an exceptionally fine attorney, and she offered us a friends-and-family rate.

"Hey, mama, what's up?" The exploding popcorn sound of her keyboard clattered in the background.

"Hi Debbie. How are the kiddos?"

"Hormonal, growing like crazy. Devouring food faster than I can cook it." The noise of her typing died down. "How's Meghan? Is she still giving you grief?"

"I dunno. I think we're giving each other grief. But listen, this is actually a business call. I was hoping you could research something for me."

"What is it?"

"Can you check on our HopNBrew contract? I can't remember it at all, and I want to know the pricing and terms. Seems like they're overcharging us. I hope I'm not stuck purchasing any minimums."

"Yup. No problem." Her keyboard rattled to life again. "Is it urgent, though? I'm buried in briefs and research right now. Big corporate case."

Patience wasn't my strong suit, but I tried to cool my sense of urgency. After all, the dollars didn't quite merit an emergency. "It's not on fire, I guess."

"Okay. I'll get back to you as soon as I can. I promise."

I thanked her and hung up the phone, then put a reminder on my calendar to follow up.

A notification pinged—my bi-weekly "New Leaders" Zoom with Jesse and Bobby began in five minutes. I scrambled to the kitchen to top off my ice water, then hurried back to my laptop and logged in.

Jesse joined first, with a sly grin, his dark eyes glinting like anthracite. "Morning, Sammy." While his thick beard, hemp necklace, and neatly ponytailed dreadlocks pegged Jesse as a Madison native, a surprisingly passionate, Type A personality lurked beneath his earthy exterior.

We chatted until Bobby arrived a few minutes late, flustered and apologetic.

"All okay?" I asked.

"No." Bobby wiped sweat from his brow, tugging a shag of his tawny hair back in agitation. His brown eyes—normally round and soulful—looked drained today. "AC is out, and the heat's making everyone nuts."

"Let me ping Marco. He can—"

"Don't bother." Bobby interjected, rubbing his slender, clean-shaven jaw. "I've already called HVAC. I know it's under warranty. Let's just get this over with."

Watching stress distort Bobby's babyface into something more fractured stirred my maternal instincts. We expected a lot from our leaders, but it was our job to provide the infrastructure. If he was suffering through a Southern summer without AC, that was on us. "Hang in there, Bobby. Crank up the fans, and eighty-six the oven-based dishes today. That will reduce heat in the kitchen. Comp cold drinks if you need to. Just keep track of it."

"Okay, hold on. Let me have 'em kill the ovens." When Bobby returned a few moments later, his anxiety still seemed piqued.

This felt all wrong. "Do you need to go? We can connect later. These meetings are supposed to help, not get in the way."

He looked surprised. "Later would be *much* better."

"Okay. Run, run." I waved him away, and he logged off. "All right. Sorry for the delay, Jesse."

I pulled up the agenda, shared my screen, and we got started. We reviewed upcoming marketing, discussed online reviews, and began tackling the P&L problems. Jesse seemed annoyed about the sales miss, though. He said most of the University of Wisconsin students had left for the summer. "Sammy, didn't you account for that in the budget?"

The subtle dig stoked my temper, but I stayed even. "Jesse, seasonality is considered, but we also plan for constant growth the first two years." I reminded him that while I handled corporate media, we expected his team to serve as brand ambassadors in the community. Summertime was perfect for this, and we discussed upcoming outdoor festivals as a great way to introduce Forbidden Brews' high-quality beer and pub fare.

I tried to help him categorize the challenges and boil them down to actionable tasks. Business was always a puzzle, and as frustrating as challenges could be at the outset, conquering a complex issue with a team could actually be exhilarating.

When we ended the Zoom, I emailed all our local leaders, asking them to avoid ordering from HopNBrew and updating them on ads that would be hitting the Forbidden Brews social media pages over the next week.

My energy was waning, but as the tasks of the day wrapped up, I remembered the early dividend I'd promised Marco. I logged into the company bank account, only to find our cash balance had plummeted further. A dull ache began to radiate beneath my temples. I scheduled the dividend transfer, then backfilled the account for both the dividend and the cash shortfall.

I fixated on the computer screen for another moment, something ominous hovering at the edge of my consciousness. When it came to working with Marco and running a company, difficulties were the norm, not the exception. But I was concerned this scattering of dark clouds might converge into a storm.

13

WATCHED

THE STALKER

Claudia circled the brewery first, confident of what she would find. Sure enough, she spotted the bike parked to a rack outside. Sammy rode around on it constantly, like some sort of hobo.

Claudia parallel parked about thirty yards from the front door of The Forbidden Craft Brewing Company, forcing the one paparazzi who'd followed her to park several cars back, with a big view of nothing.

So far, Claudia found no consistency in Sammy's schedule, but she could easily predict the woman's destinations. Always just back and forth, from the brewery to her house. Obviously, no life whatsoever.

On the plus side of this dismal bullshit, Claudia had yet to spot any signs of Gabe or his people. No security detail hovered, and as far as she could tell, Sammy hadn't left Philadelphia, despite the band touring nearby. Hardly a fitting combination of facts for one of Gabe's harpies.

In fact, after a week and a half, Claudia had yet to witness any indication this woman mattered *at all*.

The brewery's front door swung open and Sammy emerged. She unlocked her bike and pedaled off toward the main road, her long red hair flowing behind her.

Claudia considered going into the brewery, but the damn photographer would get in her face. She could swing by Sammy's house instead, but she already knew what she'd find there—the sour-face teenager and an old woman living in a garage. *What was wrong with these people?*

Poking around Sammy's life was getting stupid—and frankly a bit boring. Filming was wrapping up soon, and she definitely needed a little more action.

14

— · —

RSVP

SAMMY

Despite my increasingly concrete plans to travel, almost a week passed without the nightmare, and I could actually think about the trip without anxiety knotting my gut. *Is it finally time to do this?* I sipped my coffee at the sunny kitchen island and glanced at the stack of college brochures that continued to arrive every day from all corners of the country.

I knew that Mom—and even Meghan and her hot head—were at least a little bit right. I'd gone away to college. Then I'd taken a job in California and lived the way I wanted to. When I came back to Chestnut Hill, it was because I missed home, not because I lacked choices. Frankly, if my parents had tried to force my return, I might never have come back.

The truth of it all felt heavy on my shoulders.

I finally allowed my thoughts to drift to Gabe. I'd been so focused on researching Creekside and monitoring my anxiety that I hadn't allowed myself to truly daydream about him. Letting the floodgate crack open slightly, memories of his warm smile and alluring presence washed over me, leaving a tingling excitement behind. I absolutely wanted to spend time with him again—even if I knew better. Even if I was still a little insulted after being jilted at the rooftop bar. I took a deep breath, typed the message, and hit send before I could change my mind:

Thanks for your patience, Charlie. The July dates work for me.

A few hours later, the reply came:

That's great. Gabe asks you to meet him at La Fermata around 10am if that works. If you have any questions, please let me know or call the restaurant. They'll be expecting you.

A burst of heat spread through me. I was really going to do this.

15

ADDICTION

THE USER

He was out again. *How could he be out?* He shook the baggie violently over the mirror, but only the finest dusting of powder fell out. He wiped it up with his fingers and ran it over his gums.

He needed cash and more coke, but they'd taken his car. *His goddamn car!* How the hell was he supposed to buy more without a fucking car? Did these people not have a shred of business sense? For that matter, how was he supposed to get where he needed to go for the brewery?

Think, goddamnit. If he could just think clearly, he knew he could fix this, but the fog of need was thick in his mind.

He logged onto the computer and maxed out his last credit card on a rental car.

There. That was a first step. That was good.

He clicked a few more buttons, made a phone call, and set everything in motion. Supplies should be in his hands within the hour. Knowing relief was on the way, he felt a little calmer. He locked the office, put the most senior staff member in charge, and hurried out the door.

16

THE TAIL

SAMMY

On the big day, I got my Subaru packed bright and early, kissed Mom and Meghan goodbye, then stopped at the brewery to mount Gabe's bike to the rack on the back of the car. It was early morning, and the air was humid but not yet stiflingly hot. I dialed Creekside, North Carolina into my GPS, made sure I had snacks and cold drinks ready for the road trip, and put the car in gear. If I could get to the hotel tonight, the trip to La Fermata in the morning would be a piece of cake.

Despite the fears I'd been harboring over travel, road trips had always been fun in the past. I used to put on music, sing at the top of my lungs, call friends to catch up, or just give myself a moment to think in peace. Today could be like that if I let it. I tried to stay calm and enjoy the freedom that came with speeding down the road at my own pace, with my own thoughts and music. I put on one of my favorite Walker Smith Revival albums, and the miles peeled away easily. Best of all, despite the increasing distance from home, my anxiety didn't really stir. It all made the spacious blue sky above feel appropriate. Could I truly open our lives back up again? Could I let go of this aching fear and need to keep everyone so close?

The terrain slowly shifted from flat farmland to rolling hills, and finally, blue gray mountains appeared in the distant mist. As they grew closer, the winding freeway cut through towering stone bluffs covered in verdant shrubs and trees. Streams of water poured through crevices in the rock, evidence of recent rain.

Lulled by the beauty, my thoughts drifted to Gabe again. His deep husky voice, his rough hands, and the feeling of his chest against mine wove through my fantasies. Daydreaming, I all but ached with desire as the highway disappeared behind me and mountains rose up along the horizon. I knew I should probably stop stoking my expectations with all these wild imaginings and be more sensible, but, honestly, nothing made the miles go by more quickly. In the end, I indulged in the fantasy and barely noticed the time passing.

***

Some time later, I would learn that outside my bubble of daydreams, obscured by the ungainly bike rack, a sedan followed a few cars behind mine. For all six hundred miles of the journey.

17

CREEKSIDE

I woke up at the hotel in Creekside, well rested and glad to be done with driving for a few days. After a good stretch to ease the kinks out of my back, I opened the curtains to a bright sun climbing over mountaintops in a cloudless sky.

Twenty-four hours had now gone by, and I felt no trace of panic yet, no pressing urge to flee. I took a deep breath of gratitude—a moment of peace—then made the rounds. I called Mom and Meghan and texted Tina to check in.

Thankfully, everyone seemed to be managing themselves fine. If they were okay, I should be, too.

Thoughts of Gabe filled my mind as I dressed. I slipped on a favorite, navy-blue sundress and applied a little makeup despite the warm blush already creeping into my cheeks. Thinking about Gabe was so delicious, like a dessert I couldn't resist taking bite after bite of, whether or not it was good for me. Marveling at my body's response to the mere idea of him, I headed into the growing heat of a North Carolina summer morning and hopped in the car.

The directions sent me out of town on a sunny two-lane road. Eventually, the homes thinned out, the surroundings became wilder, and I crossed a wide, churning creek before heading up into the foothills. The road climbed a serpentine path through a blanket of forest, but the trees gradually thinned to a hedge, and field crops, apple orchards, and open pasture sprung up across gentle slopes.

When the road finally ended at a country lane, I made the final turn of the journey and started looking in earnest for Gabe's place. A few hundred yards later, a white farmhouse came into view, sitting on a wide swath of land uphill from the road, looking just like the pictures online. An antique two-story home with weathered-brick chimneys and a wide wrap-around porch anchored the property, surrounded by pergola-shaded patios. A burnt wood sign proclaimed "La Fermata ~ farm fresh wine, cider, & cuisine." I'd found the right place.

At least a dozen cars had already parked in a dirt lot surrounded by large shade trees and a split-rail fence. Groups of people milled about, wandering in and out of the old home, perusing the patio, the porch, and the grounds. I found a space and killed the engine, eager to get out and enjoy the fresh morning air.

A huge man stood up from the front stoop and ambled my way. While he wore plain clothes today, his bald head, salt-and-pepper beard, and enormous arms made him easy to recognize as one of the security guards from the rooftop bar.

I smiled and waved hello as he drew near. "Hey. I think I remember you from Philly, right? I'm Sammy."

"Hi. I'm Oscar." He nodded, all brusque efficiency, his voice a deep smoker's rumble. "Listen, there's a tour here today. Gabe wasn't expecting it. He's back at the cabins. Can you bring your car and follow me?"

"Sure. Of course."

Oscar's Jeep led me toward an inconspicuous gate in the split-rail fence. He pressed a button on his car's visor, and the gate swung open, letting us through to a long dirt road. My Subaru bumped along the dusty path, through a dense tract of fruit trees, then across a gently sloping hill covered with sunlit grapevines. The plants stretched skyward in parallel rows as neat as a pin, splayed on high trellises crafted from wood and heavy wire. After a quarter mile, we seemed to reach the edge of the property, and the dirt road ended at a collection of cedar log cabins nestled against the tree line, their ample porches facing the ripening crops. Gabe sat on one of them, picking a guitar in an armless rocking chair. He waved as we approached.

Oscar pulled away, and I once again unfolded myself from the car.

"Hey, Sammy." Gabe's foot must have healed, because he stepped down from the porch and headed my way without a limp. He gave me a strong, warm hug. "Thanks so much for coming."

He walked to the back of the car to help with my bags, only to be greeted by the clunky bike rack. "Oh my gosh! You brought the bike!" A guileless smile burst across his face. "I figured this thing was sacrificed to the forest."

He was funny—and handsome as hell.

"Well, the gods of the forest *were* angry when I took it back, but they'll have to manage. It's a nice bike." We untangled it from the rack, and I opened the hatchback to retrieve my bag.

Gabe walked me over to the cabins. "Oscar stays on the far end, but this one's all yours." He unlocked the door and dropped the keys in my hand. "Are you hungry? Thirsty? Anything you need?"

"Ugh, honestly, the only thing I need is to *not* get in another car for a while."

His face crinkled in an odd expression. "About that." He looked around, clearly uncomfortable. "I had planned to take you on a tour of the grounds first thing—walk you through the orchard and vine-yard, show you the restaurant—but there's some sort of Regional Commerce tour here this morning. I'd prefer to lay low. I was hoping to maybe drive you around town instead? Creekside's really cool, and I thought it might help you get a vibe for the area."

I struggled to keep my face from dropping but undoubtedly failed. Being smashed inside a car again sounded awful. "Um. Is there another option?"

He thought for a moment. "Well, now that you've brought an extra bike with you, maybe there is. Any chance you'd want to pedal into town? It would be a bit of a workout, which I know isn't everybody's cup of tea, but the way you powered up that hill a few weeks ago, I'm guessing you like to sweat a bit. Frankly, I've been pretty cooped up in a tour bus all week, too. I'd love to move a little."

I looked down at my short sundress. "A big bike ride actually sounds awesome. Just give me a second to change."

***

A few minutes later, we saddled up and pedaled away from La Fermata. After making the turn onto the steep road to town, the bikes picked up speed, screaming down the long incline. Cool wind blasted against the grin I couldn't keep off my face. No matter how old you are, riding a bike downhill is always a thrill. We'd have to pay it all back when we climbed the road later, but for the moment, it felt fantastic.

We reached the base of the hill quickly and crossed the creek on an old, arching, iron bridge. Gabe led the way as the town of Creekside slowly emerged, spread out across a broad green valley. Steep, wooded mountains provided a majestic backdrop behind the west side of town, and rolling hills surrounded it in all other directions, with larger mountains perched in the haze of the horizon beyond them.

As the population center drew near, evidence of tourism popped up everywhere. Restaurants, coffee shops, and establishments offering everything from hand-dipped candles to fine art lined the main thoroughfare, enticing visitors to spend money. Several shops intrigued me, and I made a mental note to come back before I returned to Philadelphia.

As the blocks fell away, Creekside College's distinctive limestone architecture began peeking above the surrounding tree line, and the offerings shifted from high-end purchases to spirit gear and bars. We turned off the commercial road and hopped onto campus, where walkways and grassy lawns surrounded huge stone buildings. Few students remained at this time of year, but we saw a handful of people going about their business, a good sign of some lingering campus life. Up ahead, the road disappeared into the hills. Gabe brought his bike to a halt under the shelter of a maple tree, and I pulled beside him to catch my breath and take a long drink.

"How you feeling?" Sweat dampened his brows.

"So much better. This is just what I needed, and the town is super cute." I took another swig from my water bottle. "How about you? Is your ankle all right?"

"Almost like new."

We continued resting and cooling off for a minute.

"Is there anything specific you want to see?" he asked. "If not, I thought we might bike over by the creek. There's a ton of shade and lots of little stands and shops. It's a nice place to grab lunch."

I popped my water bottle back in its cradle. "Sounds fantastic. Lead the way."

We pedaled back through the residential neighborhoods tucked behind the main road. Tall chestnut and hickory trees protected rows of well-kept homes, most with tidy lawns, some with quaint signs advertising bed-and-breakfasts.

Eventually, we reached the road we came in on and headed back in the direction of the creek. The soothing sound of water tumbling over rocks drew nearer as we pedaled, and before long, we turned down a wide dirt road running alongside the waterfront, blanketed on both sides by enormous shade trees. Brown water churned in the creek beyond, but its width allowed sunlight through, and its surface sparkled like magic. To the right of the lane, small creekside shacks with simple dirt parking lots abounded, offering kayak, inner tube, and paddleboard rentals. Many advertised white water rafting excursions as well. We continued pedaling, and a powerful spicy aroma filled the air as we approached a tiny house and the unmistakable scent of homemade barbecue.

Gabe brought his bike to a stop in the bare dirt lot and looked back at me. "Do you have an appetite? They make mind-bogglingly good barbecue here, and they never blow my cover." His expressive face was so funny, and the scent of smoking meat was irresistible.

"Sign me up," I said. "Sounds terrific."

***

Half an hour later, our bellies were full, and I piled praise on the chef, who would be welcome in my kitchens any day. I loved a good southern barbecue, and she had nailed it.

"You ready to climb that hill now?" Gabe asked.

I chuckled. "Not even close. Anything more mellow we can do first?"

"Actually, yeah. Come on."

He righted his bike, climbed aboard, and I followed suit. We pedaled further down the dirt lane as it veered inland from the creek. Eventually, the trees opened up along a few hundred feet of frontage, revealing a badly neglected property. Rusting structures and weeds seemed to wage a battle for dominance over the land. Gabe stopped his bike, climbed off, and walked a few steps along the edge of the site.

"You take me to all the nicest places," I joked.

"I know. It's a mess, right?"

It truly was. Dry, shoulder-high weeds and fresh green overgrowth fell away from the road, overtaking the chain-link fence and "No Trespassing" signs that kept visitors out. The unkempt vegetation crowded the acreage around a collection of dilapidated buildings.

"Do you come here a lot? What's your sign?" I asked.

"Yeah, okay, very funny." He stepped toward me. "But look, can you see it?" He squinted and took a few steps left and right. "I guess it's easier to make out when the leaves drop."

Finally, he seemed to find what he was looking for.

"Here." He planted his hands on my shoulders and nudged me over a few steps. "Stand here and look to the far edge of the property." He leaned in close and pointed a long arm over my shoulder, identifying a narrow viewpoint between the rusting structures. "Can you see the water back there? I think this land sits on a wide portion of the creek, and if you look closely, you can make out hundreds of feet of waterfront where the tree line ends. I know it looks like hell right now, but it's a decent bit of acreage, right on the creek, close to town. Always seemed like a missed opportunity to me."

The proximity of his warm body and deep, husky voice was more than distracting, but I tried to stay focused on what he was saying, on what he was showing me.

In the distance, behind towering weeds and decaying metal, a line of scraggy trees marked a likely edge to the land. Beyond it, the colors shifted, revealing a gap in the greenery. If the creek ran along the tree line, then he was right. It would be a remarkable stretch of real estate.

I tried to imagine the land with the overgrowth cleared, the metal fencing removed, and the creek frontage revealed. *Could the buildings be miraculously renovated, or would it be better to construct new ones, to optimize the view and flow? Could we salvage historic goods from the site?* As unlikely as it seemed now, the grounds could be a treasure trove.

"What was this place?" I finally asked.

He backed away from me a step. "I think it used to be a lumber mill, but I'm not sure. The old buildings look like they're falling apart, but I think it's mostly cosmetic. If you drive by in the wintertime, you can see it's really only the siding that's a mess. The structures stand tall and true."

"Hmm. Thinking about a way to get more yummy cider and wine to people?" I turned to flash a smile his way.

"Sometimes. I mean, this is so much closer to town, and tourists could bike here or stop in after a trip down the creek. Might be a good complement to what's already here and to our business up the hill."

"Have you run the numbers? Looked at it in earnest?" The gears turned in my head, and I thought about the seasonality, the likely sales, the cost of the property renovation and operations.

"No. That's not really my side of things. It's just something I like to ponder."

"You know, I used to do the scouting for our new locations. Maybe I could help." *Why on earth am I offering this?* I had too much on my plate already.

"That's cool. You guys are all over, right?"

"Mostly the East Coast and Midwest. We started in Chestnut Hill, but we're always aiming to get a foothold in new geographies. In fact, we just opened two new locations, so we're up to seven now." I grabbed a sip from my water bottle. "I had actually been planning to scout Creekside anyway. It's exactly the kind of town we like to build in. Decent population, pedestrian friendly, some disposable income—which you certainly get when you have tourists. Plus, it seems like the business climate is good."

Gabe flashed a crooked smile. "So, I invited my competition to town to drive me out of business?"

I wrinkled my nose at him playfully. "Or *maybe* you consulted me to enhance the Creekside food and bar scene. Build the economy? Attract more travelers?"

"All right, all right. Touché."

I thought of the July financials which would begin landing any day now. I did not predict good news. I wrinkled my nose and sighed. "Frankly, though, until I get the new stores straightened out, I really shouldn't even think about this. We invest a lot of capital when we start a new place, and it's never gone poorly before. Numbers so far look sideways."

"Have you put boots on the ground?"

"Not yet. I know I need to."

"Well, trust but verify, right? I mean, I come to Creekside because I enjoy it, but I also like to keep tabs on operations. Make sure local management issues don't fester unnoticed."

"You're so right." I gave the property one last look, trying to decide, but delving into this site would truly be an easy add-on to any research I did for Forbidden Brews. "You know, if you like, I could probably organize a preliminary site assessment and let you know what I find. We should be able to get some basic information about ownership, tax liens, environmental concerns—some of the first building blocks. Hopefully, that would all be public and easy to procure."

"Well, that could be really cool. Thanks, Sammy." His smile showed genuine delight.

I fished my phone out of the little pack attached to the bike, and walked the frontage, snapping a few pictures and dropping a pin for the location.

After tucking the phone away, I couldn't help smiling. "Don't you love an idea like this? People think business is such a cold, money-driven endeavor. And obviously, profitability is critical. But really, *this* is why I like it. It's interesting and creative most of the time. It's trying to bring something to life that didn't exist before, and sometimes, you get to make the world a little more beautiful while you're at it."

He stared at me, musing, then gently chucked my chin. "You sound like me talking about my music. Getting to be creative. Getting to breathe a little new beauty into the world. Those are some of the big reasons I enjoy what I do. It's why it doesn't feel like a job."

We held eye contact, a warm spark of connection flowing between us, a contemplative smile playing across his lips.

Some people seem to click with everyone they meet, but for me, it wasn't an everyday thing to feel that little tug of affinity with someone. To find a person who made sense to me and saw a little part of the world through the same lens that I did. I always found it kind of thrilling.

"Come on, Sammy," he finally said. "Let's go climb that hill."

***

It was so much worse than I'd feared. Our long joyride down would be paid back in spades.

I dropped my bike into the lowest gear, pedaling a steady, dogged rhythm, moving my front tire back and forth to create a switchback effect on the steep pavement, which seemed to attract and concentrate the sun's heat directly in my path. Trying to distract my mind from my burning legs, I counted away the strokes as I huffed out breaths and slogged up the incline. Gabe fell behind me, either for moral support or because he was struggling as much as I was.

After an interminable length, the end finally came into sight. The hill leveled out somewhat, and I saw the promise of rest and relief just a hundred yards ahead. *Thank God.*

But something moved in my peripheral vision. Gabe had pulled alongside me. He looked at me with a wicked smile, returned his focus to the road, and started to surge ahead.

He's got to be kidding.

No way was he beating me to the top of the hill with some cheap-shot, last-ditch sprint. I raised my backside off the seat to get more leverage and pumped the last of my strength into the climb. He looked back and grinned, then contorted his face in a mix of laughter and exertion and got out of his seat, too. We pumped hard all the way to the stop sign, and he beat me by inches at best.

"*Oh, my lord, are you insane?*" We were both gasping for breath, red in the face, and cracking up. I pulled off to the side of the road, grabbed my water bottle, and downed a few gulps. "I change my mind. You're a *total* predator. And you're trying to kill me. *Right now.*"

"Guilty. You got me." He seemed very pleased with himself, laughing between chugs of water, slumping over the handlebars in exhaustion just like me.

"You do know we actually have to make it another half mile to your place, right? We might not survive."

"Don't worry. Oscar will retrieve our bodies and inform our families. Is your will in order?"

I laughed and just kept taking greedy lungfuls of air, sure that any moment now, I would finally get enough oxygen.

***

A few minutes later, we staggered onto the property of La Fermata. Only a few cars remained in the dirt lot, and a last person or two trickled out of the main building into the parking area.

I climbed off my bike, leaning it up against one of the trees lining the lot. I took my helmet off and dumped a good portion of my water bottle over my head. "Oooooh. Why didn't I do that five minutes ago?"

He sidled up alongside me. "You've got a good idea there." He dismounted, clicked off the helmet, and doused his head with water as well. "Oh, that feels awesome," he said in his deep rumbling voice. He scruffed the moisture all over his head and stubbly beard and looked up again, still with that wicked grin. "I beat you."

"Oh, please! You cheated! You can't surge ahead first, then decide it's a race."

"*Oooh.* A sore loser. Wouldn't have pegged you for one of those."

"Fine. You win. Choose your prize." I rolled my eyes.

He reached over, stroked the hair back from my cheek, and gave my ponytail a gentle twist, holding onto it playfully. "Hmm. . . a prize. I'll have to think about that." He leaned toward my neck, and I squealed, yanking my ponytail from his grip.

I squirted a little more water over my head and wiped the sweat off my brow. "Come on. I think we have to walk these bikes back to the cabins. My legs won't pedal another inch."

"Yup, come on, pardner." He draped a hand across my shoulder, another on his bike frame, and we ambled toward the security gate and the dirt road. I knew he was a flirt, and in all likelihood, I was just going to get stirred up again, only to be left cold. But at least I understood him now. I could enjoy the tingling heat of his flirtatious touches without expecting anything more. I walked beside him, my body buzzing and alive.

18

In The Vines

We stopped at the cabins to get washed up, with plans to meet on his porch afterward. I got head-to-toe clean and called my mom and Meghan while my hair dried. I messaged Tina, too. Her texts had been brief and subdued the last few weeks, and I didn't want to lose touch.

I slipped back on the navy-blue sundress and comfy sandals I'd started the day in and decided to skip the makeup routine. My cheeks were still flushed and my skin glowing from exercise, which is when I felt happiest and most confident anyway. As long as I was going with a natural look, I left my hair down, the coppery waves falling past my shoulders. Gabe was already plucking a guitar on his porch when I ambled back outside.

"Oooh. . . free concert. I'm so excited!"

He looked up and grinned—and unfortunately, set the guitar on its stand. "No way, Jose. You promised you'd come look at this property with me. You get your free concert after I get my free design advice."

I pouted comically but fell in beside him. We made our way across the grounds, and for the first time, I wasn't too distracted to notice the view downhill.

Fields of grapes and fruit trees fell away in the distance, ceding space to open pastures, then to the treetops of the forest. Far below, the creek sparkled in a thin line, bordering the valley town of Creekside, which seemed miniature against a backdrop of mountaintops. Clouds drifted overhead, casting a moving mosaic of shadows over the forested green ridge of the nearest foothills. Behind them, layers of mountainous peaks faded into the horizon, before disappearing beneath a sky as bright as a robin's egg.

"Wow." I had nothing more eloquent to say. How could I have missed this view earlier? "Just wow."

"Amazing, isn't it?" He smiled, stopped, and admired it, too. "Every day, it looks a little different, you know. The light changes; the skies vary, and the colors shift from week to week. I like to stop by several times a year, just to take it in. It's one of my favorite views in the world."

"I bet." I marveled at it for another minute. "How did you ever find this place?"

"Oh, I didn't, really. The land belonged to my grandparents on the Dekker side. We grew up on the West Coast, but my mom was a teacher and missed her family. So, she'd bring my brother and me here for a month or two on summer break each year. It was more or less our summer camp."

"This must have been an endless paradise for a little kid. All that land to explore."

"Pretty much. Some of the best days of my childhood were spent floating on a tube in that creek or playing King of the Orchard with my brother."

"King of the Orchard?"

He grinned. "You know. . . climb up the apple trees, then try to knock each other down." He pointed to the scar above his eye. "Loser falls first."

"*Oh my God.* How do boys *ever* survive to adulthood?"

"Barely, Sammy. Just barely." He chuckled. "Anyway, when my grandparents got too old to manage the land, they were gonna sell it for development. So, I bought it instead. Took a while to figure out what to do with it, but I decided a business on-site would make sure it got maintained. I converted the house into a restaurant and built the cabins. Replaced some of the failing sections of orchard with grape vines. We make all the cider and wine. Buy food from local farmers to support the restaurant. It's been a fun project."

"I *love* a fun project."

"I get that impression." He laughed and nodded in the direction of the restaurant. "Speaking of which, let's keep moving. I really do want your opinion on the place."

We resumed our walk down the dirt road with that stunning backdrop at our side. Eventually, we arrived at the split-rail gate and found a single SUV still in the parking lot, its hatchback ajar.

The screen door of La Fermata squeaked open, and a tall, scrawny man in a chef's apron emerged. He glanced our way as he trudged to the lot hefting an ungainly box. "Cabin unlocked, Gabe? Got supper for ya'."

"Should be, Wyatt. Need a hand?" Gabe trotted toward him, trying to catch up, and I followed.

"Nawp, I'm good." The man loaded his SUV with the bulky cargo.

Gabe tried to peek in the box. "What's tonight's treat?"

"Italian mostly. Summer veggies are comin in. Tryin to highlight em." Wyatt closed the hatch and peeled the apron from his scant frame. He finally turned our way, dragging the crumpled smock across his sweaty forehead. "Who's yer friend?"

"Oh, my bad, Wyatt. This is Sammy. She's helping with the re-design."

"Good to meet ya'." He gave my hand a quick shake and turned abruptly, heading to the driver's-side door. "Listen, Gabe, I gotta run, but tell me if you like the dishes. Could be specials next week."

"Will do."

Wyatt climbed in his car, opened the split rail gate, and drove off toward the cabins, kicking up thick puffs of dust in his wake.

I couldn't help but laugh. "Isn't the old saying never trust a skinny chef?"

"Pff. That man's a sorcerer in the kitchen."

"I'll believe it when I taste it."

"Yes you will."

***

Gabe guided me through his grandparents' old home, now a restaurant that blended modern, rustic, and homey vibes. We sampled everything like Goldilocks: nibbling at appetizers, perching on the barstools, lounging at the outdoor tables. I busily snapped pictures and took measurements while he described the current customer experience and what he really wanted it to be. He hoped for a setting where people could feel connected to the mountains and each other. A place where folks could rest while enjoying delicious food and wine. Of course, the restaurant also had to be enticing enough to coax tourists and locals to make the drive from town. La Fermata was thoughtfully laid out, but nothing was ever optimized. We could surely find ways to better align the design and his vision. After logging impressions and recording a few voice memos on my phone, I promised to provide ideas once I could think it through.

I tucked my phone back in my pocket as we walked out the old farmhouse's front door. "I know you don't have the work product yet, but taking measurements and doing the consultation is probably enough for a free concert, right? I bet you're just dying to play 'Shivering Bridge.'"

"Is that your favorite?"

"One of them."

The breeze blew a wisp of hair across my eyes, and Gabe peeled it away gently. The casual gesture sent sparks across my skin. *How were his hands always so warm? And charged?*

"Well, I happen to like playing 'Shivering Bridge,' so you're in luck. Guitar's at the cabin though. Why don't we walk back."

We crossed the empty parking lot alone, with only the cicadas and a hot July breeze keeping us company. The bustle of activity at Gabe's property had finally died down. Even his ever-present security was out of sight.

"Where's Oscar?" I asked.

"Wherever he wants to be. Once the visitors are gone, he's off duty."

"*I'm* a visitor."

He flashed me a playful grin. "*You* don't count."

We strolled down the long dirt road toward the cabins, passing through a grove of apple trees before entering the vineyard.

The view never waned in its beauty. Rows and rows of climbing plants, heavy with fruit, surrounded us on the brightly lit hillside. "You know, I've never actually seen grapes up close on the vine like this. And I lived in California for a while. Pretty silly."

He stopped, looked at me, surprised, then reached for my hand. "Well, let's not waste another moment. Come, my lady." He led me through a break between the fields, up the gentle slope of the land.

We climbed through soft grass into what was clearly a working portion of the farm. A pop-up canopy stood between the fields, shading a cooler and a few camping chairs. In the distance, tractors and attachments rested beneath an open pole barn.

"Are the field crews here today?"

"They were earlier, but Oscar gave them the afternoon off. Really, the whole operation is supposed to be shut down when I visit. Bit of a miscommunication today."

We turned down one of the rows, where vines stretched above our heads, creating a sense of shelter. Thin tendrils reached for the sky, nearly translucent in the sunlight, and bundles of plump fruit hung in a kaleidoscope of shades from chartreuse to pink to violet.

I took a cluster of grapes in my fingers. "What variety are these?"

"Cabernet. They're ripening right now. That's why the colors are so mixed up. But they'll turn a deep bluish purple by harvest time." He pointed to the next field. "The grapes up ahead are chardonnay. They ripen gold with hints of bronze. They're always changing—and always pretty."

We reached the end of the row, where a gap between the fields allowed a clear view down the hill and across the valley to the mountains. I leaned forward against the slanted wooden post anchoring the end of the trellis, letting my hands brush against the soft leaves and tendrils of the vines. How could you not stop and admire such a spectacular landscape?

When I turned after a moment, I found Gabe studying me intently. He held his hands up at eye level, his fingers forming an imaginary viewfinder. He squinted one eye closed and tilted his head to look through it. "Now *that* is a *very* pretty picture." He dropped his hands and shook his head gently. "Marco's a lucky guy."

What a strange thing for him to say. Why would he look at me like that then comment about Marco? "Wait. What makes Marco lucky?"

"Well, probably lots of things, but to have you as a wife is what I meant. I hope he appreciates it."

My world stilled.

He thought I was married to Marco? What on earth had I said to make him think that?

I tried to recall our conversations, and memories flitted through my mind: Gabe asking me about our partnership as we sipped wine by the fire light, Marco's angry reaction when he found us squeezed together by the brewery offices.

Is this why Gabe had twice walked away from me when his hands were practically on my body? Was his rejection of me at the rooftop bar all a misunderstanding?

If so, it was time to clear it up. "Gabe, Marco is *not* my husband."

"Husband. Partner." He gestured with his hands as if to brush away the difference. "Whatever you want to call it. I respect existing relationships."

Had he wanted me the whole time? Was he just deferring to what he thought was a marriage? I wet my lips as heat and anticipation skittered through my belly.

"Gabe—" I worked to keep my voice steady—"Marco's my partner, but only in business."

Gears turned behind his eyes.

"He's marrying his boyfriend this fall. Gabe. . . I'm *single*."

A sly smile crept across his lips, and his eyebrows crooked up. "Well, this day just got better."

Oh my God.

Weeks of lust I'd been trying to tame broke loose, surging freely through my body. The atmosphere took on a palpable charge, and my senses sharpened.

Gabe leaned against a trellis post, bathed in afternoon light. Golden warmth illuminated his skin and highlighted blond wisps of color in his light brown hair. The clusters of grapes around him all but glowed. *He* all but glowed, for that matter.

"Come here, Sammy." His voice was low, husky.

Keeping my distance from him was a challenge. Drawing near was simple. All I had to do was stop resisting. I crossed the soft grass until I was close enough to feel his body heat.

Gabe traced his fingers, light as feathers, up my arms, across my shoulders, and along the sensitive skin of my neck. Then he cradled my face in his palms and lowered his sun-warmed lips to mine, gentle but sure.

It felt like the dawn breaking—like a flourish of brilliant color bursting over the horizon.

I leaned into his kiss, pressing myself against the hearty planes of his chest as his hands sifted through my hair. An exhilarating wave of pleasure enveloped me as Gabe's tongue twisted against mine—demanding, taking, drawing me in.

His hands explored the contours of my body, but their exact path was a mystery, because beneath their roving touch, all my cells roared to life at once, swarming fizzy and weightless beneath my skin. My fists were in his hair, and we were clasped tightly enough together that I felt every pulse as he stiffened against me.

When we moaned at the same time, all gentleness melted away. Suddenly, the hem of my dress was over my hips as his strong hands cupped my ass. He hauled me against him—too hard—and we stumbled back into the trellis, laughing as broken grapes splashed our skin.

My fantasies on the long drive to Creekside had been *wildly* deficient.

I hadn't imagined the taste of wine on his tongue or the thrill of his powerful response to my curves. Hadn't fathomed the feeling of being pinned against Gabe's body in the lush vineyard or just how consumed I would be by the fire of his touch.

My hands moved with hunger and impatience over the muscles of his sturdy arms and back, down the sides of his chest, over the curves of his backside. I was becoming impossibly aroused, and the evidence of his desire pressed urgently against my belly.

"Dear God, do I love this dress," he mumbled, his hands everywhere: under it, over it, stroking my body through the thin fabric.

I stepped back, ready to burst into flames. If my lack of clarity earlier had caused us frustration, I could make up for it now.

"You like this dress?" I stepped out of my sandals and pulled the garment's thin straps past the edge of my shoulders. "Hope you're not attached to it." I let the entire thing fall to the earth, and stood beneath the open sky, wearing only a tiny thong and a light coating of freckles.

His erection strained against his jeans. "Here, let me help you out there." He tugged my panties off quickly, gripped my waist in his broad hands, and pushed my back against the grapevines at the edge of the row.

My eyes fluttered open, taking in paradise—an endless vista of fields, hills, and light.

His tortuous kisses trailed down my neck, my breasts, my belly. "Hold on to the trellis, Sammy."

I did as he asked, grabbing the vines and wires—whatever I could get ahold of.

His kisses dropped even lower, and pleasure exploded through my body.

I laid my head back against the grape leaves, curling my fingers tightly around the vines and wires. The blazing southern sun spread a feverish heat across my breasts, and my mind emptied of everything but overwhelming sensation.

Gabe's relentless attention continued as I melted into a limp, senseless tremor of need.

His skilled tongue and broad fingers had me teetering on the edge, but not crossing it, and the sweet torture continued until I finally just begged. "I need you in me... *Please*... I need you in me to come."

Gabe didn't hesitate. "Yes, ma'am."

He took off his shirt like it was on fire and wrangled the shoes from his feet. After retrieving a condom from his jeans' pocket, he dropped the remainder of his clothes to the ground. "You have a good grip on that thing?" His voice was raspy, urgent.

"Yes." I tightened my hold as he boosted me up with a grunt.

A moment later, we were locked together, the furnace of his body merged with mine. I leaned back into the vines for support as he tested a few tentative, shimmering strokes. Our balance held, and soon, when he seemed confident he wouldn't hurt me, he drove into me with more power. As the exquisite sensation unfurled, his grunts and my cries of pleasure followed his rhythm. I wrapped my legs around him, holding onto the trellis for dear life while he powered into me greedily, filling me up.

"So close," I gasped. "I'm so close."

He immediately picked up steam, rocking my body back and forth into the soft grape leaves.

My mind completely left me—replaced by friction and pull, muscle and power, give and take. And heat. So much heat. A rising, throbbing pleasure expanded inside me as I edged toward oblivion.

Gabe heaved erratic breaths and moaned garbled expletives to the heavens.

At the sound of his voice, so thick with want, I finally shattered, breaking into a million quivering pieces, unable to hold back my screams.

Gabe's entire body tensed as he drove away the last of his desires. He gave a final hard push, a deep guttural sound escaping him.

When he collapsed against me, and gravity took the burden of my weight back, we clung together against the trellis. He buried his face in my hair, his stubbly cheek resting against mine. His heart pounded through the wall of his chest, and our bodies rested, overwhelmed—rendered temporarily unmovable by release.

Time slipped by as we found our way back to the world, and eventually in the distance, a creature rustled through the vines. Only the sound of our breathing followed, still slightly labored.

"It's just a deer or a fox," he finally mumbled. His body was a motionless weight against me.

A thought found its way to the surface of my pleasure-drunk brain. "Could that deer or fox be named Oscar?"

That got his attention. He craned his head up and looked around. "Um. . . I don't think so, but maybe we should get dressed just in case."

***

We made our way back to his cabin at a leisurely pace. When we arrived, we freshened up, then Gabe met me on the porch with two bottles of cold cider in his hands. He popped the tops off and handed me one. "Here you go. One of our bestsellers. A hard pumpkin cider. Good stuff."

We plunked down on the rocking chairs and took long sips. The cider tasted like a fall festival—like apples, pumpkins, sweetness, and spice, with just enough bite. After a busy afternoon in the Southern heat, it was perfect.

Halfway through our drinks, I remembered the rest of the world. "Can you give me a minute?"

I ducked back into my cabin, checked my texts and emails to make sure no emergencies had arisen, and for a moment, marveled that it actually hadn't been hard to get through the day. I had been so certain that anxiety would keep me from ever leaving Philadelphia again, but it didn't seem to be the case. I sighed with deep relief, then double checked my text to Tina from earlier in the day. She had merely replied that she was fine, tied up with cub scouts, and would talk to me later.

Content that all was right with the world, I returned to the porch to enjoy the afterglow and the changes in the sky as the sun sank below the mountains, melting into a sea of color.

19

DESSERT

"So, I'm not sure what you like? Wyatt left a vegetarian lasagna and some sort of elaborate risotto." Gabe sifted around in the fridge. "Um, if you're lactose intolerant, I think we're screwed."

"No, we're good. I eat everything. You pick."

He turned on the oven and put the lasagna in before coming back to join me at a small wooden table nestled between a kitchen and sleeping area in the efficiency-style cabin.

Though small, it was a beautiful space. The log walls were a rich, deep cedar, almost the color of whiskey, and matching wood floors created a feeling of all-over warmth. A sumptuous king-size bed abutted the rear wall, and soothing acoustic music emanated from a simply furnished kitchenette. At the center of the dining table, a short hurricane glass sheltered the dancing flame of a candle. Gabe retrieved cloth napkins and simple silverware to make a setting for two.

"Thanks for dinner," I said.

"Thank Wyatt. I'm just the slide-it-in-the-oven guy." Gabe grabbed a few more bottles of hard cider from the fridge. He popped them open, handed me one, and eased into the chair opposite me. "You know, you really surprised me today with the whole 'being single' thing."

"And yet you had a condom handy." I grinned.

"Hey, I said I was surprised." A devilish spark lit his eyes. "Doesn't mean I wasn't hoping."

"Well, I might have been hoping for a few things, too. So, I'm glad you were prepared."

He squinted. "But didn't you tell me you and Marco started the brewery when you found out you were pregnant?"

"Oh, well, that's true." *So, that was part of the confusion.* "But that's just when I found out about Meghan. She was conceived when I was living in California."

"And Marco wasn't in California?"

"No. He was at a hole-in-the-wall microbrewery in Philadelphia, building our future product line."

"Got it." He leaned back in his seat and took a swig from his bottle. "Is Meghan's father involved today?"

"Unfortunately, no." I shrugged. "Honestly, though, I get it. We were both so young and got rich quick. Weird things happened."

"Hope you didn't rob a bank." Gabe raised his eyebrows in mock concern.

"We did *not* rob a bank," I said, amused at the silly comment. "We were just out of college, working at a startup in Silicon Valley. The jobs paid poorly—mostly equity compensation, which I didn't even understand at the time. If you had roommates though, the paychecks were enough to live on, and you could work on cutting-edge stuff, which was exciting." I shifted in the chair a bit, my legs tight and aching from the morning bike ride. "Anyway, the product we were developing sold for an absurd sum of money, and that's when we learned what equity comp was. I mean, we were literally eating ramen noodles for dinner when we found out we were rich as Midas."

"Hmm. Not a rough start to your career."

"Stupid lucky is more like it."

"And you moved back to Philly?"

"Crazy, right? I had a golden ticket, and I chose to go home." I shrugged. "But I really missed my family, and I figured, with that much in the bank, I could take some time to see what was next, maybe get a master's degree."

I rubbed my neck, thinking of the best way to say the next part. "Meghan's father, on the other hand. . . he took off. He said he'd hit the jackpot and wasn't going to waste it. When I called to tell him I was pregnant, he didn't even respond. He just hung up. I'm guessing spit-up and diapers weren't part of his lottery-winning-lifestyle vision. Anyway, I never heard from him again."

"That's really shitty." Gabe's voice sounded sincere. "And what a shame. Look what he missed out on."

"Yup. Meghan's a great kid. Anyway, it's ancient history. What about you and Trevor's mom?"

He picked at the label on his cider bottle. "That's a bit of ancient history, too. Her name's Summer. She was sort of a groupie, who became a serious girlfriend. When we found out she was pregnant, we got really excited. Starry-eyed about the idea of a new life. We both got cleaned up, quit partying, bought a portable crib for the tour bus. We had lots of ideas about how it would be." He sighed heavily, shifting his weight in his chair. "After Trevor was born, though, she went right back to using. I tried to get her help, but she didn't want it."

He crossed his arms in a defensive posture. "I don't really like to think about it. . . but, when he was eighteen months old, I found him trying to climb out of his crib in a room where she was passed out, a pharmacy's worth of pills spilled on the floor." He looked me in the eye. "That was the last time she saw him for a while."

Chills skittered up my bare arms. "Sounds pretty scary." I couldn't fathom a parent with substance-abuse issues trying to raise a toddler. It was hard enough to keep them safe when you had all your faculties. It would be impossible if you were impaired.

"It took a while to figure out how it was going to work. I had a lot of childcare help on tour for a few years, and eventually, Summer got herself cleaned up. Got married. Became steady and stable." He leaned forward on the table, rubbing the back of his neck. "By the time Trevor started school, we settled into a routine. She kept him during the school year. He would come with me over the summer. It probably helped that the whole band sort of grew up over the course of those years. Marriages. Children." He leaned back in his chair. "Maybe a concert tour isn't the ideal place for a kid, but we managed to keep things reasonably family-friendly. It worked out."

I smiled at him. "Sounds like you went on quite a journey when you became a dad. Trevor's lucky he had you."

The sky had fully darkened outside, and the wonderful scent of the warming lasagna grew stronger by the minute.

I thought of the million things I didn't know about him yet. "Where do you live when you're not on tour? Here in North Carolina?" I set my elbows on the table, propping my chin on my hands.

"No, I just visit occasionally. . . I guess the place I've always considered my permanent home is on the Columbia River Gorge in rural Oregon—near the town of Hood River."

I couldn't imagine *considering* a place my home. "You don't seem so sure."

"Well, lately, that house is getting spooky quiet. My brother and parents have moved away, and Trevor's not around much anymore. Makes me wonder what I'm doing there sometimes."

"You're used to seeing Trevor a lot?"

"For sure. When Summer got straightened out, she moved to Portland to be close. Her home is maybe an hour away. So even during the school year, Trevor would come stay on weekends if I was home. We'd go windsurfing or hiking or try some crazy home improvement project. And he hated math, which I'm good at, so I was sort of his unofficial tutor. By senior year, though, he just wanted to spend time with his girlfriend, and now, he's off at college. So, if I don't have guests, the house feels. . . I don't know. . .kind of hollow." He shrugged.

Just thinking about it was a knife to the chest. "I can't imagine."

"Well, get ready girl, 'cause it's coming. Do you think a lot about your next chapter? What you'll do when Meghan heads off to school? I mean, presuming she's a college-type kid."

"Oh, she definitely is. I'm sort of hoping she'll stay close, though. There are so many great schools in Philly."

He tilted his head. "Is that what *she* wants?"

"Um, I'm not sure." I could barely be honest with myself about it.

"Okay." Gabe eyed me skeptically. The music strummed in the background, and he took a swig of cider. Then he set the bottle down and clapped his hands with finality. "Well, onward. Let's talk about something more fun. What do you wanna do tomorrow? The mountains await, and it's supposed to be a gorgeous day."

Grateful for the change in conversation, I bought right in. "Any recommendations?"

"Oh my gosh. The hiking around here is epic, and whitewater rafting is super-fun, if you're feeling adventurous. A cousin of mine has a horseback riding place a few miles away, too. She takes you through the woods and past little waterfalls. Or we could go for a drive—"

I shot him a look.

"Oh," he chuckled. "I forgot. The lady does *not* want to sit in a car." He shrugged. "Well, any of that sound good? Or do you wanna aim for something more mellow?"

With such an amazing menu of options, it was tough to choose, but the creek in town looked so appealing today—sunlit and vibrant. "You said you liked to go tubing in the creek when you were a kid. Do you still enjoy it?"

"Sammy, it's one of my favorite things ever. You wanna have a float day?"

"Yeah."

"Done. . . I love it." He stretched his well-muscled arms over his head, cracking his back. "So, how dedicated are you to the anti-car vibe? Wanna bike down to the creek again? Burn off some energy first?"

"Well, I dunno." I squinted my eyes at him playfully. "Are you gonna pull a cheap shot on the way home again? Beat me at a race I don't know I'm in? Cheaters are so uncool, you know."

"Nope. I'm gonna beat you fair and square. You're going down, girl." His diabolical grin crinkled the crow's feet around his sparkling, butterscotch eyes. I would never understand how men consistently grew sexier with age, but they sure did. The candlelight flickered a golden radiance across his sun-kissed skin and his eyes shone like polished amber. To me, he was luminous.

An electronic timer went off, prompting Gabe out of his chair and snapping me out of my revery.

I got up to help. "What can I do?"

He pulled the steaming lasagna from the oven and took a quick peek beneath the foil, uncovering it to cool. "Do you want a salad? I think there are some in the fridge."

I took a look and pulled out a few prepared plates of dark leafy greens covered with berries, cheese crumbles, and nuts. I found a jar labeled "Vinaigrette" and set that on the counter as well.

We munched the salads while the lasagna cooled, then dove into the gooey pasta. The al dente noodles were steaming, the vegetables were fresh and flavorful, and long strings of melted cheese trailed behind our forks.

"Oh, my lord, Gabe. This afternoon with you was pretty amazing, but I think I might run off with your chef."

He smiled. "Yeah? Well, you're no slouch yourself, but that cognac-aged porter you served me at your brewery a few weeks ago? I dunno, I might have to run off with your brewmaster."

"Well, my brewmaster is Marco. So have fun with that."

We laughed and dove back into the amazing food.

When dinner was over, we cleared the dishes, and Gabe found the dessert his chef had left—a flourless chocolate torte covered in fresh raspberries and decadent curls of dark chocolate.

He set it on the table, along with a small dish of whipped cream, and pried the cork from a tall, dark bottle. "Do you like port?" He poured a small glass for each of us.

"It's a great sip."

"Hmm." His gaze on my face simmered, and I felt a blush creep into my cheeks. "Sipping is one way to enjoy it, but I've got another idea."

He scooched his chair toward mine and dipped the cork in his glass of port. He stroked it down the sensitive skin of my neck before pressing open-mouthed kisses against the trail of sweet wine.

The luscious pull on my skin radiated pleasure, and I lay my head back as the magical sensation unfurled. Coupled with the buzz of the cider, the coziness of the cabin, and the comforting draw of Gabe's company, it felt borderline hypnotic.

When he pulled away, I breathed a heavy sigh, opening my eyes. "So, that's how you enjoy port? I've been doing it wrong." I dipped the cork in my own glass. "I should practice."

I traced the cork down his throat and lavished kisses along the sweet sheen of liquid it left behind. His skin was warm, and the luscious flavor of caramel and dark berries spread across my tongue.

Everything about him was enticing—magnetic—and I scooted onto his lap to get closer. I continued kissing his neck until he exhaled a soft groan, his hands caressing my figure. I put my lips to his ear. "I like to hear you make that sound, you know."

His eyes took on a drunken quality, and he grabbed the cork to spread more port on me. His mouth was more insistent this time—a warm, demanding tug that shot electricity to all the right places.

"You know, I hear port goes well with chocolate." I plucked one of the chocolate curls from the torte. After softening its edges in the candle flame, I stroked a rich, sugary trail along the most tender part of his throat.

His eyes fell closed, and he grunted with satisfaction as I worked my mouth across his skin.

Anticipation simmered in my blood.

"You know, Gabe, these whiskers are hard to work around. I think I'm gonna need access to some smoother flesh."

I got up and carried the candle and the chocolate torte to the bedside table. He caught on quickly and followed me with the whipped cream and a glass of port, the cork bobbing gently on its surface.

"That t-shirt and jeans aren't gonna work. Can we get a little more skin showing?" I tugged at his top, and he helped lift it over his head while I worked at the button and zipper of his jeans.

Our clothes were off in a flurry, and he pushed me down on the bed, his erection digging into the flesh by my hip bone.

"Un-uh. Wait," I said as he sucked kisses down my neck. "I think it's still my turn."

He'd selflessly turned me into a puddle of illogical craving today in the vineyard. I wanted to make him lose control, too.

I rolled him onto his back, then reached for another chocolate curl. After warming it in the candle flame, I traced the melting sweetness beside the short hairs of his happy trail. Unhurried, I followed the chocolate's path with my tongue—from the yielding flesh of his belly to the throbbing pulse of his hard-on—allowing my hands to explore the contours and ridges of his sturdy frame while I took my kisses lower. I smeared a dollop of whipped cream on him and slid him in my mouth.

The groan he emitted was louder than before, and his hips lifted slightly. His cottony sheets tugged beneath my knees as he squeezed and knotted them in his fists.

I surrendered myself to pleasing him, relaxing and taking him in, focusing on his sounds and the response of his body. He was warm and full in my mouth, and my free hand wandered, stroking and cradling every sensitive inch of him.

He grew more and more delirious. *"Fuck. . . Sammy. . ."*

His breath accelerated and grew heavy, and his muscles started to twitch and tense. He was getting very tightly wound up, and I knew I had to shift gears soon if I didn't want this to be over.

And it couldn't be yet. I needed more.

Releasing him gently, I worked kisses from his belly to his throat, letting my breasts dangle against his skin. I brought my hips astride his and rested myself gently against his cock.

"Sweet Jesus," he moaned. He reached in the bedside stand for a condom and rolled it on.

I eased him into me, then gripped the wrought iron headboard, so we could rock together in slow, easy waves.

Sex in the vineyard had been all kinds of things: frenzied, impulsive, mind-melting. But it hadn't been an opportunity to savor. I was merely lucky to have remained upright, to have kept a grip on the trellis. Here, though, on a soft mattress, I could enjoy the luxury of his body.

And a luxury it was. He was a thick, intoxicating, aching heft inside of me.

My nipples were in his mouth, one by one, and his hands consumed my curves. I concentrated on a steady rhythm, despite the electricity that flickered beneath my skin and the shimmering dissolution that merged my cells and nerves.

I fought for time to enjoy him: the terrain of his rugged shoulders, the fine scruff of hair on his chest, the feeling of his thick torso between my thighs. His was not a show business physique, not a ropy mass of unyielding muscle. Rather, it was manly and real, with softness around the edges, some bulk to squeeze—hearty and tangible in a comforting way that showed he walked the same ground, indulged in the same earthly delights we all did. I couldn't get enough.

'"Sammy. . ." He brought his hot breath to my ear. "So good."

Rough and raspy around the edges, his voice sizzled like fire inside me. His sexy, comforting timbre had been my companion for years. But now, it was a deep, breathy whisper between us. It was my name on the tip of his tongue.

He lifted his hips into me, and a rising tide of sensation eroded the tether between my mind and body.

I struggled to hold out, to enjoy the sound of his mumblings, to absorb the feeling of him a bit longer.

But Gabe was full steam ahead and growing frantic in his touch. He massaged my ass, my breasts, everything within reach before opening his eyes —determination set in his features. Then he licked his thumb and anchored it between my legs, pressing firm, wet circles against my most sensitive nerves.

It was a mainline, bullseye, direct hit to my nervous system, and I lost it. My brain unraveled and my hips took on their own life.

"*Yes…*" Gabe strengthened his grip on my ass with his free hand. "*Yes… Go crazy.*" He brought me down hard against him again and again.

All control disappeared.

I raised my voice, shouting incoherently. The world disintegrated into a bucking, crazed, uncontrollable shaking until my nerves finally detonated, and a flood of pleasure gushed through me.

He kept on, powering into me brutally, before coming with an inhuman moan.

I collapsed forward on his chest, with the thunderous beat of his heart in my ear.

Except for the pounding beneath his ribs and deep, huffing breaths, he was motionless. "Fucking amazing," he muttered.

"Yeah…" Every cell in my body buzzed, heavy as lead, and I kissed his chest, my brain lost in a fog.

When I could eventually move again, I rolled off him, staring in a daze at the candlelight dancing across the ceiling.

He was so much more than I had expected. In every respect. His body was perfect for me, and his touch was confident and attentive. Plus, he was funnier than I remembered. Playful and intelligent. And—by some miracle—our conversation was so normal. So easy and down to earth. Even if nothing else good came from the trip, this feeling now—being sexed into utter bliss by such a stellar specimen of a man—it would be enough.

When our bodies finally settled, Gabe got up and fetched a couple forks from the kitchen counter. We passed the chocolate torte back and forth, finishing a last few bits of sweetness before we were too sated for anything more.

Gabe rose to turn off the lights at that point, came back to bed, and blew out the candle. He spooned my naked figure. "Thanks for coming all this way, Sammy." He buried his nose in my hair.

"Thanks for having me."

He murmured a sleepy chuckle. "I'll have you *anytime.*"

We laughed, and he pulled me tight against him.

I'd been cold my whole life, always sleeping in a frothy pile of comforters, but he radiated warmth, and I snuggled in.

If there were problems in the world, at that moment, I couldn't imagine them.

20

Still Shots

THE OPPORTUNIST

Absolute gold.

The photos were so much better than anyone could hope for. Maybe a tiny bit grainy in spots, but the people were identifiable, and the explicit details were everywhere. In some shots, you could practically measure his girth, and her grooming regimen left nothing to the imagination.

Maybe the content was enough to piss you off a little. After all, who knew she was such a slut? By the same token, at this point, who cared? Why bother working the rest of your life? For that matter, why struggle at all? This is the way it was done.

The email path was already secure, and the list of demands drafted. All that was left to do was hit send.

<h1 style="text-align:center">21</h1>

FEVER

SAMMY

The cheerful, trilling jabber of songbirds announced first light, piercing my slumber. I squinted in the direction of my dormer windows, only to find an unfamiliar space. Light floated through faint dust motes, filtering in from the wrong side of the room.

Gabe's cabin.

The mattress shifted as warm muscles wrapped my torso and a firm body pressed heat into my back.

It all returned in a rush as I stroked his arm gently, reveling in the contact.

While my brain bumbled awake, I gazed at the subtle shifts in morning light washing over the knotted grain of the cabin's cedar walls. Gabe adjusted his position again, turning over to nuzzle the pillows, and a muted snore ruffled the stillness.

I closed my eyes once more, stealing a few more minutes of nirvana in the cozy cloud of his bed.

My morning mouth begged for a toothbrush, however, and I badly needed a restroom and shower. Before long, I could no longer ignore the plea of biology. I snuck out from beneath the comforter, got dressed, and slipped back to my unlocked cabin.

A hot shower released the kinks in my back and loosened the tight knots in my legs. After a thorough steaming, I set a pot of coffee to brew then dressed in shorts, a strappy blouse, and yesterday's sandals.

The plan was to spend another day here—to float in the creek and maybe go over design ideas if I could draft a few. That meant twenty-four more hours of outdoorsy, artsy time with Gabe.

Heaven.

The irresistible scent of coffee permeated the cabin, and I checked my phone and booted up my computer while it finished its noisy percolation. I'd missed no texts from the prior night, and there was nothing new today so far, but it was still early.

I took my laptop and a steaming mug out to the cabin's porch, where I could enjoy the view while I worked. Humid air hung across the dewy vineyard, and low angles of morning sunshine filtered through the crops. Carolina Wrens continued their warbling gossip, and a construction crew of woodpeckers hammered hollow, echoing drills into the towering treetops of the surrounding pines.

I cracked open my laptop and sipped coffee, thinking through a few to-dos. The brewery merited at least a little attention, so I checked network security, moderated the social sites, and took a quick peek at how the July numbers were landing. Sales were still poor and expenses were still elevated. *Dang it.* I truly had hoped to see progress.

Maybe Gabe was right. I should get boots on the ground in Madison and Charlotte. More than a day had passed since I left home, and I still felt good. Strong. Maybe I could pull it off. Actually, now that I thought about it, I might be able to squeeze in a Charlotte visit before returning North. The brewery could easily be within a couple hours' drive of La Fermata

The idea was enticing, but for now, I refocused on Gabe's restaurant. *One thing at a time.* I opened my favorite design software and roughed in La Fermata's existing patio, porch, and indoor areas, as well as the approximate surrounding acreage. I transcribed my voice memos into notes in the margin and uploaded the photos I'd taken yesterday, pinning them to the software's bulletin board feature for reference.

Footsteps on the porch signaled someone else awake, and I looked up into Gabe's sleep- crinkled face. He raised his coffee cup in a simple gesture of cheers, then eased himself onto a rocking chair. He set his coffee on a small wooden side table and laid the guitar across his lap. "Mind if I join you?"

"Sounds perfect."

Gabe plucked idly at the strings, circling around a melody I hadn't heard before while I gathered photos and product links for design inspiration. Eventually, he played "Shivering Bridge", and I shot him a warm smile. Then he strummed another favorite of mine, "Eight Lilies." *Gorgeous.*

The sun slowly rose higher in the sky, casting away shadows and basking bright, nourishing light across the vineyard. After a while, Gabe stood up and stretched, then walked over and took a peek at my computer. "When do I get to see?"

"Not much to look at yet. Just gathering ideas." I tilted the computer his way. "But I'm thinking there might be two ways to go, and one would require very little capital. I'm guessing you don't need to blow your budget on this."

"Well, that's good news," he said.

"How do I share the designs with you when I'm done? I don't think I'll have them finished today."

"Oh, Charlie's your man for sure. Just call him, and he'll set everything up."

That stung.

We're not intimate enough to swap phone numbers yet? Or emails? Disappointed and frankly a little ticked, I turned my attention back to the screen. In fact, I snapped the laptop shut and picked up my coffee instead. Why give him free labor if he couldn't even trust me with an email address?

He leaned against the post of the porch then, studying me. "By the way, Sammy, I think you should know—this must be a world record."

I cut my eyes to him as I blew on the surface of my topped-off mug. "Oh yeah? How so?"

"Well, as far as I can tell, you're a fan of my music, right?"

"Um. . . *yeah*. I mean, this free performance I've been getting all morning is gonna be the highlight of my year, I'm pretty sure."

"Oh, *really?*" He raised an eyebrow. "*This* is the highlight? I might need to drag you back to bed and change that."

I was still annoyed, but heat rose to my cheeks anyway, a deep blush no doubt coloring my face. I sighed. "Fine. I stand corrected. . . And pleasured. There are indeed better experiences from the trip."

"That's more like it." He playfully tugged a strand of my hair. "Anyway, like I was saying, I think this is a world record for the most time I've spent around a fan without being asked to take a selfie."

Interesting.

"Well. . . " I blew on my coffee, considering the best response. "A picture would be fun. . . but I didn't think you'd appreciate being asked."

He tilted his head. "So you didn't ask?"

I shrugged.

"Well, you're remarkable in all kinds of ways, aren't you?"

"Not remarkable. Just enjoying your company. I don't need a photo op."

"Well. . . you might get one anyway." His expression was amused. Irresistible. "Because frankly, at this point, I think *I'd* like a selfie with *you*. I want a way to look at your pretty face after you drive away and leave me."

Such drama. I rolled my eyes. "I'm sure my departure's your biggest concern."

"Hey, you don't know. Maybe it is." He stretched his hand my way. "Come on. Indulge me."

I set down my mug, took his hand, and let him lead me to the grape vines. He put an arm around me and pulled me gently against him. He leaned his lips close to my ear. "To help preserve my sweet memories," he whispered.

The warm strength of his body stirred my blood. Staying angry when he held me close was too great a challenge. I gave in, at least for the moment. I laid my head back against his shoulder and hugged the arm he'd wrapped around my waist while he snapped a few pictures.

They turned out lovely, in an early-morning sort of way. Our hair was messy. I wore no makeup. Our smiles were relaxed, and the morning light was soft. Perfect really.

"Can you send them to me?" I asked.

He froze, his finger hovering over the touch screen. The look on his face told me plenty.

"Ah, let me guess, *Charlie* will send them to me." I made no effort to hide my annoyance and displeasure.

"Look, I'm happy to send these. I trust you with the photos. But it's got to be through Charlie. That's just a rule."

Nothing he said made the situation any better, and I leveled a hard gaze at him.

He scoffed. "Sammy, do you have *any* idea what happens when thousands of crazy people get access to your email? Or your cell? Or your *address* for that matter? People get angry, relationships sour, and this stuff gets released. Makes it very hard to function. So, this is just how I operate." He crossed his arms defensively.

"You don't trust me yet."

He sighed heavily, his frustration obvious. "I do. But I've trusted a lot of people, and I've been burned. A lot." He kicked at the dirt. "Look, I won't deny I've had fun, but, sometimes, I wish I'd found a more permanent relationship before all of this happened. Because the problem is, everyone in my orbit wants something sooner or later: money, fame, a ticket around the world. Or sometimes, women just want a fantasy and not a flawed, sweaty, idiotic guy. It's just been over and over again."

I was about to fire off a retort when my cell phone rang. "Hold on, Gabe." I took a few steps away for privacy and answered.

Meghan's voice came over the line. "Hey. Sorry to bug you."

I turned my gaze to the distant mountains and walked a few paces farther away. I didn't want my irritation with Gabe bleeding into my conversation with my daughter. "Hi, sweetie. I was gonna call soon. How's it going?"

"Fine. Do we have a key to Grandma's cottage?"

She knew better.

"We do. . . but you're not allowed in there when she's not home. You know that."

"She's home. She wants ice chips for her fever. So, I just need a key."

A flutter of nausea rose in my gut. *Why would this happen the one day I'm away?* "She has a fever?"

"I guess."

"Meghan, since when? She was fine yesterday evening."

"I dunno. She texted a little bit ago. I'm sure she's okay."

"Can you put her on the line?"

"Well, I *could* if you would tell me where the key is."

"Did you knock?"

"*Of course* I knocked."

"She didn't come to the door?" The humid morning air was suddenly difficult to breathe. "Can you see her through the window?"

"Yes, Mom. Relax. She's just sleeping. Are you gonna help me or not?"

My heart splashed frantically, and the world accelerated around me. My brain scrambled to keep up.

"Mom?"

What was she asking for?

"*Oh my God. Are you flipping out? I knew* you would do this. I shouldn't have called."

"*Wait, Meghan!* Don't hang up."

"Well, am I wasting my time?"

"I'm sorry. What do you need? Just tell me again." *Come on, Sammy. Listen.*

"The key. Mom, I *need* the *key.*"

"A key?" *Oh. To the cottage. Where was it?* It was so damn hard to breathe. *Think, Sammy, please.* "There's a spare on a Temple University keychain in my desk drawer."

Meghan's footsteps pounded up the stairs. The stiff wooden slides of the drawer whined, and papers shuffled.

"The center drawer, Mom? Or down in the filing cabinets?"

"The middle drawer. It should be *right* there."

I tried to stay present, but images of Mom flooded my mind: alone, red-faced, limp on her bed.

"Mom, there's nothing here but files and papers and junk."

Rationally, I knew this wasn't cause for panic. If Mom was in bad shape, she would have called me, not Meghan. She would have asked for more than ice chips. I clung desperately to that reality, tried to get oxygen.

But my internal alarm system didn't give one fig about rationality or reason. Panic was screaming bloody murder in my body, and my mind was descending into a muddled, whirring chaos.

What's real, Sammy? Please think! Is there another spare? Should she call 911?

At the thought of sirens, a tingling rush of blood drained from my face, and a fainting swell of lightheadedness left me wobbling. I grabbed the trellis for support.

Please body. Please chill out.

I tried calming words—tried every trick I'd been trained to use—but my brain's betrayal raged against me. My heart beat manically, and my stomach retched, burning my throat with bile.

Oh, God. Not that. Not here.

"Meghan, I'll call you back. Go pound on that door. *Wake her up!*"

The firestorm in my body was not backing down, and I knew I had minutes at best.

I ran back to the porch, grabbed my computer, and dashed into my cabin. A voice called behind me, but I only saw the route to escape. I tossed clothes and shoes in my bag, grabbed my purse, then looked around in futility—unable to remember what I needed, or what might still be in the cabin. I couldn't get air in my lungs, and I knew it would only get worse. I gave up and sprinted out the door.

"Sammy, what the hell's happening? *Slow down.*" Gabe suddenly swam into my field of vision. He squeezed my arms gently in his hands. "Slow down so I can help. What's wrong?"

I couldn't think clearly to explain— couldn't breathe—and I was aware of what a ridiculous mess I was. Acutely embarrassed, I ran to my car and fumbled with the driver's side door lock, struggling to get in. Hot tears spilled down my cheeks. This was the worst-case scenario, and I refused to vomit in front of him. *Absolutely refused.* But I didn't have much time.

"Sammy, stop. This is crazy!" He gripped my arm gently.

I needed to respond, but I couldn't get enough air for words. "Let me go," I finally gasped.

He did.

My hands shook as I stumbled into the driver's seat. I cranked the engine over, backed away from the cabins, and fled down the dirt road.

One hundred yards past the front gate of the property, I pulled over and threw up, sobbing and spitting sour acid on the roadside.

Why did this keep happening?

I knew there was nothing wrong. I knew everything *had* to be fine, but my body didn't care. Millenniums of primitive instinct were bathing my brain in chemicals that collapsed every bodily function into an overwhelming urge to flee. I was a prisoner to my own stupid chemistry.

I wiped my mouth on the back of my hand, got back in the car, and sped away, turning onto the long curving road that would lead me down the mountain and far away.

***

One other driver fueled up at the ancient gas station, but aside from his shuffling footsteps and the comforting sound of the burbling creek, everything was quiet. After my breathing finally calmed, this was the first pull-off I'd found, and I'd stopped to let my brain unscramble. The tears and nausea had subsided, and rational thoughts reemerged.

I closed my eyes to concentrate. *Take stock, Sammy. What's actually happening?*

I scavenged for facts: *Mom has a fever. Meghan's home with her. Mom needs ice chips. Her cottage is locked.*

My daughter needed to get into Mom's cottage. That had to be the first priority.

I dialed Meghan, and she answered quickly. "Mom. Are you okay? Sorry I was a jerk."

"I'm fine. Did Grandma answer her door?"

The muffled sound of Mom's raspy voice carried from the background. "Hand me that phone, Meghan." After a pause, Mom came through loud and clear. "Sammy, what's going on? I asked for ice chips, for Pete's sake, and Meghan says you're completely out of sorts."

"I'm calm now."

She coughed. "Good. You should be."

"Mom, how high is your fever?"

"Barely over one hundred. Nothing drastic. Sharon's sick, too. We played tennis this week. I'm sure I caught the same thing she did. It's not a big deal."

"Do you wanna call Dr. Hurwitz?"

"No, Sammy. I don't. I feel a little cruddy, but that's it. Meghan's here to help if I need anything."

"Okay." It was barely ten a.m. Even with stops, I should be able to get home by sunset. "Listen, I won't be home 'til eight or so. I'll call Tina and get her on standby."

"*What?...*" She coughed again. "Sammy, don't be silly! We're *fine.* Stay in Creekside. Find the best piece of property you can. Don't give up. This is *good* for you."

From her perspective, I'm sure it was a reasonable suggestion, but I didn't think my pride could bear returning to Gabe's right now. Plus, what if there was another update? What if Mom took a turn for the worse or my brain spiraled into hysteria again.

It wasn't workable.

"Thanks for the encouragement, but I think coming home is the right thing."

"Well. . . Sammy. . . don't do it for *my* sake."

I squeezed my eyes shut. *Who would I be doing it for? Meghan? Mom? Me? Or would it be the wrong choice for all three of us?* I had no idea anymore. All I knew for sure was that I needed to get back to my family—to the people I was responsible for.

"Thanks, Mom, but I'm coming home. Have Meghan call Tina if you guys need anything immediate."

"Are you sure, Sammy?"

I wasn't. "No. . . But it's what I'm doing. Love you." I ended the call.

I took a deep breath and wiped my nose one more time, trying to center myself. *What's next, Sammy?* Tina, of course. I need to get Tina on board.

I dialed her number.

She answered after a few rings, sounding haggard. "Hey, Sammy. . . Oh, Noah, *honey, no! Icky! Icky!. . .*"

"Everything okay over there?"

"The dog just puked. On the carpet. . . *No, Noah! Stop. . .* Hold on." She breathed more heavily, and noises crashed and clicked in the background. "Okay. Thank God for baby gates. Doing alright?"

"Not entirely."

"Worse than dog barf?"

She could still make me laugh. Even with tears and snot on my face. "Maybe not."

"That's what I thought." She slurped something, almost certainly coffee at this hour. "Listen, kinda nuts right now. Need something?"

"Well, I'm out of town, and Mom has a fever. I was hoping you could be on call 'til I get home."

"You're out of town?"

"Yeah."

"By yourself? Or did you finally go with Marco to check on construction?"

"Construction's done. I'm not with Marco. It's just me."

"Well, Sammy, that's great! I'm so happy for you!" Cabinets banged and running water shooshed in the background.

"Thanks. But I'm coming home. Can Meghan and Mom call you if they need something? I won't arrive 'til tonight."

"Sure. . . Where are you?"

"Um, down near the Smokies." It pained me to give an incomplete answer, but I wanted to respect Gabe's wishes. "There's a good expansion opportunity here."

"Wow. That's awesome! And of course I can help."

"You're a lifesaver." I really hadn't been keeping up with her as well as I should. "How are things with Andrew? Any developments?"

"*Ugh*, not remotely enough time for that topic. Listen, I've gotta go, Noah's doing the potty dance."

"Oh, run, run, run! Thanks, Tina."

She hung up.

Hearing Mom's voice helped so much. Knowing Tina was available for disaster coverage made a big difference, too.

I realized my mouth tasted horrible, and I rummaged through the car for my water bottle.

No luck.

Great. One more casualty from the trip, likely left back at the cabin.

I went into the gas station and bought some water and a sandwich, too. A little nutrition should help even me out.

I settled back into the driver's seat, rinsed my mouth, and put the food aside for a moment.

Ok, Sammy. Anything else? What else is real?

Unfortunately, one more big thing loomed. I just had a panic attack in front of Gabe and had run away with no explanation.

Tears of frustration leaked out, and I leaned over the steering wheel in defeat. I took another swig of water and blew my nose, wishing this would all just end.

I tried to comfort myself with the positives. After all, I'd managed to leave Philadelphia. In fact, I'd made it nine hours down the coast and another thirty-six hours after that before a minor meltdown that, in all fairness, was triggered by an *almost* reasonable fear. This was progress. Maybe not great—but progress.

My phone rang. I swiped my wet eyes and saw it was Charlie calling. *Should I let it go to voicemail?* It rang again while I hemmed. And again. Tempted as I was to avoid the call, I realized if I wanted any kind of ongoing relationship with Gabe, I had better pick up.

I caved.

"Hi, Charlie."

But it was Gabe's deep voice that answered. "Hey, Sammy. Charlie patched me through. Look, I'm worried about you. Can we come pick you up? Seems like you shouldn't be driving if you're so upset."

I prayed I didn't sound as wretched as I felt. "It's okay. I pulled over. I'm much calmer now."

"What happened? Who on earth called?"

I sniffed. "It was Meghan. Mom has a fever and wasn't answering her door. Meghan couldn't find the key. I think I have to get home. Sorry for the change in plans."

"Do you need to call 911? Is it bad?"

"No. Mom woke up. We talked. She's stable for now."

He was quiet a moment, and his next comment came out at half-speed. His voice was hard and uncertain—like there was a lot more on his mind than he was saying. "Sammy. . . I don't understand why you ran off."

Be careful here.

I knew I hadn't shared enough to make sense of my behavior, but what could I say? That Dad had died on the phone with me, begging for help? That I'd been out of town and unable to save him? That my brain set off five-alarm fires every time I got too far from my people, especially if there was trouble? It was way too much, but saying nothing would be worse. I had to share at least some of the truth.

I didn't see any choice other than to count on him being a real person who could cope with real human being stuff.

"Listen, I'm fully aware my behavior was unreasonable." I paused to muster courage. Gabe seemed to wait patiently. "The truth is. . . my dad died a few years ago. The circumstances were traumatic, and I was out of town when it happened." I took one more deep breath then plunged in all the way. "Anxiety attacks have been a problem for me ever since, especially if I try to travel or if something's wrong with my family. I know that's not good, but it's just what happens." My voice was cracking, and I fought to hold it together. "I'm embarrassed, and I'm really sorry." I felt so vulnerable, so raw.

Gabe's husky voice regained its softness and betrayed no alarm. "I'm sorry your mom is sick. Sorry about your dad, too." He was quiet for a moment, as though he was collecting his thoughts. "As for the panic, I'm sure it's awful, but listen. . . I'm twenty years into parenthood, and I've spent a few decades on the road with messy, complicated, human beings. So, it stinks that you're dealing with this right now, but please don't feel embarrassed."

It was an unexpected bit of compassion, and I felt new tears coming, but these were the good kind.

22

A SOURCE

THE ENABLER

Claudia answered on the first ring. "Hello?"

The silky sound of her voice sent warm throbs of blood to Oscar's groin. "Hey, it's me. Got something for you."

"Good. Hit me."

The phone connection was solid—no static like sometimes happened when Gabe dragged him up to the mountains. "You know that woman at the bar in Philly? The one you asked about? She was in Creekside the last couple days. Name is Sammy."

"Is that right?" Claudia's voice sounded almost casual. "Who would've guessed."

"Yup, came here yesterday morning. Didn't leave 'til today."

"Thanks. That's an important tidbit, Oscar." Claudia was quiet for a beat. "Do you think she's a vendor or something?"

"Well, she went into his cabin last night and didn't come out 'til morning. So, unless she's selling skank, I'd say no."

"Wait. She spent *the night* with him? Like, *in his bed*? What the hell is his *problem?*"

"I dunno." He put a hand between his legs, cupped the pulsing thickness. "Poor taste, I guess, if he's passing *you* up."

"Well, at least *one* of you has a brain."

"That's not all I've got."

"No. Certainly not. . . but Oscar, you *have* to let me talk to him."

"No can do, babe."

"Oscar, those promos kick off soon. I *need* this."

"Claudia, relax. Lie back. Why don't you let those pretty tits loose from your bra. Tell me how they feel."

She was quiet.

"Take care of yourself, C. Feel good. I wanna hear it."

Her voice dropped to a sultry note. "I *do* appreciate the updates."

"I know you do," Oscar breathed. He eased back in bed and put the phone on speaker.

She started in a whisper, and Oscar turned hard as a pile driver.

Was this wrong?

Maybe.

But what harm could it really do? Claudia might be a little nuts, but keeping her around meant job security, and she was just feral enough to be a fucking dream weaver in bed. Besides, it's not like he was putting the golden goose at risk. Hell, the most dangerous thing Claudia had ever done was reveal that tight, gorgeous body to Gabe and hurt T.J.'s precious feelings.

What total pansies.

When a hot snatch like that spread her legs, you'd be an idiot to pass it up, and you sure as hell didn't whine when it moved along. Access to quality pussy was the best perk of the job, and unlike those limp-dicks, Oscar knew how to enjoy it. As long as Claudia posed no real threat, he'd lap that shit up like the delicacy it was.

He laid his head back on the pillow as Claudia detailed exactly what she imagined doing to him. "Yeah, baby. Make me *real* glad I called."

He closed his eyes and let the crazy girl give him an afternoon to remember.

23

The First Threat

SAMMY

Mom's fever was already coming down the next morning and seemed to need only chicken soup and time. She wasn't quite herself yet, but she was back at her cottage, reading a novel, which I took as a good sign. Plus, she had cut flowers from the garden that morning for her kitchen table. That meant she was at least feeling good enough to go outside, another encouraging indicator.

Meghan had been remarkably kind since I got home. She sat next to me at the kitchen island, nursing an elaborate coffee drink with whipped cream and caramel. She was in full lounge mode this morning, sporting a t-shirt and pj bottoms, with her long red hair tied up in a scrunchie.

"Meghan, you did a great job keeping Grandma comfortable yesterday. I'm so proud of you."

"Sure. What else would I do?" She spooned the whipped cream out of her mug, licked her lips, and shot me a side-glance. "So. . . How was North Carolina?"

"Well, I managed to leave the state, and the world didn't fall apart. You held down the fort here like a champ."

She rolled her dark, espresso eyes. "Yes, but how *was* it? Was the town cool like you thought? Are you gonna open another brewery?"

"Oh. Actually, the town was great. Really pretty and all surrounded by mountains. A nice downtown shopping district, too, and a big creek for rafting and boating. Maybe we can go there sometime."

She mimed shock, grasping a hand to her chest. "And leave the state twice in one decade? No!"

It was my turn to roll my eyes. "Look, I know you're cooped up, and I'm trying, Meghan. I wanted to see if I could do this without falling apart, and it sort of worked."

She finished the whipped cream and sipped her drink while I munched on my cereal. I remembered something I wanted to float past her. "Actually, I'm thinking I should go check on a couple of the new breweries soon—Madison and Charlotte. Would you like to come? We could explore a little, and I could teach you how to do an ops visit, how to root out problems."

"Seriously?" Her face stilled. "Yes, Mom, please. I'd love that."

Meghan's high school offered great business classes, and she excelled at them. It would be a huge missed opportunity if I didn't involve her more.

We finished breakfast, rinsed off a few dishes, and I climbed down the back porch stairs to check on Mom.

Shoppers Challenge chattered from the TV as she snacked on tea and honey toast. The color was back in her cheeks, and she had lots of questions about the trip. I settled into a chair and happily filled her in—at least the parts I could share.

She asked for more toast, and I made her a nice stack, with plenty of butter. She munched, and we continued to talk, but when the final round of Shoppers Challenge started, she unceremoniously kicked me out. "No more jabber. Gotta see who wins."

I kissed her on the forehead and hustled back to the house, past the empty spot in the driveway where Meghan's car had been just a few minutes ago.

***

I climbed the creaking stairs and settled in at the little desk in my bedroom to try and catch up. Running through my IT to-dos first, I noticed the tablets I had ordered for Cape May arrived, and I emailed Griffin the instructions for getting them synched up to the point-of-sale system. I checked our social media management platform next. I'd received feedback on some of the negative comments from local management, and I left replies I hoped were gracious and accommodating. We had no big promotions this week, so I sifted through the pictures submitted by staff instead and posted some of the best images, along with a profile on one of our chefs. We liked to make personal connections with the communities and found the candid photos and personal stories generated a lot of engagement.

I was almost ready to log off when I noticed a direct message in my inbox. I clicked it open, anticipating another complaint or a recipe request—which we sometimes got—but not expecting what popped up on the screen:

BACK OFF BITCH! HE IS NOT YOURS! DON'T MAKE ME TAKE ACTION. YOU WON'T LIKE IT!

I stared in shock. *What the hell?* The account had no profile picture and was simply called Gabriel's Grrrrl.

Confusion, anger, and fear all bubbled inside me, the entire message making so little sense that my body couldn't figure out how to react. First, as far as the public was concerned, I didn't even have an acquaintance named Gabriel. Of course, an intimate connection existed now—one that could conceivably threaten someone—but there wasn't a soul alive who was aware of it. Even if someone had seen us in Creekside or at La Fermata, they wouldn't know who I was, let alone that I was associated with Forbidden Brews. I stared at the screen a while before finally closing the laptop, baffled.

I picked up my phone to text Gabe, then remembered I didn't even have his number. Peeved, but seeing no other option, I sent a text to Charlie, letting him know about the threat and asking for Gabe to call me.

***

An hour later, I had showered, put everything away from the trip, and was generally getting my life back in order when the phone rang.

"Hey, Sammy." Gabe's low, comforting voice came over the line.

'Hi." I wedged my empty suitcase into the overstuffed hall closet, then returned to my bedroom. "Thanks for calling."

"Meant to call last night, but we had a little chaos here. You made it home safe and sound?"

"Yeah. Trip was fine, and no worries about calling. We were running around helping Mom yesterday anyway."

"Is she feeling better?"

"Much. Her fever's already broken. She should be back to herself in no time."

"Really glad to hear that. . . Hold on." A muffled conversation filtered through the background and Gabe was quiet a moment before returning his attention to me. "Thanks for waiting. . . Charlie messaged me. He said something about a threat?"

I explained what happened, and how it made no sense.

"Okay, actually, that's interesting. Can you send a screenshot of the DM to Charlie? We're trying to piece something together over here, and it might help." I heard him converse with someone again. "Um, listen, we've got a bit of a situation, and I need to talk with you about it." He sighed heavily—maybe stalling—before finally spitting it out. "Someone got pictures of us."

"Crap." So much for keeping our connection private. I knew how much he hated this stuff. "I should have said something. I kept thinking you were a bit obvious with the helmet off at the barbecue place."

"No." A strange tone entered his voice. "The pictures aren't from the barbecue place."

"From town? How would anyone know it was you? Our heads were covered, and we were zipping by pretty fast on those bikes."

"Sammy, they aren't from our bike ride in town. The pictures are from the farm. It's you and me in the grapevines."

A chill swept over my skin. "Please, tell me you mean they got hold of our selfies."

"It's not the selfies." He paused for a minute before forging ahead. "And I'm sorry, but they're pretty graphic. Whoever took these had either an excellent camera or a really good vantage point."

"Are we recognizable?"

"Unfortunately, yes. You can make out our faces pretty well. In fact, there's an awful lot you can see clearly. It's practically stop-action porn."

I shut my eyes. This just couldn't be happening. I thought about Meghan—what she would learn about relationships and risk-taking. About what I was actually doing on a trip I said was for business. She barely spoke with me as it was. This could make it a thousand times worse. "I'm gonna be sick."

"Look, we're doing what we can on our end, but they're asking for a substantial sum of money to keep the photos off the internet."

"Should we just pay? I can pitch in—or heck, I might be able to cover it. If those photos see the light of day, I can't imagine how Meghan will react. Or Mom. Or for that matter, the drunk patrons at the brewery. Or the Chamber of Commerce. Good God."

"Sammy, paying won't stop this. They'll just come back to the well again. We need to catch and capture."

"Are you going to the police? I mean, this is extortion, right?"

"We're trying to handle this in-house for now. Sometimes, legitimate photographers will exchange money to keep photos out of the press, so it's conceivable this is a paparazzi. All things being equal, I'd rather not have this in the public domain at all just yet."

"Can you send me what you got, so I know what I'm dealing with?" Something occurred to me. "And actually, Marco's fiancée, Ian, is a private investigator. He's very good. Maybe he can help." The prospect of Ian seeing what Gabe had described was awful, but it seemed better than the whole world downloading it.

"I'll send it." He blew out another deep breath. "But, Sammy, can you turn on your video? I want to talk face-to-face for a minute."

I clicked the video button, and his face appeared on the screen with a hard set in his eyes and a seriousness in his features I hadn't seen before. He was still at the cabin, and a few security folks I didn't recognize were exiting behind him. *Had they seen the pictures, too?*

"What is it, Gabe?"

"I need to ask you something." He closed his eyes and pinched his brow with his fingers before finally looking up at me. "Listen, this kind of thing isn't common. Yet, it's happening now. Right after you drove halfway down the coast, then dropped your dress under the open blue sky. At the end of a crop row, no less, where the view goes clear to the valley. You know, you said some of your businesses were doing poorly." He looked downright pissed. *"Are you shaking me down?"*

I stared at him, dumbstruck. In the corner of the screen, I saw the shock and disgust register on my face, but right behind those emotions a healthy dose of anger waited to explode. *He was handing me some sort of celebrity catastrophe, then laying the blame at* my *feet?*

So mad I couldn't speak at first, I closed my eyes, attempting to rein in my temper. Finally, I released my words in a careful cadence. "You think *I* did this? For *money*?" I took a few more deep breaths. "Gabe, I came all that way because I wanted to visit the town and help you—and because I wanted to spend time with you." My words sounded clipped and angry, which was about as close to calm as I could get at that point. "And I *dropped my dress*, as you say, because I wanted you badly, and I wasn't sorry about that until this very moment." Oh, how I regretted it now. On so many levels. "As for the money. . . Are the new stores struggling a bit? Maybe. But, I've got *millions* invested in business real estate and plenty of that Silicon Valley cash still in the bank. I neither need nor want a single red cent of yours!"

I paused to take a breath but had definitely not finished. I could see my face on the screen, my dark eyes boring into him, my mouth in a severe tight line. "And I have a seventeen-year-old daughter at home. You really think I would risk her seeing something like that? *This*, for me, *is a nightmare*!"

He seemed remarkably unmoved. "Yes, but those photos would never reach her eyes if you were the one who controlled them."

I was so furious I was practically shaking. "Look, just send me the damn pictures and emails and whatever else you have. That way, I can actually *do* something about them, if you won't!"

I disconnected the call and chucked the phone at my bed covers. *What a complete ass!* I couldn't believe I'd gone all the way to North Carolina to spend time with him. To share his bed! *Such a total waste!*

I prayed the photos weren't as bad as he described. If they were, I'd find a way to squash this. Whatever it took. With or without his help.

I paced back and forth frenetically, too riled up to figure out next steps. I finally threw on some running gear and headed out the door. If I didn't burn off some anger, I was going to snap.

24

—·—

A Little Help

The emails eventually arrived. I didn't recognize the sender, but there was no mistaking the contents. I read through the demands and braved the photos. Dozens of them. If it were even possible, they were worse than I had feared. Just like Gabe had warned me, it was stop-action porn. In full color. Us kissing; me taking off my dress; my naked, freckled body against the vines; him clothed with his mouth on me; my bare breasts in the afternoon sun; Gabe stripping naked; and finally, my legs wrapped around his back. No graphic detail spared. No mystery left to the imagination.

Horror show. Absolutely awful.

Powerlessness was the foe. I needed to do something. I called Marco's fiancé, Ian, and asked him to come to the house.

***

An hour later, I'd checked on Mom again, and Ian sat at my desk, scrutinizing everything. He still had the physique of an active Marine, and his classically handsome face, framed by a short blond buzz cut, was normally sunny and full of smiles. This morning, however, he was all business as he gazed critically at the images. It was humiliating to have him see all this, but I didn't know what else to do. Most importantly, I hoped he could help. The world of secrecy, people sneaking around, and long-distance photography was his day-to-day.

"The pictures are shot from somewhere downhill. What's downhill from this, Sammy?"

"Lots of grape fields, apple orchards, a few country roads. Actually, you can see all the way to the town in the valley, but it's very, very far away." I buried my head in my hands. *What had I been thinking?*

"Could anyone have known you would be there?"

"Honestly, I don't know how. Gabe's very private, and I didn't tell anyone exactly where I was going."

"Hmm." He thought for another minute. "Even if no one knew, this is still Gabriel Walker's property, right? He's sort of a big celebrity. Was there any kind of media presence?"

"Not that I noticed. The property is a few miles outside of town, and the road he's on is quiet. I presume I'd have noticed if extra people were loitering. Plus I don't think he's in Creekside that often, so I doubt paparazzi would camp out or anything."

"Was anyone else on site?"

"Not while these were taken, as far as I know. Gabe did have some staff at the property early in the day, but I think they were away. A big group had also toured the restaurant on site—but I'm pretty sure they were all gone as well. The parking lot was empty a few minutes before all this happened."

"Okay, let me see what I can do. The best thing would be if you could forward me the email, photos and all. If you're not comfortable with that though, just send the email body."

"I'll send it. Just don't show anyone, okay? I'm pretty mortified."

"Sammy, I would never share anything like this around. And that's both personal *and* professional code."

Ian was like the younger brother I never had. He was probably insulted I'd even asked. "I know you wouldn't. I trust you. I'm just having a bad day."

"Understandable. Listen, can you ask the team that sent this for any technical details they already have? IP address of the sender, that sort of thing?"

"I will. And thank you so much, Ian. I'm grateful for the help."

"I'll do what I can, Sammy." His expression shifted a little. "I wish I could tell you this would be a slam dunk, but I'm actually not sure how much we'll have to go on. Email can be tough to trace, and I don't have a lot of contacts in North Carolina to leverage. I promise I'll try though."

When I stood up to walk him out, he grabbed my arms to stop me, then simply wrapped me up in a warm hug. "I'm sorry this is happening to you, lady. You're such a good person."

God bless Ian. He was many of the things I loved about Marco—sharp, hardworking, creative—but with less attitude and more softness. Plus, with his strong frame and big heart, he gave amazing hugs. I squeezed him back fiercely. "Thanks, Ian. I don't know how I can repay you."

"Well, I do have one idea." He stepped back from me, a mischievous smile curling the corners of his mouth.

"Oh yeah?"

"When all this is done, and I save you from certain doom, you're letting me cook you an amazing dinner. Then, over a *very* large bottle of wine, you're going to spare no detail in telling me exactly how you wound up al fresco with Gabriel Walker in his vineyard. Deal?"

"If you fix this, Ian, I'll tell you anything you want to know. Well. . .almost anything."

"All. The. Details." His schoolboy grin was as wide as his face.

He spun on his heel, obviously pleased with himself, and headed down the stairs. He was almost at the front door when something occurred to me.

"Hey, Ian," I called, running down the steps to catch up. "Can I ask you something?" I paused for just a moment, choosing my words with caution. "Is Marco alright? He's been really short-tempered and high strung lately. . . and he asked for an advance on his dividend."

Ian's face froze. A cloud of concern moved through his features. "He asked you for money?"

"Well, he asked me for *his* money, just early. Said it had something to do with the wedding."

Ian covered his ears and closed his eyes, shaking his head playfully. "Oh! Don't tell me then. I know he's planning something just perfect, and I want everything to be a surprise. I'm so excited!" His broad smile gleamed.

"I'm sure it will be epic. Marco always nails stuff like that. But what about his mood? Has he been cranky at home?"

"Sammy," he sighed. "He's always cranky." He looked at me obligingly. "It's not his most endearing quality, but nobody's perfect, and it makes his good moods that much better." He reached out and stroked my cheek gently. "You know Marco. He gets himself wound up. He'll calm back down soon. Don't worry." He gave me a quick kiss on the cheek, promised to call soon, and headed back into the world.

25

THE MEND

After a few days, Mom seemed to be healed. She had played a set or two of tennis and had weeded her cut flower beds until all you could see were colorful blooms.

I, however, had been sleeping terribly. I spent my nights staring at the ceiling, unable to shut off my brain. I just needed those photos to disappear. Permanently.

Paying the photographer off might stop their release, but Gabe seemed confident that was the wrong choice, one that would ultimately lead to more demands. Requesting assistance from the police might help a lot, but I'll admit I didn't relish the idea of those photos becoming public record—it might be a solution as bad as the problem. I had no idea if Gabe was doing anything, or if he was just stuck on blaming me. Ian was my only resource, and I couldn't think of anything else. My mind spun in circles.

So far, Ian only had a few insights to share. He was pretty sure the photos had come from a high-quality smartphone, not a long-distance lens. He'd triangulated the nearby roads, and they all seemed too far away, given the number of pixels and the quality. So, he was thinking whoever had taken the shots must have been on the property somewhere. Obtaining the IP address had been a dead end, and he hadn't found any traceable data in the digital images. No useful contacts in North Carolina had turned up, and Ian wasn't sure how to get more information without police support and warrants. He was more apologetic than anything when he provided the update. He didn't think he had useful results to share.

And so, I stared at the ceiling and simply lost sleep, which meant I spent the days in an exhausted fog. I was starting another morning like this, shuffling around my kitchen in a stupor when a text arrived from a new number:

I'm sorry. I've been an ass. I'm sending this from my cell phone, so you have my number now. But Sammy can we talk? -Gabe

I stared at the screen. I was too groggy to process it, let alone face that conversation. The whole situation really wasn't okay.

When the coffee finished brewing, I took my mug to the front porch swing.

What on earth had happened to my life? I'd met Gabe only a few weeks ago, and already my world was upside down. Pictures of me having sex? Extortion? Accusations I was a criminal? Ridiculous. This wasn't how I liked to start relationships, to say the least.

I picked up the novel I'd been savoring and read for a few minutes, idly watching the neighbors start their day. The elderly man next door talked to himself and cursed at the cat who wound between his legs while he retrieved a newspaper from his driveway—probably the last one still being delivered in the entire neighborhood. At seven in the morning, the mom across the street was scolding her toddlers as they joyfully shredded the marigolds in her front garden. *Poor woman.* And here I sat mulling over my ridiculous mess. Just a cross section of real people, bumbling our way through life.

I watched their mornings unfold for as long as I could, but it was a busy day, and, eventually, I got moving.

***

After loading laundry and dishes, I snuck away to my computer to finish the work-related tasks that had been so horribly interrupted with all this craziness.

The July numbers should have landed, and I pulled up the financial statements. As expected, they did not look good. Expenses were far worse than they had been in June, and the balance sheet was wonky, too. I immediately dove in.

The cost of goods sold was up again, but, oddly, capital expenditure had increased as well. I downloaded all the transactions, checking first on anything purchased from HopNBrew. A virtual avalanche of invoices filled the screen. HopNBrew orders had multiplied, not decreased, and the purchases had expanded to high ticket items: dishes, appliances, barstools. All were absurdly priced. None of it made sense, and with asset purchases on the list, I was thinking that Charlotte couldn't be the sole driver anymore—their freshly built facilities wouldn't need upgrades for years. *Had I misworded my email to the franchise managers?* I dug up the message and reviewed it. To me, the language seemed crystal clear.

My brain reeled. I did appreciate our leaders finding creative solutions to procurement problems; however, this was the opposite of helpful. It needed to stop now.

I sent another email to all locations. No one was to purchase from HopNBrew until further notice. A block on the HopNBrew URL would help as well. It wasn't a foolproof solution to shutting down orders, but it would at least prevent employees from accessing the website through internal hardware and routers.

I logged into our bank account to check today's cash balance and couldn't believe what I saw. We had never experienced negative cash flow like this before. *How was it possible?* I poured more money into the account again and called Debbie, hoping she had found something on the legal side.

"Debbie Ryland, Esquire," She sounded a bit distracted.

"Hi, Debbie. It's me. Just following up. Did you get a chance to check on that HopNBrew contract?"

"Oh, I did. Hold on. Let me grab my notes." I heard a few keystrokes and waited. She must have been reading through everything. "Ah, yes. So, Sammy, I don't see any record of a vendor agreement. So, if they're overcharging you, a contract isn't the problem."

"Thanks. That's a relief, I guess." I thought a bit, but the situation still didn't make sense. "Debbie, something feels off about this. Orders are growing rapidly. I'm trying to shut it down operationally, but can you see what you can find about the company? The pricing defies logic."

"I can, but I'm still a bit buried with that big corporate case, and it's covering the bills right now. What's your timeline?"

I sighed. We truly did have plenty of money in reserve. Nothing was on fire. I just really, *really* did not like this trend, and if the new breweries failed completely, the broader financial implications would dwarf any troubles from a few cruddy months of expenses.

"Debbie, it's not wildly urgent, I guess. I've communicated with the local managers and told them to cease ordering activity. I've blocked the URL, too, but I'd like to know what other options I have for stopping it completely."

"Okay, let me see what I can find. I promise I'll squeeze it in as soon as I can."

"Thanks, Debbie. I appreciate it."

We ended the call.

I pushed back from my desk, rubbing my temples in peace for a moment, but subtle sounds disturbed the quiet of my room. I looked over my shoulder and found Meghan hovering in the doorway, dressed in her soccer jersey. She had a weird habit of lurking like that.

"Something wrong, Mom?"

"Oh, just a Forbidden Brews problem I can't quite figure out."

"Please let me help. You'd be surprised what I can do." She took a few steps into the room, trying to see my laptop screen.

She looked so earnest, and truly, I had more to accomplish than I could get through. The reality was, Meghan was as smart and as organized as anyone I knew. "I tell you what, sweetheart. I'd be happy for your help this time. There's a company we're having issues with, and I don't have time to sort it out. If I got you a Forbidden Brews login, would you be willing to compile the invoices for one of our vendors? I need them organized in a database, so I can make sense of them."

"Mom, you won't be disappointed. I'll kick butt at this, I promise." She smiled broadly, the eagerness plain on her face. Meghan made little effort to hide her emotions. It wasn't fun to be around her when she was angry, but when she was excited, it was impossible not to feel caught up in the moment, too.

"Thanks, sweetie. I'll get things set up for you. We can go over it after soccer tonight."

"Sounds awesome." She looked at her watch, and her eyes got big. She dashed to her room, grabbed her soccer bag, and hustled down the stairs. "Gotta run!" she called from the first floor. "Warmup's in fifteen minutes."

"See you there," I called after her. "Drive safe!" The front door had already shut.

I watched her pull down the driveway, grateful to finally have an interaction that ended on a positive note. If involving her in the business was what it took, I should have no problem amping that up.

***

Meghan's team took a tough loss that afternoon, in part due to a penalty kick she'd missed.

When we got back to the house, she threw her soccer bag on the ground, and wrenched off her dirty cleats and shin guards, leaving them in the middle of the kitchen floor. She stormed out of the room to get a shower before I could stop her, but I left her mess where it was. She could perfectly well clean up after herself.

Thirty minutes later, the scent of onions, oregano and simmering Bolognese had drawn Meghan back to the kitchen, but she was no friendlier. I made her pick up her dirty soccer gear before serving up pasta and fresh salad at the kitchen island. She grouched her way through dinner with Mom and me, then slammed her plate into the dishwasher before heading back upstairs.

Single parenting meant picking my battles carefully, and I didn't take the bait this time. "Boy, she's a delight when she's had a bad day, huh." I looked to Mom for a little sympathy.

She arched her eyebrows and dried the dripping pot I handed her. "Too bad she can't keep her emotions in all the time, like you and me."

I scrubbed remnants of Bolognese from a saucepan and rolled my eyes. *Why did Mom always have to be so reasonable?* It was very irritating.

When we finished the dishes, Mom headed back to her cottage to finish the book she was engrossed in, and I took a glass of wine out to the front porch, ending my day where it began. The air had cooled, and twilight was darkening the sky from rose to amethyst. Crickets tuned up their songs for the night, and I rocked gently on the swing, sipping a Malbec.

The garden across the street had been rightly decimated. The toddlers had won their battle against the marigolds. I thought again of the mom who had raised her voice at them this morning, remembering what it was like to spend every waking moment keeping a little one alive and never having time to do anything for yourself. It must have been last-nerve frustrating to have those little munchkins rip apart the one shred of beauty she'd had time to plant in the world. I probably would have raised my voice, too.

My thoughts turned to Gabe. He should never have accused me of something so awful, but what had he been through the last couple decades? How many people had tried to take advantage of him or betray him? I sighed, thinking through my own million faults and remembering the kindness he'd shown after my panic attack.

No relationship could survive without a little grace. Or a lot. We were all so fallible.

I finally set down my wine, picked up my phone, and dialed his number.

He picked up after a few rings. "Sammy?"

"Hey."

"Thanks for calling."

"Thanks for your text."

It was quiet a beat, and I didn't fill the space.

Gabe finally did. "Listen, I've been thinking a lot about this mess. I haven't figured out the right path yet, but I'm pretty sure I was a jerk the other day. I owe you an apology."

"You were stressed."

"Yeah." He grew quiet again as the first fireflies blinked to life in the yard. "But the truth is. . . I'm struggling with this. I'm not sure what to do."

He was struggling? My days had not been a picnic. "Yeah, blackmail's new for me, too." The words came out clipped and irritable.

"*Shit*. No, I mean. . . Look. . ." He huffed out a sigh. "The thing is. . . trust is non-negotiable for me. It's really important, but my instincts for it clearly suck. I keep getting six months or a year into a relationship only to find out I'm not with the person I think I am. So all I can do is watch for red flags, and they seemed to be flying everywhere."

I shook my head. "I get it. New people are always a risk." I sipped my wine and rocked gently on the porch swing. "Heck, the last guy I was involved with turned out to have a long-distance engagement he didn't bother to mention. And for Pete's sake, we were introduced by friends. I would have considered that pretty good insurance."

A car drove by, its headlights illuminating the yard for a moment. Otherwise, the neighborhood was still.

"Look, Gabe, I struggle with this too. It always makes me nervous to let someone new into my life. I choose as well as I can, but in the end, it's a roll of the dice. I have to decide if I'm going to take a chance or not."

"And how do you decide?"

"Ask honest questions. Get to know people. If they're friends of friends, it helps, but obviously that's not foolproof."

"Okay, fair enough. I like that." He paused, maybe collecting his thoughts. "Can I ask *you* some questions then?"

"Yup."

His voice was steady and even. "Sammy, why did you really drive all the way down to Creekside? What do you want to get out of a relationship with me?"

I found myself shrugging, even though he couldn't see me. "There's nothing I wanted to get out of it. I'm attracted to you. I enjoy your company. I simply wanted to spend time with you." I took a breath. "And if I'm being fully honest, I also wanted to see if I could be away from my family without falling apart. It *almost* worked."

"It stinks that your mom got sick."

"Yeah." The lights grew dim in my neighbors' homes as kids were tucked in for the night and adults retreated to the quiet of their family rooms. "Look, you seem kind and intelligent. You're easy to talk to and incredibly talented. I just wanted you. Plain and simple. There's no other agenda."

"I want you, too. But I've got another question." His voice took on an edge. "I want to know how much trouble your company's in."

Back to the money again.

"Well, first thing. It's my company, not me. Forbidden Brews is an LLC. So, if everything went down the tubes, it would be really sad—a lifetime of work lost. But my personal finances are separate and protected." The temperature was dropping, and I considered retreating inside. Meghan was home, though, and I didn't want her to hear our conversation. "Anyway, I don't think collapse is on the horizon. In the past, we've always managed to right the ship when things got rocky. We'll do it again."

"So, you're not facing bankruptcy? You're not in financial peril right now?"

"No." I swirled the wine in my glass. "Look, I'm not a tech mogul or anything, but I haven't truly worried about money in a long time—not since that Silicon Valley windfall. My home is paid off. My daughter's education is covered. Even without cash flow from the breweries, I've still got enough invested that—as long as I'm not wasteful—my little family will be fine. . . for the rest of our lives.

Ironically, I'm usually the one in the relationship who's worried about this—being used as a meal ticket, I mean."

"One more thing we have in common, I guess."

"Pretty lucky problem, huh? We'd be almost insane to complain about it."

"You're probably right." He didn't sound convinced. "But almost everyone's moral compass starts to bend when enough wealth is at stake. Makes genuine interaction pretty questionable. So, I dunno."

Dusk had disappeared into night. The porch light was off, and I rocked on the swing as the sky grew darker, sipping the Malbec. He remained quiet.

"Listen, Gabe, all I can tell you is the truth. I love my family. My business is exhausting but fulfilling. I have lifelong friends, and I'm financially secure. I'm not trying to shore up any gaps in my life. Like I said, I just wanted you, and I wanted to spend time with you. That's all."

"Past tense?"

I sighed. "I don't know. I mean the *wanting* you part. . . that's not past tense. But I don't care for drama—*at all*—and this is some pretty ungodly drama. Plus, are you even doing anything about these photos? I got the impression you were ignoring it and blaming it on me. So I've been floundering around trying to solve it on my own—embarrassing myself in front of my friend Ian. I feel frustrated and pretty pissed, frankly."

"I *swear* we're trying, but we're not making much progress. Whoever did this covered their tracks well. There's very little we can glean from the email."

"That's what Ian's telling me, too. I'm glad you're trying. I thought you were abandoning me with it."

"God, I'm making a mess of everything, aren't I?" He exhaled. "I wasn't abandoning you. I promise we're trying." He was quiet a moment. "And, Sammy, I could tell you I don't come with any drama, but I'd be lying. It's not usually bad like this, but I can't exactly claim my life is normal either. I wish I could tell you otherwise."

It wasn't what I wanted to hear, but at least he was being open and truthful. Maybe that's as much as anyone could ask for. I tried to let go of my anger. "Well, I obviously come with some issues too. You've had a front row seat to that, and you were amazing about it. I think I owe you some understanding in return."

I heard knocking in the background, a faint conversation, then Gabe was in my ear again.

"You don't owe me anything, Sammy. Listen, I want to get past this. You're so bright and accomplished and warm. You're creative and practical at the same time—which is pretty much what I live for." He paused and his voice dropped. "And good God. . . when I think about our time together at the cabin. . . I practically sweat."

Heat shot through me, and I sat up straighter on the porch swing. There was no denying the physical memory of him. The sensation of his body was still with me—it had been since I'd returned home. "Yeah, me too." Stars were emerging low in the sky, under the dark eave of the unlit porch. I took a deep breath. If we were aiming for honesty, I may as well go all in. "The truth is. . . I can still *feel* you, Gabe. *Right now.* I can't even describe how it's been making me ache."

He blew out a long breath. "Seriously?"

"Yep."

"You're *killing* me."

I could hear the desire in his voice, and my whole body felt alert again—heated, taut, and attentive.

"Listen, we take the stage soon, and I need to get warmed up, but can I call you after the concert? We could talk more, and I would *really* like to hear about this aching."

I did hate drama. But an honest, intelligent, gorgeous, mature man? That I could take quite a lot of. I wanted to tell him about the aching. In fact, I wanted to hear the groaning sound he'd made at the cabin when I'd had him in my mouth. I wanted a lot.

I set my misgivings aside—decided to keep rolling the dice. "I'll answer if you call, Gabe. There are definitely details I could share."

"Promise me you'll hold those thoughts, Sammy. I'll call as soon as I can."

***

The dense plaster walls of my aging home earned their keep that night, and most nights thereafter.

Sometimes our calls remained chaste, a time to decompress. It was nice to talk with someone who understood the trials of raising a teenager and running a business, and I was certainly content to listen to him unpack his day. Some nights he was weary—worn out from being on the road and interacting with so many people. Other nights, he was ebullient with energy, overflowing from a set of music that worked and a joyous crowd that poured out their appreciation. I gladly listened to him regardless of what kind of day he'd had, and I was always happy to finish the night with a little comfort and spice.

Unfortunately, all the cozy tuck-ins in the world couldn't clear away the worries that kept me awake, nor could they do anything to quell what loomed on the horizon.

26

DESPERATION

THE USER

He crouched behind the desk.

Were they here?

Something had clattered in the tasting room, but the place was locked up. They shouldn't be able to get to him.

He listened to the emptiness and looked down at his hands, counting off ten solid digits, healthy and sound. They'd been threatening to take his fingers! He instinctively curled them in protective fists. *Why didn't they just bring him the product and fuck off?*

The money wasn't coming in fast enough. No matter how much he tried.

He'd attempted to reason with them, offering them interest on the debt. *Could they not understand the concept of a goddamn investment?* They had to know he would be good for the cash eventually.

Getting up from behind the desk, he checked the baggie again. He shook the last bits of powder out of it, lined the particles up on the mirror, and snorted them. But he knew that meant he was out again. He was always out. He wiped his nose and swept away blood. *Shit!*

He grabbed a napkin from his desk and applied pressure, staining the pale cloth red.

He was so frustrated he could scream, but if he did, they might find him.

It didn't have to be like this. He just needed enough money to get them off his back—and he needed more stuff.

But it all needed to happen faster. A lot faster.

27

Escalation

SAMMY

My phone rang around noon while I was at the brewery, floating between positions, covering for people who hadn't shown up for their shifts. I glanced at Gabe's name on the caller ID, asked someone to handle the hostess station for a second, and stepped into the narrow hallway by the offices.

I put the phone to one ear and covered the other to drown out the racket. "Hey."

"Hey," Gabe said. "Can you talk?"

"Wish I could, but the lunch rush is a madhouse. Can we catch up tonight?"

"No. Sooner would be better. I know you have a busy day, but I'm afraid I have to disrupt it a bit. I'm sending a security detail to Philadelphia—Oscar and a woman named Lucy."

"Wait. What?" The noise level in the restaurant was absurd. I shoved open the screeching side door and stepped onto the blacktop. "What did you say?"

"We received another email. This one contained some threats. We're taking it seriously, and we're sending Oscar and Lucy your way. You'll like her."

"Hold on. Go back. Did you say *threats*? What kind of threats?"

"Why don't you call me when you have more time. The team should arrive in a few hours. I'm hoping you can be home by then?"

"Gabe, you're scaring me."

"Sammy, I don't want to panic you. We're just being conservative. Call me when you get home, and I'll fill you in. See if you can gather Meghan and your mom, too."

The sun reflecting off the blacktop suddenly felt stifling, the August air thick. My thoughts swarmed. Meghan might be at a friend's. Mom could be anywhere. *Should I leave now?* The staff could figure things out without me.

Wait...

No. No.

I forced a deep breath and tried to focus on what was actually happening. What was real. There were threats. Help was coming. I was filling in at the brewery—a public place with lots of people around. Gabe said nothing was urgent. *Come on, Sammy.* My head felt light, but I kept my breathing even. I was determined to stay present.

"I need to hand off a few things off here. I'll be home as quick as I can."

***

As soon as relief arrived, I hustled to the house and called Gabe from the front porch, hopefully out of everyone's earshot. "Gabe, what in the world's going on?"

"Hey, Sammy. There's been a development." His voice was low and measured like usual. "We've reached out to law enforcement."

A switch in tactics. "The police? I thought we were keeping the pictures private."

"Ideally, yes. But the message we received contained a threat—a death threat in fact. So, at this point, we believe we're dealing with a criminal—not a paparazzi. We don't think we should take any chances. Is your mom home? Is Meghan? We do have a plan."

I plopped down on the porch swing and tried to make sense of what he was saying. "A *death* threat?"

"Unfortunately, yes. Our blackmailer must think we need a nudge."

"Do you think it's legitimate?"

"I think we don't want to find out the hard way. We're gonna treat it seriously, take all the necessary steps, and not risk it."

"But don't you need all your security there with *you*? You're the one who needs protection. This doesn't feel right."

Silence.

"Gabe?"

"The threat wasn't directed at me." He huffed a breath. "I'm truly sorry, but they seemed to be referring to you."

"*What?*" My brain locked up. Couldn't compute it. It made no sense. "But I'm a nobody. How's that even possible?"

"We don't know, but you said you received a threat online, so maybe there are things we haven't figured out. Maybe it's connected."

"What, exactly, did the message say? Can you send it to me? Maybe I can ask Ian to look at it."

"I'll forward it. But I'll warn you. . . whoever sent it is good at covering their digital trail."

I squeezed my eyes closed as the news sank in, the first tentacles of genuine fear slithering into my heart. The threat of those photos being published was child's play compared to the possibility of violence. "Gabe, this has to stop. I can't have anyone coming near my family. I'll cover whatever they're asking for."

I looked around at the rickety 1920's window frames and the flimsy door locks. I'd never even worried before about the security of my home.

"If paying would make it stop, we would've done it a long time ago." He sighed heavily. "Handing over cash tends to fuel the fire."

I put my head in my hands, trying to think through the implications. "All right. I think Meghan and Mom are here, but I'll make sure before Oscar and Lucy arrive." I remembered the number of chairs in my kitchen, the number of beds in the house. "I'm not sure how the sleeping arrangements will work. I only have one extra bedroom, and it's small. Someone might be stuck on a sleeper sofa or blow-up mattress. I hate subjecting people to that when they've traveled so far." The idea of Oscar's enormous physique on the tiny pullout couch seemed impossible for both the man and the furniture.

"I know you'll be crowded tonight, but I think we can make it better." He took a breath. "Listen, we have a couple days' break right now, then we play the Big Riff Festival for two nights. The venue's on the Columbia River Gorge, just a few hours from my home in Oregon. Look, I know you all have existing commitments, and this isn't easy. But given the stakes, we think your family should join us, if possible. Our security is here, we have plenty of room, and it's very secluded. Oscar and Lucy can accompany you here via private plane, and I promise it won't be a prison. There's plenty of acreage to explore, and you can come backstage for the concerts. We can turn it into something good, Sammy. Plus, Trevor and his friends will be here. They're a little older than Meghan, but they'll include her. She shouldn't be bored."

The festival was relatively new but had quickly become the stuff of legend—a week-long campout with guitar-centric headliners at a spectacular outdoor venue. A backstage pass would be surreal, but I had hoped to get down to Charlotte. Plus, Meghan had soccer practice, and this was the week of Mom's tennis tournament.

But did any of that matter now? Did anything but our safety count at all? And even if we could up and leave, how was I going to explain all this to Meghan and Mom? If I did, they would know I had lied, at least a little bit, about my North Carolina trip. I stood up and paced. I needed a plan—and quickly.

Gabe wasn't giving up. "Please, Sammy. I'd rather have our security together, and I'd feel a lot better knowing you're here. We just need to give the police a few days to track this down."

"I know you're right. It's just a lot to process." I sighed and tried to make sense of the news. "Listen, I know you've gone to a lot of expense and planning. If it's the right thing to do, then I'm sure we'll come. But I need to think for a few minutes, figure out how this can work."

"I like where you're headed, Sammy."

The fan on the air conditioner kicked on, rumbling the sweet sound of relief from the August heat.

"Besides—" his voice dropped a notch— "I have a few more bottles of port. Maybe you could help me enjoy them."

I thought for a moment about what exactly he could do with the port. Thought about his lips on my neck and my body. Even through the fog of fear and stress, his suggestive voice and my vivid memories of the cabin in North Carolina were enough to send ripples of desire through my body.

"A few bottles of port sound amazing. Let me talk with everyone, and I'll get back to you soon."

We said our goodbyes, he disconnected, and I scrambled to prepare some very strange conversations.

***

"Sammy, I'm *not* going anywhere." Mom stood on the front stoop of her cottage in a tennis skirt and visor, ready to hit the shower.

"Mom, I know this is bizarre, and I'm sorry I didn't tell you more. I was trying to protect his privacy. But this is real stuff. A death threat. I think that's more important than a tennis tournament."

"Honey, I'm not going to live in fear, and it's time you stopped doing that, too."

"I'm not living in fear. This is a perfectly rational concern. I need to know you're safe."

"Samantha Louise. . . look at me." She waited until my gaze was squarely on her face. "I'm not sure you see me clearly anymore, sweetheart. Do you really think I'm a frail, elderly woman? I'm the president of my garden club. I play tennis three times a week, and I've got a big group of friends here." She shook her head. "You know, sometimes, I think you still believe I moved in here so *you* could protect *me*." She let the words hang in the air and stared me down for a minute. "Did it ever occur to you that I'm here to keep an eye on you and Meghan? That I'm not living in this beautiful, converted carriage house for my own sake?"

I was too stunned to say anything.

"That's right, sweetheart. And you know what? You're getting stronger. Those nightmares hardly ever happen anymore, and you're getting ready to leave the state for the second time in a month. I believe in you, and you need to start believing in me." She took off her visor and wiped beads of sweat from her forehead. "Sammy, if you and Meghan want to go, then go. It will probably be good for her to get away, but I'm staying here. Plus, you said there would literally be an armed guard with me, right?"

"Potentially. I don't even know if that can happen for sure. I'd need to talk to Gabe."

"Well then, talk with him, please, because Sharon's sixty-fifth birthday is next week, and the tennis tournament starts in two days. I'm not leaving." She took a chug from her water bottle. "Now is it okay with you if I hit the shower?"

I sighed. "Of course."

"Good. 'Cause I'm definitely a bit funky." She tromped through her doorway, leaving me with one more complication to sort out.

***

The conversation with Meghan was pretty much the opposite.

"Wait. *Seriously,* Mom? You know Gabriel Walker? Like, since when?"

"Meghan, that's really not the point."

"I know, I know. But *come on*, I'm dying here."

I gave her an abridged version. "I met him when he was in town for a concert. He wanted my help with some landscape designs for his restaurant in North Carolina, and things sort of evolved. Anyways, it's a mess, and someone has it out for me."

"Hold on. *That's* what you were doing in North Carolina? I can't believe you didn't tell me you were visiting Gabriel Walker! *Ooh*, and actually. . . you kind of lied. But *OMG, this is amazing!*" She was going from her dresser to her desk to her closet, manically grabbing belongings and stacking them on the bed. But then she stopped, a look of alarm on her face. "Wait. Why is someone mad at you? Is he married? Are you a *home wrecker*?"

This was going to take forever. "I'm not a homewrecker, and no, he's not married. I did lie a little—to protect his privacy—but, please, focus. Look, I'm sorry about all of this—"

"*You're sorry?*" Her face was glowing with joy. "You're taking me to the West Coast to see concerts from backstage and meet Gabriel Walker—and you're *apologizing*?"

"Meghan, listen, if we do this, you can't go all fangirl on him. Understood? I'm serious—no photos, no selfies, no social media of any kind. Got it?"

"I mean, I can tell Marnie at least, right? And surely, I can post a *tiny* bit to Instagram."

"It's actually better if people don't know where we are, sweetie."

She looked at me like I had lost all reason. "Seriously? The most interesting thing to happen in my entire life, and I'm not allowed to tell anyone?"

I just stared at her, unyielding.

Her shoulders slumped, and her face finally sagged a little. She plunked down on her bed, defeated. "You know, sometimes, you're a very big buzzkill, Mom."

"Oh, yeah?" I challenged her. "Well, Gabe's son and his friends will be there. So, how's that? Is your buzz alive again?"

"Oh my God. Trevor Walker? He is so hot! I'll have my stuff ready in ten minutes. Coach Clint will understand. *Oh my God!*" She shoved me out of her room, bursting with all the joy and exuberance of a kid on Christmas morning.

***

I called Gabe. "Well, I'm two for three. I'm ready. Meghan is packed and pretty much waiting by the door, but Mom's digging in. She refuses to go."

"Oh, okay." I could practically hear him thinking as the seconds ticked by. "Do you think she'll come around? I know you get worried when you're separated."

"Unfortunately, I don't think she will. So, I don't know what to do. I can't risk Meghan's safety just because Mom won't budge." I decided to ask the question. "I know you wanted everyone together, but is there any way Oscar could stay here with Mom while Meghan and I travel to Oregon with Lucy? I know she'd be safe with him." I prayed he would say yes. I had no ideas for a backup plan.

He was quiet for a moment. "I think that can work. No one is getting past Oscar, and Lucy can definitely handle bringing you and Meghan here."

"Oh, that would be great. Can we call it a plan?" My fingers were still crossed.

"It's a plan. I can't wait to see you."

28

THE ARRIVAL

The Gulfstream G550 powered over the deserts of Eastern Oregon before descending through the clouds above the forested outskirts of Portland. When we touched down at a small airport outside the city, it was the first time in my life I felt sad about a flight ending. The private plane was set up like a lounge, with a pantry full of treats and an ample bar. Meghan and I had reclined in plush leather seats, while she chatted away uncharacteristically. I could stretch my legs out as long as I wanted, and we could walk around freely most of the time. There had been no crowds to cope with at all.

Lucy turned out to be an excellent companion. While Oscar had been the fifty-something, gruff, bullish smoker I'd remembered from Creekside and the rooftop bar, Lucy was young, refined, and personable. She had skin the color of smoky quartz and natural hair she wore in a short afro. Her dark eyes sparkled when we talked, and her laugh was easy. But I didn't mistake her easy disposition for lack of strength. With her thick, muscular build, I imagined she could give Oscar a run for his money—if there were ever a fight.

When the Gulfstream finally came to a stop, Lucy guided us to a waiting black SUV on the tarmac, where I was pleasantly surprised to find Charlie behind the wheel.

"Hey, Sammy" A youthful grin lit his face. He grabbed my bag and popped it in the trunk. "Good to see you again."

"Great to see you too, Charlie. Thanks for picking us up."

"You bet." He extended a hand to my daughter. "And you must be Meghan. You look just like your mama."

After the pleasantries, we got settled and navigated off the tarmac. The SUV traveled through the outlying neighborhoods of Multnomah County, then onto freeways similar to those in any other U.S. city. Before long, however, the exits spread out, and the scenery shifted from urban to wild. When the SUV pulled off the highway, we climbed to an older two-lane road that hugged the low mountains south of the Columbia River Gorge, and a panorama opened up beneath us.

I had read about this place and seen pictures, but I was not fully prepared for the beauty of it. Sweeping vistas of blue water, green trees, and hazy mountains emerged, stretching for miles, looking peaceful under a bright sky scattered with drifting white clouds. In the distance below, the waters of the broad Columbia River shimmered beneath the wind and sunlight. Low, forested mountains made their way nearly to the edge of the gorge on both sides, and waterfalls punctuated the landscape, as melted ice from faraway peaks tumbled toward the river below. Pull offs abounded, and cars crowded the small lots as eager visitors clamored to experience the splendor up close.

We drove east past the tourist turn-offs and several small towns before travelling through a more remote area. After a few miles, Charlie turned onto an unmarked road. He paused after several yards, pushed a button, and a gate closed behind us. The road wound its way up a steep grade between tall Ponderosa pines on what must have been private land. I rolled my window down as we climbed and tasted the temperate air of the Pacific Northwest, the scent of evergreens tickling my nose. Eventually, the road turned sharply, and a break in the trees opened to reveal a rambling home perched over the edge of the world.

The modern, dark-gray house looked to be a story-and-a-half tall, but the hill cut away steeply behind it, and I realized there could be other levels below. The expansive structure had sleek lines, large windows, and a black roof covered in solar panels. The parking pad out front was enormous, and I imagined the home was designed to occasionally host crowds. Meghan and I grabbed our bags and followed Lucy to the front door.

She punched in a key code. "Come on in, guys."

While the façade of the house was shaded by conifers, light filled the interior. Floor-to-ceiling windows ran the length of the great room opposite the front door, framing an unparalleled vista. The Columbia River glimmered at the base of the gorge, and the surrounding mountains now looked like mere foothills as the snow-capped peak of Mt. Adams rose above them on the horizon. A huge sectional couch invited visitors to linger, and a well-appointed kitchen peeled away to the right, providing any cook who worked there with awe-inspiring views.

We were setting down our bags when Gabe walked down a set of floating stairs. His gaze filled with instant heat when he saw me, and a knowing smile crept across his lips. He crossed the room, and the hug he gave me set my nerves ablaze. "So glad you're here, Sammy." He stepped back. "And you must be Meghan. Nice to meet you." He offered his hand.

Meghan took his hand in both of hers and gawked, her eyes sparkling. "Wow, I can't believe it's really you. We listen to your music all the time." She kept shaking his hand, a mile-wide grin stuck on her face.

"Thanks for coming. I know the circumstances aren't ideal, but I think we can have a great time anyways." He patted her hands.

She did not let go. "It's just so pretty here. I mean, we have mountains and stuff out East, but I've never seen anything like this, and I can't believe your view. Your home is incredible."

"Thanks. The area's spectacular. Tons of waterfalls. Trevor and his friends will have to take you to see some of them."

She still held his hands, evidently too starstruck to notice. Gabe looked over at me, uncertainty flitting across his features.

"Meghan? Sweetheart? Do you think maybe that's enough?" I asked as gently as I could.

She glanced at me, then back at Gabe, and finally to her hands, still wrapped around his. "Oh! Crap!" She released her hold and stepped back, casting her eyes down in embarrassment. "God, could I *be* a bigger idiot?"

"Now come on, you're not an idiot." The worry disappeared from his face. "Sometimes people get excited. Look, if I didn't have fans, I'd have to get a real job. So, thank you."

Meghan's smile returned, and she stared at the big picture windows. "This really is so gorgeous."

A happy chaos of noise interrupted her comments. A pack of boisterous college kids emerged in straggling succession from what must have been a basement stairwell. Multiple, simultaneous conversations bounced through the group as they walked toward the kitchen in a jumble of backslaps, swearing, and laughter.

"Trevor," Gabe called out. "Can I ask you to come say hi?"

One of the young men stopped and looked our way. He broke away from his friends and reluctantly ambled in our direction. He had his dad's height and bone structure, but his hair and complexion were darker, contrasting with bright green eyes. Honestly, he was a strikingly handsome human being.

He looked us over skeptically.

"Trevor, this is my friend, Sammy, and her daughter, Meghan. I told you about them. They'll be staying for a few days. It would be great if you could make Meghan feel at home."

"Yeah, cool. Hi." He shook our hands and looked at Meghan. "Um, we're just grabbing snacks and hanging out in the basement if you want to come down."

A pretty brunette wandered over and claimed Trevor with a hand around his arm.

He gave her a quick smile. "Oh, guys, this is my girlfriend, Pria. Pria, these are my dad's friends. Meghan's gonna hang with us."

"Oh, thank goodness." She reached around my daughter's shoulder for a quick hug. "We're outnumbered, and I swear the boys only want to eat chicken wings and nachos. Wanna help us find something better?"

Meghan glanced at me, and I nodded. "I'll take your bag to your room. Go unwind a bit."

I watched her follow Trevor and Pria into the kitchen. "I bet I won't see her again for at least a couple days."

Gabe chuckled.

"Sorry she didn't keep her cool."

"Don't worry about it. Come on, I'll show you where we can set Meghan up."

One of the first-floor hallways led to four ample bedrooms, and we dropped Meghan's suitcase off in an unclaimed room. Then Gabe picked up my suitcase and led me up the floating stairs.

"The master and one extra bedroom are up this way." He set my bag down at the top of the steps. "You can settle in wherever you're most comfortable."

I hadn't thought everything through yet, and the kids were within line of sight. "I'm not sure Meghan knows exactly what's going on. Is it okay if I put my stuff in the guest room for now?"

"Sammy, you can set your suitcase on Mars if you want. I'm just so damn relieved you're here."

***

The kids eventually drove off to explore one of the big waterfall attractions, and we decided to hike around the property. While the back of the house looked out over a steep, untraversable hill, the front of the house sat on more level ground, and several trails led away from the parking area and driveway.

Gabe took my hand and led me to an uphill path. Ponderosa pines and oaks rose high overhead, shading a sprinkling of lanky dogwoods stretching for light.

He gave my palm a gentle squeeze. "Was your flight good?"

"In that *jet?* The flight was awesome."

"Not a bad perk, right?"

"Not at all."

We trekked up the path as it cut in and out of the tree line, sometimes ducking beneath the soaring canopy and other times catching glimpses of the Columbia River and the surrounding mountains. He really did live in the most spectacular places.

"Are you excited to have a break for a day or two?" I asked.

"Of course. It's a quick break, but it's always nice to do what I want for a bit." He shrugged. "Obviously, the circumstances could be better."

We kept a steady rhythm as we pushed uphill over the dry ground, scattering pebbles and leaf litter in our wake. The fresh smell of spruce and pine scented the air.

"How have you been doing with all of this, Sammy? I know it's been a long week."

"Eh. During the day, I'm too busy to think about things, but late at night, I can't seem to shut off my brain. I wish I could fix this." A tree had fallen across the path, and we took turns stepping over the huge trunk. "How about you?"

"Same." His deep voice remained steady. "During the day, we're warming up and getting ready for shows. I'm too occupied for it to cross my mind. Once it gets quiet though, after we talk, I guess I'm like you. I just wish none of this had happened."

I was sure he hadn't meant it to sound hurtful, but the words stung. I let go of his hand and walked a few steps. "You wish this hadn't happened?"

"Well, I mean, of course not. Blackmail's not really on my wish list."

We both stopped, and he studied me quizzically, wrinkling his forehead. Then realization dawned on him. "Oh, wait. . . Sammy, I mean the photos and the extortion—I wish that hadn't happened. I wasn't talking about spending time with you." He took both my hands and gave them a reassuring squeeze. Then a more crooked smile crept across his lips. "And I *definitely* wasn't talking about getting freaky in the grapevines. *That*, my dear, is a memory I like to revisit often." He tilted his head playfully, licked his lips, and shamelessly stared me up and down. "Hmm. . . in fact, I'm imagining it now."

"See, whereas I can barely remember." My voice dripped with sass. "What happened, again?"

"Come on, let's go find something to hold onto, I'll show you."

He pulled me into the woods, backing me up against the thick trunk of a towering pine. He tickled a light caress down my sides and closed the space between us. "I would be more than happy to reenact that, you know." He paused and glanced up into the trees. "Actually, though, maybe not here. The pine sap's a bitch to get off your skin." He took my hand again. "Come on. . . There's something I really do want you to see."

Gabe led the way up the path. We walked until our legs ached before the trail descended and the land ahead seemed to disappear. The faint sound of crashing water drifted to us. "Is that what I think it is?"

"Yeah," he said. "Just watch your footing. The path is safe, but don't stray from it, okay?"

We walked the last several yards to an overlook, and I stared in awe as the cliff opened up below us, revealing a vast expanse of sheer rock. Pine trees and lichen softened the edges of the stone, something green growing anyplace life could get a foothold. A thin waterfall fell from the center of the cliff and tumbled hundreds of feet to the valley below, splashing through brilliant prisms of sunlight.

"Wowza." The sheer awe of it was overwhelming. "Is this here all the time? You can come see it whenever?"

"It's here pretty much year-round."

I watched him stare with contentment at the breathtaking spectacle. "I love that you enjoy things like this."

He twirled a ribbon of hair that fell over my shoulders. "It's a sad man who can't see the beauty right in front of him." His hands slipped to my waist, and he pulled me his way. "It's really good to have you here."

"It's good to be here." I nuzzled in. I had forgotten how good he smelled. His woodsy scent called up a flood of memories.

He brought his lips to mine, and the kiss emanated a fever through my blood. I leaned in closer, letting my body press into his, stroking the contours of his shoulders. His mouth was like a drug, melting my nerves from the inside out. When I groaned and shifted my weight, my feet slipped on the dry ground, sending pebbles scattering to the cliff edge.

Fast as lightning, Gabe stabilized my torso. "Whoa, my God. Don't do that." He pulled me a few steps away from the edge. "You know, the whole point of this week is to avoid near death, okay?" He shook the image out of his head. "Do you attract trouble?"

"Not normally."

"You're gonna have to prove that. *Please.*"

I laughed at the absurdity of it all.

"Come on, let's get you away from there." Gabe wrapped his broad, rough hand around mine, squeezed gently, and led me back beneath the pines.

***

When we got home, the kids were sprawled across the sectional in the living room, scheming ways to procure dinner. Gabe's chef had a personal commitment in Portland and wasn't scheduled to return until later that night, so I went foraging in the kitchen. The pantry was exceptionally well stocked with dry goods, cans of gourmet vegetables, cooking oils, seasonings, and vinegars. Plus, the fridge and freezer were chock-a-block full of healthy produce and good cuts of meat. I took a quick mental inventory and got an idea for dinner. The simple act of cooking would be a good way to wind down from an otherwise bizarre couple of days, and it would prevent anyone from needing to make the long drive to town.

I was leaving dust on everything I touched however, and a quick glance at my clothing inspired me to clean up before handling food any further. I changed out of my hiking togs, washed my face and hands, and pulled my hair back in a ponytail. My favorite black sundress would be the go-to tonight. Made from a stretchy fabric, with a halter top and a gently flared skirt, it was one of those things that looked cute but felt as comfortable as a t-shirt.

I wandered back to the kitchen, past the now-empty great room (the kids tended to scurry when boring grown-ups wandered in), and got busy. I started the chicken sautéing in garlic and butter, then made a paprika cream sauce, and eventually mixed everything together with artichoke hearts, sun dried tomatoes, and spinach for flavor. While the chicken simmered, I generously doused potatoes with olive oil and seasoning then slid them in the oven to roast before tossing together a quick batch of green beans almondine.

I called and talked with Mom while I worked, and she recounted her busy day to me. She'd gotten the final seeds set up for the tennis tournament and had prepped goody bags for all the participants at a friend's house. Oscar was evidently staying out of her hair, but she admitted it did make her feel safer knowing he was nearby. I caught her up on our travels, but it was late on the East Coast already, and Mom was yawning. I let her go. "Talk to you soon, Mom. Love you."

At some point during my call, Gabe had emerged from his room and sat on the sofa, plucking his guitar. He caught my eye and got up. "What can I do to help? You've got quite an operation going on."

"Oh, it's all done. The potatoes just need to cook. I was actually gonna put my feet up. I was hoping you'd keep playing that pretty song."

"Yes, ma'am. Best deal ever." He picked up his guitar and flashed a grin at me.

I sat opposite him and opened my novel while he played a finger style tune. The music was gentle and intricate, and, after a minute, I set the book down to listen more carefully.

"That's the same melody you were playing at the cabin, isn't it? It's lovely, you know."

"Thanks. Just something I'm noodling around with."

I listened to the meandering notes and subtle harmonics. The tune was moody but still had a feeling of lightness and ease. *Remarkable.* "How do you *do* that?"

"Play guitar?" He chuckled. "You wanna learn some chords?"

"No. I mean, how do you create these songs? It's always been such a mystery to me. Music is like a language I understand but can't speak. I can't imagine how anyone writes it."

"Oh, well, let's see." He plucked a few strings together. "Sometimes I'll start with a few chords I like and play around with an articulation of them—altering a few notes here and there. Like, this song started out with this little riff."

He played a short series of notes finger style, then repeated it. It was a tiny fraction of the song he'd been playing. "When I find something that sounds good, it sets up a key, a mood, and based on that, I work on progressions—chords and notes that go well with it. I might work on lyrics at that point, something to capture the feeling of the music. That might lead to structure for the song: verses, a chorus. If I get that far, I'll usually share it with my bandmates, see how they respond. What the bass line might be, how the vocal harmonies, percussion or horns might add layers to it. It's always a collaboration. In the end, writing a melody is easy, but getting an entire song to come together in a way that makes people really feel something? That's the trick. Certainly doesn't happen every time." He looked my way, sheepish. "I know that's boring for most people."

He may as well have been describing alchemy—some sort of magical recipe that transformed humble components into a thing of treasured beauty.

"It's the opposite of boring, Gabe. And for the record, I hope this little melody becomes something. It's gorgeous."

"Thanks." He smiled and turned his attention back to the instrument.

I relaxed and enjoyed the majestic view and exquisite music while the warm spicy smells of simmering food and roasting potatoes filled the house.

Eventually, the aroma was enough to rouse the masses, and the kids began to emerge from the basement. Even Charlie and Lucy stepped away from their monitors in the office to check in on the kitchen situation. When dinner was ready, everyone served themselves heaping plates of food, then headed back to their digs. Meghan gave me a quick grin but otherwise seemed content to hang with the big kids, and I was glad to see her enjoying some freedom.

I put things away so I wouldn't have to worry later, then Gabe asked me to make a plate and follow him. He led us to a balcony outside his bedroom, a secluded perch atop the covered back deck. A bar-height cafe table with sleek lines and cushioned seats made a comfortable place to land. The hill fell away sharply below the home, and the resulting view stretched endlessly, with few signs of civilization in sight. Clouds had moved into the region, covering much of the sky and obscuring some of its color, but we could still watch hints of sunlight finish their descent into the mountains. We dug in to enjoy our dinner.

"This tastes awesome, Sammy. Thanks for cooking. That's above and beyond."

"I don't mind at all." I enjoyed the warm food and the Oregon Pinot Noir Gabe poured as the clouds shifted East, revealing hints of rosy color where light peeked through. Even under the pall of a heavy sky, the splendor of the gorge seemed boundless. "Boy, if you spend all your time around cheering fans, I bet this place is an amazing haven from the fray."

"As long as there's someone to enjoy it with, it's hard to beat."

At the cabin in North Carolina, Gabe talked about the house growing quiet lately. I could only imagine the depth of the solitude you'd feel if you found yourself alone out here.

As we ate, the western edge of the sky darkened from warm colors to a dusky twilight, and after dinner, Gabe really did open a bottle of port, making it hard to keep a straight face as we sipped and watched the night descend. The balcony light was on, and little bugs buzzed around its glowing beacon in the darkness. Eventually, fireflies winked in the trees below, and the quiet chirp of crickets rose around us in a soothing song.

We talked about his recent tour stops, about Trevor's friends, and about our families. We were well into our second glass of port, and the night sky had darkened to an inky black when Gabe paused the conversation. "Sammy, I need to say, I really am sorry for what I did this week. I gave you terrible news, then piled on with accusations and made it worse. I'd take that back if I could."

I looked over at him. "Well, I'm sorry I ran away from the cabins in North Carolina." I shrugged. "Turns out we've both rack up some scars in life. You're more than forgiven. Truly."

He stood up, walked behind my chair, and massaged my shoulders. "You deserve some relaxation." His hands were strong, broad, and nimble. Sensation emanated in waves every-where he stroked my skin.

"Unnnh." My head lolled forward.

He continued to work my muscles, loosening the kinks in my shoulders and neck.

"That feels incredible." My whole body softened, becoming pliable in his hands.

"Come here. Stand up. I can do better."

I was eager to do anything that continued his magic touches, and I followed Gabe to the deck railing.

He stepped behind me, pressed his hands against my neck, and began to work his warm fingers against my muscles again. He deepened the massage, kneading the flesh behind my ears and rubbing his fingers along my hairline. He loosened the tight sinew in my neck until I had no words. Then he gradually shifted to long firm strokes across my shoulders and down the length of my arms and back, the halter neck and open back of the sundress baring my skin to his touch.

The heat and electricity built up on my body. I tried to turn to him, to kiss him, but he held me in place.

"Just stay there, Sammy. Let me make you feel good."

He brought his body against my back, and planted slow, deep kisses across the sensitive skin of my neck. I leaned my head against his shoulder, luxuriating in the charge of his touch, my heart rate rising. He roved his hands to my hips, then up the front of my body, crisscrossing my belly, caressing my ribs, and sliding beneath my halter to cup my sensitive breasts in his warm palms. He grew hard against me.

I stilled his hands with my own. "Gabe."

"Mmh?" He continued to kiss my neck.

His mouth was a wonder of the world, and my brain was melting at the edges. "Gabe. . . outside gets us in trouble."

He gently pulled one of his hands free and moved it lower, beneath the hem of my dress, scattering spells across my thighs. "There's no trouble for miles, Sammy."

Logic was evaporating from my system, as his fingers found the lacy edge of my panties, teasing me through the thin fabric.

"Gabe. . . really. . . we should go inside."

He finally paused. His chest rose and fell against my back. "Wait here a second, okay?"

He disappeared into the bedroom. A click sounded from the door in the hallway, and the bedroom lights blinked off. His footfalls crossed the carpet, then the outdoor lanterns went dark. Only his dim outline showed when he rejoined me on the balcony, sliding the screen door shut.

We stood beneath a profound blanket of night.

I leaned my hands against the barely discernible railing, looking out into the inky landscape. Heavy clouds obscured all but a few scant stars and peekaboo views of a silver, crescent moon, hanging low in the western sky. The river wasn't visible except for the moon's fleeting reflection on the water. The foothills and mountains that should have dominated the horizon remained hidden. I saw no streetlamps, no lights from other homes, no passing cars. Twinkling fireflies and the night sounds of the insects were the only hints life still surrounded us.

Gabe stepped behind me again, leaning his warm body against mine, wrapping his sturdy arms around my torso. "See. Nothing for miles," he breathed. The hypnotic strength of his hands found my curves. "Still wanna go inside?" His magical mouth moved to my neck again.

What do I want? I want him. I want this pleasure, this peace, this utter escape from everything. "You, Gabe. You're what I want," I whispered.

He slipped his hands under my dress, and a laugh burst out near-by.

Kids' voices drifted to us, and lights blazed on from the covered deck below. A door slammed shut. Conversations peppered the air.

"Ugh." Gabe's hands stilled on my thighs. He collapsed his forehead against my shoulder.

I turned to him, keeping my cheek close to his. "Inside," I breathed. The hearty bulk of his body pressed against mine. "Inside will be just as good."

He led the way to the bed, and we *did* make it good.

The way he moved inside me reminded me why the mere thought of his touch could boil my blood. . . why the memory of his heft stayed with me long after our time in Creekside.

Our phone calls hadn't gone to waste either—we had both paid attention. He found my triggers with ease, and I said the words I knew sent him sailing. He pounded me in waves until my muscles grew limp, my nerves exploded, and our pleasure crashed around us in earth-shaking tremors.

Later that night, lulled by release, I finally drifted into a solid sleep, no longer searching in the dark for answers that didn't exist.

29

— · —

DISCLOSURE

THE STALKER

Claudia's phone rang as the evening sky in Los Angeles turned vibrant shades of pink and orange.

"Hey, Oscar," she answered.

"Hey, babe. Got another update for you. This one's juicy."

Claudia watched traffic clash in the streets below. Sometimes, everything in life was a tangled mess. "What is it this time?"

"So, get this. He flew Sammy and her kid to his house in Oregon."

"What?" This was moving in the worst direction. Bile stirred in her gut. "I'm really starting to hate her."

"Yeah but hang on. It gets better. I'm stuck here—with the old lady."

"Stuck where? . . . *In Philadelphia?*"

"Yup. Grandma refused to go. There's been a death threat, and the other two took off, but she stayed."

"With *you* as bodyguard?"

"You've got it."

"Ooooh. . . I think I finally know how to squeeze where it hurts." Claudia's mind raced with possibilities.

"Whatever Claudia. Nobody's gonna *squeeze* anybody. I just thought you'd get a kick out of it."

He was always blowing her off. *Did he not get it?*

"No, Oscar, wrong again. I've been stuck on location all week, getting nowhere, and this is finally a chance to apply some leverage. It's too easy to pass up."

"Relax, C. Why don't we move past this crap and get to the good stuff? That will make you feel better." He practically panted into the phone. "Are you wearing a skirt? Something that can slide up?"

She had no patience for him today. "*God*, Oscar, you can be so clueless. The news you just gave me? That *is* the good part of this call. I've been looking for a way in, and you're finally giving it to me."

"No, I'm not."

"Like hell you aren't. You owe me."

"Oh, that's bullshit, Claudia! We're settled up at the end of every call."

"Not even close. Listen, when I get there, just stand down, okay?"

"*Stand down?*" Oscar's rumbling voice lost its playful edge. "*Are you crazy?* Listen, we can play spy games and have our happy endings on the phone, but this isn't some public concert venue. *Do not* come here. You'll blow my cover."

"I'll go where I damn well want." Claudia was so sick of men who thought they owned her. . . who thought her needs didn't matter.

"Don't fuck with my paycheck!"

"You're fucking with mine!"

"You listen to me." Oscar steamed angry breaths into the phone. "If you show up here, you're not getting anywhere near that woman. I *will* do my job."

"I'll enjoy seeing you try." Claudia hung up, killing the line before he could get another word in.

30

Headed to the Canyon

SAMMY

The next morning, people ambled through the kitchen for orange juice and coffee as the household slowly awakened. Gabe's chef was hard at work, whipping up a cheesy, vegetable-rich frittata. The smell of something buttery and cinnamon-laden filled the house, and a huge dish of fresh fruit brightened the kitchen island. What a wonderful luxury.

Gabe was on the back deck playing guitar, singing, and sipping coffee with Trevor and his friends. I was on my way to join them when Meghan sauntered in. I hadn't caught up with her since we arrived.

"Hey, sweetheart. How's it going?"

She looked more relaxed than I'd seen her in a while.

"Mom, it's so good." She sighed, filled a coffee mug, and stirred obscene amounts of cream and sugar into it. "Trevor's friends are amazing."

"Oh yeah?"

"Yeah. A few are studying music or medicine, but several of those kids are in business school out here. Do you know how many good programs are on the West Coast?" She sipped at her coffee. "UC Berkeley, Stanford, Pepperdine, UC San Diego. They go to school—*and live*—right near the mountains and the ocean and. . . all of this!"

"Meghan, we have mountains and oceans on the East coast, too. We practically lived at the shore on the weekends when you were little."

"I know, but it's not the same. I mean these are big mountains, national parks. It's different, and you know it."

"Well, the scale is grander, I'll give you that."

We picked at plates of fruit while we chatted, the heavenly scent of baked goods growing stronger.

"Wanna go hang with everyone outside?" I asked. If I stayed in the kitchen, I might start drooling.

Meghan didn't miss a beat. She hopped off her barstool and led the way out to the deck, where Trevor was holding court, explaining the itinerary. "We'll head over to the amphitheater in the early afternoon. Everyone needs to pack their bags for a night or two."

We settle in as he went on. full of excitement. I couldn't believe the front row seat we were getting to all of this.

"It takes maybe four hours to get there," Trevor continued. "We'll be allowed to hang backstage and listen to the warmup, but we can also hike around or take bikes out on the grounds if we want to. The tour buses pack a dozen of them. It's super cool. Plus, The Sloping Crux plays the first couple nights before my dad, and Baja Gravy headlines after him over the weekend. So, they may turn up for a duet or something. It's kind of epic."

The Sloping Crux was Meghan's favorite. She would lose her mind if they showed up.

"Are we camping there?" asked one of his friends.

"No, we'll head out to private property afterwards. My dad rents a bunch of RVs, and we'll just party and hang out." His rakish smile indicated that this festival had quickly become a relished tradition. "Welcome to Wonderland."

***

A few hours later, our heavily laden bus rumbled beneath the Sam Hill Memorial Bridge's weathered steel trusswork as we crossed the Columbia River into Washington state. I sat with Gabe in the middle rows; Lucy held vigil near the door, and the kids crowded all the way to the back, reveling in the day ahead.

The ride was long and crossed a landscape that shifted from the lushness of western Oregon into something more arid and sparse as the miles slipped away.

Where the bare skin peeked out from my shorts, Gabe doodled lines across my thigh with his strong fingers.

I tried to concentrate on him rather than the thrilling heat of his touch. "You know, I never asked you. Do you get nervous before your concerts?"

He shifted in his seat to look at me and shook his head. "Not for a long time now. Actually, the longer we're at it, the more I'm just myself up there. We're putting on a show, of course, but how I'm feeling is just however I am that day—cranky or excited or whatever. We feed off each other, too—the vibes from the band and the crowd, the quality of the music—it all has a big impact." He smiled. "The Canyon is almost always awesome, though. It's other-worldly."

"I can't wait. I was supposed to attend a concert there back in college, but I got sick and missed the road trip. The Columbia Canyon Amphitheatre is a bucket-list item for me."

"Oh yeah?" Curiosity shone in his eyes. "What else is on it? Where do you want to go?"

I thought for a minute. "Lots of places, I guess. I've seen plenty of the states, but I haven't traveled much internationally. The Galapagos has been on my list and maybe Costa Rica or Belize. I'd love to hike in Switzerland someday—the pictures look so pretty. In fact, I've seen very little of Europe so far. And a safari would be amazing."

I gazed at him, bemused. "Do you still have a bucket list, or have you sort of been everywhere?"

"We've been a lot of places, of course, but there's an entire crew on the clock when we travel, so we usually can't linger. Honestly, there are still entire continents I've not explored, and that's pretty enticing. I like to get outside my comfort zone and reset my expectations of what's normal. Keeps your brain from getting stagnant." He scratched at the stubble along his jaw. "I guess if I was making a list, I'd say South America, the Caribbean, and Africa are places where I'd like to spend more time—cultures with a lot of musical tradition. Sometimes we do try new tour stops to explore a little. Build in a break afterward. Maybe we should consider that for next year."

"That's a fun thing to think about."

"One hundred percent."

It had been so long since I'd seriously contemplated travel, but the idea of exploring the world again was a rush. Meghan only had one more year of high school, and I was a business owner, so I could set my own schedule in some ways. I realized how my life could open up if my anxiety didn't get in the way.

He placed his broad hand on my thigh, stroking it gently. "You know, I don't know where things will be with you and me this fall, but we *do* have some tour dates in Europe. Maybe you could come see a few shows. We could stick around after and knock an item or two off of your bucket list. Could be fun."

"That sounds pretty great." It sounded *more* than great. Could that really be my life again? Traveling? Seeing new people and places? Getting to spend more time with Gabe? I hoped so. Mom could probably keep an eye on Meghan if I decided to join him on trips.

On that thought, I realized I hadn't called Mom yet, and I asked Gabe to pardon me while I gave her a quick ring. She was hustling out the door when I reached her, so I had to be content with just a quick assurance that she was doing well and things at the house were uneventful.

As long as I was checking in on my life, I took a few minutes to sift through emails, too. A few from our Nashville and Madison locations merited a response, but they were easy to handle. Still nothing from Debbie on HopNBrew. I wondered if I should be a little pushier there. I drafted a follow-up note.

I was still typing when a Zoom notification pinged my phone: my biweekly conference with Jesse and Bobby. *Crap.* The bus offered limited privacy, but skipping wasn't an option. I found an empty row of seats, plugged in headphones, and logged in. Jesse was already online, and his wicked smile told me more than any general ledger could.

"You're looking happy."

"We had a thirty-minute wait on Saturday." His dark eyes reflected an almost lascivious pleasure. "People literally lined up to come inside. I'm so stoked."

"That's great news!"

"The summer fairs were a hit. I took your advice, and we served Bru Burgers and flights at 'Madison Gathers' and the 'Lake Mendota Flavor Fest.' I think it worked."

"Keep your foot on the gas, and build on this, Jesse. You've seen what outreach can do. Keep it up!"

An uneven section of pavement bounced me.

Jesse chuckled. "Are you on a bus?"

Whoops. "A little road trip."

"Where are you going?"

I angled the camera more carefully. "I'll fill you in later, if that's all right. Any other issues? Are the glitches in the point-of-sale system ironed out?"

We talked technology, lingering to brainstorm over a few more challenges, before wrapping up the call.

Despite the meeting running long, Bobby never showed, and I realized we hadn't connected face-to-face in almost a month. Charlotte's air conditioning outage had interrupted our last Zoom, and he had declined our follow up. Plus, this little journey to the Pacific Northwest meant delaying my plans to finally pay him a visit.

I still remembered the battered look in Bobby's brown eyes when we last spoke, and guilt twisted my heart. Antsy to stay engaged and help, I scheduled a one-on-one with him for the following week and decided to call as well. A minute later, I had only a voicemail to show for the effort.

I sighed, frustrated at my inability to make even a sliver of impact there. In reality, though, there was little I could do from a tour bus in the remote wilds of Washington state. At some point, I simply had to trust the professionalism and competence of our team. Forbidden Brews would be sunk without it anyway.

I blew out a breath and moved on, checking on the company's social media accounts. I'd need to make another post soon, just to maintain engagement and stay in people's feeds. The algorithms seemed to demand a constant presence, but I didn't want to rush a bad post. Better to wait until I could crack open my laptop and design something of quality.

Reassured that I'd done what I could to keep Forbidden Brews on a decent trajectory, I put my phone away, rejoined Gabe, and tried to focus on the day ahead.

The hours of travel slipped by, and we passed remarkably few towns. It was still hard to get over the unfathomable vastness of the western U.S. The sky was wide and blue here, with low mountains hugging the distant horizon in so many directions. Dry expanses of terrain alternated with regions more blessed with rain, where fields of vegetables and row crops veiled the earth.

As the afternoon stretched toward golden hour, we finally exited the freeway and made our way to the amphitheater grounds, where we turned down a long, paved road. Fences separated the road from campgrounds jammed with RVs, and clusters of temporary structures dotted the landscape. As we went deeper into the property, the mountains loomed closer, and earth scattered with silvery sage sprawled around us. Finally, the road made a sudden descent, revealing the stage ahead as well as the full beauty of the famous gorge.

The spectacle of sunbaked cliffs looked as though the Creator had crossed the majesty of the Columbia River with the vastness of the Grand Canyon and painted it all under an impossibly wide sky. We exited the bus, meandered to the rock's edge, and marveled.

After a few minutes, Gabe leaned down and gave me a quick kiss. "We need to go get ready for the show, and I'm guessing the kids will take off on bikes. Can I introduce you to a few folks, so you're not bored?"

It turned out there was no need.

One of Gabe's drummers, Dylan, was ambling our way. "Hey! The famous Sammy! Good to see your pretty face again." He smiled wide and introduced me to the petite brunette by his side. "This is my wife, Piper."

"Hi, Sammy." She gave me a quick hug.

"Hear you guys are having a spot of trouble," Dylan said.

"I'm sure it's stressful," Piper added. "But I promise: these things almost always blow over."

"That's what we're hoping for." I shrugged. "But at least this trip came out of it, and I'm excited about the concert. Those are good things, right?"

Dylan punched Gabe's arm playfully, his smile devilish. "Notice she didn't mention you, big guy. You being lousy company again?"

Piper tsked. "Dylan, knock it off, you'll scare her away." She gave me a pointed look. "Don't mind my husband, Sammy. Gabe's great."

A blonde, pony-tailed woman approached the fringes of our circle, chattering into a headset. She tapped Dylan's shoulder. "Dylan? Gabe? Time for sound check."

"Thanks, Ellen. Got it."

Piper took hold of my arm. "Go on, guys. Shoo. I'll show her the ropes."

The guys disappeared to get ready, and Piper guided me to the catering cart. We helped ourselves to cocktails and hors d'oeuvres before settling in together at a picnic table beneath a white canopy near the edge of the canyon.

Halfway through our drinks, sounds rose from the stage. At first, there was just a cacophonous, halting jumble of chords as the band tuned up and sampled the sound mix. Eventually, though, everyone must have synched up, because the first true notes of music lifted into the atmosphere.

The rich bass vibrated my ribs; the sweet sound of the guitar set a captivating melody, and the drums drove a rhythm directly into my bones, so that I couldn't help but move.

It was going to be one hell of an evening.

31

—·—

Intruder

THE ENABLER

Sometimes, Oscar had the best job on the planet. He had staked out a perch on Sammy's front porch swing, where he could keep an eye on the street and smoke as much as he liked. . . maybe even browse a little porn. Practically a fucking vacation.

Sunset always brought out the mosquitoes, though. When he felt the first bite, he considered retreating indoors. The motion-sensitive cameras he'd mounted along the fence line monitored things better than he could anyway, once it got dark. He toggled through the cameras on his smart watch and took comfort. Everything was working as it should.

A car pulled up across the street and parked. No one moved for a minute. Then Claudia emerged from the driver's-side door and made a beeline for the carriage house.

Oscar stubbed out his cigarette and scrambled down the porch stairs in a flash. "Freeze, Claudia. Not another inch." He unholstered his Sig P220, holding it discreetly at his side. An ornamental cherry tree sheltered him from the neighbors' view, but he'd still prefer not to flash the gun around.

Claudia paused, then simply changed course, approaching Oscar instead.

"Claudia, get your hands where I can see them. I'm not fucking around."

"Relax, Oscar, I'm harmless." She lifted her tiny hands up subtly, just to the height of her ribs, and continued walking toward him.

"You need to leave."

"Oh, come on. When's the last time I could get near you without Gabe's people shooing me away." She took a few steps closer. "I just thought maybe you were tired of all the phone sex and might like to enjoy me in person again."

His heart picked up pace. Even in the dimming twilight, she was spectacularly beautiful. Her face was all slender, symmetrical angles, and her blonde hair fell like silk down her shoulders. Her wide-legged linen pants cinched snugly at her waist. If he tugged the drawstring, he imagined they would fall right off. She clearly wore no bra beneath her camisole. In his mind, she was already naked.

He tore his gaze away from her nipples. "Get lost, Claudia."

"Oscar, I'm not armed. I'm just here for fun." She eased toward him. "Why don't you frisk me? See for yourself, so you can chill out."

He tried to control his breathing but was failing. He knew what lay inside those pants was tight as a fist.

She drew close and placed her hands on his chest. "Go ahead, Oscar. Check me for weapons. I want to see what happens when you do it." She dragged her fingernails toward his waistband, then slid her hand in his pants, gripping him gently. "Come on. Show me what happens."

The cherry tree obscured the neighbors' view, but Kate was home. He really should chase her away.

She started to rub her hand in mesmerizing circles. "I know what you need, Oscar," she breathed. "No one should keep you from what you need."

His brain lost focus.

Using his free hand, he felt around Claudia's waistband and stroked the firm curves of her ass. *No weapons there.* He patted her pockets—nothing but a lighter. He needed to check her ankles too. She could have anything concealed in those baggy pants. He tucked the Sig into his waist holster and bent to stroke both hands down her toned legs.

She lunged for the gun.

"Goddamnit, Claudia!" He grabbed her tiny wrist in his giant paw. "What the hell?"

"I'm just playing Oscar. Relax." She laughed at him. "Seriously, you should see your face."

He finished feeling up her legs. He could see goosebumps through her top. Nothing could hide there. She was unarmed.

He led her to the porch, peeked through the door to make sure Sammy's mom wasn't inside, then hustled Claudia up the old wooden stairs to the second floor.

On the landing outside Sammy's bedroom, Claudia stripped off her cami, baring her round, plump breasts. The last of Oscar's blood rushed from his brain to his groin. She pulled the drawstring on her pants, and they fluttered to the floor, just like he thought they might. She wore nothing else.

Oscar picked her up in a fireman's hold, carried her into Sammy's room, and barely made it to the bed.

***

Afterward, he lay beneath her, drowsy, his heart still pounding. He glanced at the nightstand and saw his pistol. From this position, Claudia could grab it before he could—if she wanted. His wallet and phone sat on the opposite bedside table, and he began to realize just how stupid this was. Slowly shifting his body, he moved from under her, picked up the pistol, and eased out of bed.

She propped herself up on her elbow. "You're getting up?"

"You need to go, Claudia. This was fun, but you need to split."

"Not yet." She looked around curiously. "So, is this where she sleeps? Surprised she let you in here."

"She didn't. But I'm not sleeping on a fucking twin mattress." He found his underwear and pulled them on. "And she didn't let you in, either. Get dressed. You need to get gone."

Claudia slipped out of bed and perused the simple white room, peeking in drawers and lifting up picture frames. "Ugh, could she be any more plain?"

Oscar crossed to the opposite bedside stand and tucked his wallet in the drawer. "Claudia, seriously, the old lady could come in any time. You've *got* to leave. I have a job to do." He picked up his phone and checked the security cameras—no notifications.

Claudia opened Sammy's closet door and stepped inside, rifling through the hangers.

"Come on. Get out of there, Claudia. You're starting to piss me off."

A moment later, she emerged. "Look, Oscar, the ugly girl has silk scarves. What do you think we should do with these?" She walked languidly to the bed and laid upside down on it, so her head was near the footboard. She held a scarf in each hand and grabbed the posts. "If you're so worried, why don't you tie me up? I can't do any harm then. Plus. . . I think I need some more attention. I'm not quite done yet."

Oscar froze in place. Claudia *needed* to leave, but he couldn't stop staring at her. Couldn't stop imagining all the things he could do with her bound up.

She released one of the scarves, licked her fingers, and stroked them down past her belly. "Well, I guess if you're not going to help me, I'll help myself." She let her legs fall gently apart, revealing silky pink flesh.

Fuck.

All of a sudden, Oscar couldn't think of anything he'd rather do than tie her up. He walked to the foot board, grabbed the scarf, and lashed one of her wrists to the bedpost. Then he crossed to the other side of the bed, stilled her busy hand, and tied it up securely as well.

"Well, Oscar—" her pale blue eyes shone wickedly— "I guess you can do whatever you want for as long as you want now. But try to finish me off this time. I shouldn't have to do it myself."

Oscar didn't wait another moment. He tore off his underwear and did exactly that.

***

"Oscar?" Claudia wriggled beneath him. "Oscar, wake up. You're too heavy, and I need to pee. Get up."

He could barely move. He was incredibly drowsy, like he'd been drugged. He reached up, loosened the scarves, and let her go. "Bathroom's in the hallway," he mumbled.

Darkness had settled over the room. The old, wooden bedroom door closed with a bang, and the bathroom door in the hallway clicked open and shut.

A hazy, seductive shroud of sleep weighed on Oscar, and he dozed in the margin between dreams and wakefulness, his nerves tingling with pleasure, his face buried in Sammy's comforter.

The back door chimed.

Holy shit. Oscar bolted upright. *Had he fallen asleep? What had he done?*

Oscar leapt out of bed and yanked on his pants. He zipped them carefully and fumbled around for his pistol before racing into the hallway. The bathroom door was closed, and the light was on, but that didn't mean anything. Someone was clattering around in the kitchen, down in the room with the giant butcher's knives. If it was Claudia, he couldn't risk it. He raced down the stairs shirtless, still reeking of sex.

Sammy's mom was crouched on the kitchen floor, foraging through the cabinet under the sink. He didn't see anyone else. "You okay, ma'am?"

"Yup. Just out of dish soap." She stood up and pivoted, taking in Oscar's disheveled appearance.

He looked down at his scruffy, naked chest and realized what a mess he was. "Sorry, ma'am. I was napping and heard someone down here. Just wanted to make sure you're okay."

"I'm fine, of course." She caught herself. "Well, I guess not *of course*. I do appreciate you checking in on me. Death threats. . . Can you believe it? What a crazy world."

She looked him over more closely, tilting her head with concern. "Sure you're okay? Looks like you've had a good spook. Why don't I make us a pot of coffee." She turned on the faucet and started to fill the carafe.

How could he get out of this? *And where the hell was Claudia?* "No thanks, Kate. Can't sleep if I drink that stuff."

"Oh." She shut off the water.

"Why don't I walk you back to your cottage? Make sure you're good and settled for the night."

"All right." She dumped out the water, retrieved the detergent from the kitchen counter, and pinched his cheek. "You're a gem, Oscar."

Keeping his pistol low and out of sight, he followed her out the back door. He inspected the old carriage house but found no trace of anything amiss. He checked the window locks and took comfort everything was secure, for now.

"Good night, ma'am." He locked the door on his way out, then took a few strides to Sammy's back door, creeping cautiously into the kitchen.

***

Claudia couldn't believe her luck. *Could the old woman have better timing?* With Oscar downstairs, she could finally poke around the room freely. She rifled through Sammy's stuff and snatched a photograph or two, before deciding to leave something behind as well.

She sat her naked bottom on Sammy's office chair and grabbed a piece of paper and a pen. *It was always nice to leave your host a thank you note, right?* Using big capital letters, she scrawled quickly, digging the pen into the paper.

YOU FUCK HIM IN HIS BED. I FUCK SOMEONE IN YOURS. GET AWAY FROM HIM OR LIVE IN FEAR, YOU CUNT!

She placed Oscar's sticky, disgusting condom on top of the note, folded it in half, and slid it under a file folder in the desk drawer, leaving a little corner peeking out.

Would that do it? She *did* want it to be found soon. Looking around the desk for a moment, she saw something the little love-starved woman couldn't resist. She plucked the pink highlighter from a cup of pens and colored a big pink heart on the exposed corner of the paper. She could just see the pathetic bitch finding it, drawn to that stupid pink heart like a fly to a pile of shit.

Claudia shut the desk door, put the pink highlighter back on the desk, and continued to search the room. Checking for anything useful, she hunted through the rest of the drawers, the bedside tables, and Oscar's backpack—

Oh my God! Jackpot!

Her heart racing, she pulled on her clothes, tucked the best treasures in her pockets, and sprinted down the stairs.

***

Oscar inched back into Sammy's empty kitchen and listened intently, keeping as still as startled prey. Faint noises reverberated from the walls. The cellar stairs creaked and popped. It could just be the sounds of the house. He hadn't learned them yet.

"Claudia?" Oscar's low, rumbling voice echoed in the space.

She didn't answer.

Other than the kitchen, the first floor was unlit, and Oscar gripped his pistol tightly. "Claudia, I've got my Sig drawn. Don't do anything stupid!"

Still nothing.

Oscar eased his way into the dining room and flicked on the lights.

Empty.

Shadows swallowed the family room beyond.

He swept his gun in a wide arc and raised his voice. "Claudia, answer me, damnit! Where are you?" He stepped to the window, lifted the blinds, and surveyed the dark street.

Her car was gone.

Oscar shoulders slumped. *Way too close. Such an idiot.*

He tucked the gun in its holster and trudged back upstairs, with the leaden gait of a body suddenly drained of adrenaline.

Collapsing into Sammy's desk chair, he logged into his laptop. He confirmed the camera feeds were still working and watched recent recordings flash through the screen. Claudia appeared in hyper-exposed, night-vision images, dashing down the porch steps and driving away.

Definitely gone.

He deleted the clip and went through the last few hours' footage, erasing anything incriminating.

With that done, Oscar finally examined his surroundings, realizing how many things looked out of place. Sammy's dresser drawers hung ajar, and his backpack was splayed open. His jacket lay discarded on the floor.

God damnit.

He racked his brain. What had he stored up here? He felt the Sig in his waistband, then hustled to the bedside table and yanked the drawer open. His wallet was still there, but were his credit cards? His ID? He leafed through the billfold, found the contents intact. He located his passport next.

What else? He walked back to the dresser, picked up his watch and slid it on.

He surveyed the flat surfaces in the room. Had he left anything else up here? Prescriptions? His tablet? Had he brought his second piece?

Oscar's skin went cold. *Holy shit!*

Oscar ripped open every compartment of his backpack and tore through his jacket's inner pockets.

No Glock.

Is it still in Oregon?

He usually traveled with both guns, but this was supposed to be a quick trip—out and back. He barely brought a change of clothes.

If they were still at Gabe's, maybe Lucy and Charlie could check his duffle.

No. No way.

They would lose all respect for him if they thought he couldn't keep track of his firearms.

Had he stashed it? Oscar scavenged the room, rummaging through shelves and cabinets. He was furious with himself, and downright livid with Claudia. *That psychotic witch!*

Wrist-deep in Sammy's desk drawer, his fingers struck slime. He pulled out the pink-heart note, still oozing with DNA. When he peeled it open, his condom slid down the insane scrawl of Claudia's handwriting.

His world shifted.

Harmless? He'd thought she was harmless?

The dominoes tumbled through his mind.

She'd implicated both *of them. She was crazier than a rabid, shit-house rat!*

A horrible thought surfaced through his shocked fury. Just because Claudia had left the house didn't mean she would stay gone. And if she had his Glock. . . *Fuck!*

His heart jackhammering, Oscar flew back downstairs. He burst onto the front porch and stalked the lawn.

Claudia's car was nowhere to be seen, and the street was quiet.

Oscar considered resuming his stakeout on the porch swing, but Claudia could be anywhere. She could slip through a side yard for all he knew.

Oscar crept down the dark driveway toward the carriage house and peeked through the moon of windows on Kate's door. She was lounging in a recliner, reading by the light of a dim lamp. He gently tested the knob.

Still locked.

He backed away and checked his phone, reviewing the camera activity from the last quarter hour. Claudia hadn't reentered the property since he'd wiped the recordings.

Oscar lit a cigarette and took a few drags, mentally scrounging for options. The glowing edge burned halfway to the filter before he resigned himself to the consequences of his shitty judgment.

There would be no sleep tonight.

He went inside and grabbed a throw pillow and afghan from the couch before exiting the back door again. A decrepit chaise sat on the patio, and he scraped it across the concrete until it blocked Kate's door. He laid it almost flat, then settled his considerable frame on it for the night, stubbing out his dead cigarette and lighting another.

Oscar breathed the nicotine deeply and blew out thin, curling trails of smoke, watching them evaporate into the night.

Anger thrummed in his blood.

That Glock was on the grid.

More than a decade ago, Oscar fired it in defense of a client. Forensics teams had pored over the scene, logging the minutia of death and violence in the permanent public record. The unique etchings Oscar's Glock left on a bullet were enshrined in the NIB-IN database. If Claudia shot anyone, the ballistics would lead law enforcement right back to him.

Gabe would know.

His career would be finished.

The police would be all over him. *Good Lord. . . it would all come crashing down.*

Oscar seethed like a building storm, his thoughts spiraling. On the one hand, he refused to regret the night. That kinky shit with Claudia would inhabit his fantasies forever, a sparkling souvenir from fucking the crazy bitch.

But there were limits to the entertainment of an unhinged woman, and she'd crossed a bright red line with the theft of his .357.

As the night stretched on, Oscar's consciousness warped, stretched beyond reason by fatigue. He imagined endless hor-ror—the worst scenarios. Spilled blood. Shredded organs. The carnage of wasted lives due to his carelessness and the psychotic behavior of that deranged woman.

His anger boiled for hours, slowly reducing into something hard and unforgiving.

Because as best as he could figure it, if Claudia had stolen his Glock. . . he was gonna kill her.

32

FIRST NIGHT AT THE CANYON

SAMMY

From the comfort of the billowy hospitality tent, a small crowd of family and friends absorbed the vibrancy of the concert while the fiery skies of sunset transformed the Columbia River into a shimmering expanse of gold. The drummers propelled an irresistible groove, and the crowd swelled with excitement as well-loved melodies and rich, reverberating chords filled the atmosphere. The concert stretched for hours as the world beyond the blazing, high-wattage stage lights gradually melted into a deep, black night.

When the set finally wrapped and the encores were complete, the band came offstage, reconnecting with loved ones before ducking into trailers to refresh.

Gabe appeared after a bit, his hair damp and his face glowing. "Man, I am so pumped! Tonight felt awesome!"

"It sounded awesome! Really, really amazing!" I gave him a big kiss.

He lifted me off the ground, swinging me around for a moment. "Damn, I love the Canyon." He took my hand. "Come on, Sammy. Let's go find everyone. It's time to celebrate."

***

W e sat near the front of the bus again and watched as the kids stumbled in. They clattered and laughed their way to the back seats with Meghan right in the mix. She glanced our way as she passed by, noting my hands in Gabe's. Her eyebrow shot up, and she tried to hide an amused grin as she followed the pack.

After a mercifully short drive, we pulled off the road onto a dirt path cutting between vast groves of cherry trees, their wispy branches disappearing into the night just beyond our headlights. We continued through the dark landscape until the land opened up. A half dozen RVs circled a wide swath of grass, their awnings twinkling with string lights.

We parked and waited as Trevor and his friends unloaded cargo from the belly of the bus. By the time we retrieved our bags, the lights in the kids' RVs were already shining, portable gas firepits had been cranked to life, and music filled the cooling night air.

Gabe turned on his phone flashlight and headed away from the crowd. "My RV's over here."

"I'll follow you."

We walked through the grass for longer than I expected, and I stopped when the kids' music began to fade, scrutinizing the firelit party in the distance. "Gabe, where are Charlie and Lucy?"

"Um, they stay back near the kids." He followed my gaze. "Why? Would you feel safer if they were with us?"

"No, it's not that."

This was more spread out than we'd been at Gabe's place, and discomfort squirmed in my gut. I could make out Meghan's profile. She sat with a cluster of girls, but the blond boy I kept seeing her with throughout the day was right at her side. "Who's the boy that's been hovering so close to Meghan?"

He squinted in the kids' direction. "You mean Connor?

"The blond. On her left."

"Yeah, that's Connor. Trevor's neighbor growing up. Sweet kid, really. I think he just finished high school."

I stared at the faraway scene, deliberating. Gabe knew these kids. But I didn't.

"You're worried about Meghan?"

"A little." Even though she would be a college student soon, exposed to hordes of new people, living with the freedom to exercise all kinds of bad judgment, I still felt uneasy. The kids were cracking open beers when we'd walked away, and I had no idea what else would be passed around. Inebriation never produced terrific judgment in anyone.

Gabe tilted his head. "You know I've got Charlie and Lucy all over this, right?"

I met his eyes. I didn't *know* anything.

"Sammy, I didn't think to say anything before, but we're aware Meghan is underage. She'll stay in Lucy's trailer, along with any girls who go overboard. . . Period."

I nodded.

"Look, it's a party and we give the kids some latitude, but the team knows: nothing happens on this property that could cause actual harm. . . or leave me liable."

Another strange aspect of his world. At times, I worried about what happened at my home when I was away, but I'd never hired a team of professionals to manage it. "I guess you've thought through this already."

"Motto's simple. Have fun. Be safe." His smile twitched in the glow of the flashlight. "Avoid idiocy."

I chuckled. "How's that working for you?"

A spark of humor lit his eyes. "Better with the kids than with me, evidently."

His levity was infectious. "You're funny, you know that?"

"Sometimes." He squeezed my hand, bouncing on his heels. "Come on, Sammy. All's well, and I'm starving."

We finished our trek toward the twinkling lights of Gabe's RV and stepped inside to find surprisingly posh accommodations. Dark wood cabinets and gleaming stainless steel surfaces accented a kitchenette, and plush leather seating surrounded a table for four. A luxurious sleeping area lay along the back wall, and open windows let in the cool night air.

Gabe dug foil containers out of the fridge and sifted through bottles lining a well-stocked bar. "Hungry? Anything to drink?"

"We munched appetizers at the Canyon, so I think I'm okay. But I'll join you in a nightcap."

He heated up a plate in the microwave and poured us both a short glass of Irish whiskey over ice, then sat down and dug in.

I could only imagine how much he needed to refuel. "You guys crushed it tonight. That crowd was so full of energy."

"Yeah." His infectious smile was full of excitement. "Did you have a good time?"

"Are you kidding? The venue lived up to the hype, and the concert was genuinely epic."

He grinned and wolfed down a few more bites before chattering away again. "Man, I'm amped. I love a night like this–when the band vibes, the crowd is charged, and the venue is so pretty. I can't describe it."

"I could feel it. I'm bubbling, too." I sipped the whiskey while he ate, savoring notes of caramel and the warmth it spread through me. Despite being in the elements all evening, the night air drifting through the windows was so enticing and fresh, and I just didn't want to be cooped up yet. "You know, when you're done, why don't we go sit outside? That's as good a place as any if you're energized."

Gabe agreed, and when he finished, we grabbed the whiskeys and a portable speaker and headed out the door. The temperature had dropped a bit, but it was still wonderful outside. We settled into camping chairs with an outdoor rug at our feet and string lights overhead.

"Hmm. . . hold on. Check this out." Gabe stood and turned the string lights off, plunging us into darkness. Then he rolled the awning back, revealing a brilliant spectacle of stars. With last night's cloud cover gone and no light pollution from the amphitheater, they shone from every corner of the sky.

"Wow. . ." It was so much clearer than anything I'd seen in Philadelphia.

"Just wait. Keep looking." He came to stand behind my chair.

My eyes adjusted slowly, and the contrast of the inky sky against the bright pinpricks of light became clearer. Layers of fainter stars gradually appeared behind the brightest ones, until a sparkling blizzard of distant suns filled the sky. The faint cloud of the Milky Way whispered into focus, stretching in an ethereal ribbon across the heavens. "It's overwhelmingly gorgeous."

"Pretty spectacular." He squeezed my shoulders, then came around my chair, bursting into a grin. "I've got to *do* something though. Should we go hang with the kids? They've got some campfires, and I could grab my guitar."

I studied him. It was such fun seeing him all wound up and joyous. "We could go hang with the kids for sure, but one other idea. . . do you like to dance?"

He laughed. "Are you kidding? Of course I do."

I connected my smartphone to the speaker and cued up a band I loved to listen to when I was cooking or enjoying cocktails at night. The sounds of a keyboard, guitar, upright bass, and drums poured out, and a woman's rich, full voice filled the night. The music rocked and swayed, a soulful blend of classic sound, jazz, and rock.

Gabe held out his hand to me, and I stood to join him. He spun me around to the mid-tempo rhythm, his fingers warm on my skin. His body was no less captivating this way than any other time. His strong shoulders and chest made me want to stay close, and when the music slowed and he pulled my hips against his, heat and arousal wound a sinuous path through my body.

We kept dancing and taking breaks to sip our drinks, letting the music wash over us. Before long, the magical sky, the stirring melodies, and the warmth of the whiskey produced a glow in me so strong I couldn't remember any pain at all.

In fact, I realized everything was a little too soft. Evidently, whiskey plus appetizers-wasn't going to cut it. The last thing I wanted was to go over the edge and miss out. I asked Gabe to give me a minute, and I fumbled my way inside to down some water and a few bites of food. Once I felt steadier, I made my way back outside, sat on a lawn chair, and laid my head back. I turned my eyes to the sky, enjoying the music's jazzy, lilting beat.

A moment later, the first one blazed by. "Oh my God, did you see that?"

"No. What?" Gabe's eyes followed mine, and another sizzled by. "Whoa!"

I tried to make my brain work, but it was foggy. "Gabe, what's the date?"

"August eleventh. The festival is a week later than usual this year."

"Oh my gosh, I can't believe I forgot." I looked around at the dark skies and felt like I'd won the lottery. "The Perseid meteor shower is tonight. It's always strongest the night before Tina's birthday. I can't believe I didn't connect the dots. Hold on."

I popped into the RV again and brought out pillows and blankets to cushion the thin outdoor rug. Meghan wouldn't want to miss this either, and I shot her a quick text:

Perseids meteors! Look up!!

We lay down and settled our heads on the pillows. The meteors would peak before dawn, but with the sky so dark, we could still catch an impressive show. Brilliant streaks of light raced across the sky at unpredictable moments, like little, thrilling gifts from the universe. The music played, the stars dazzled, and the night continued to feel like a soft, glowing, living thing.

We watched the celestial display as the songs ticked by, but the ground was admittedly hard. Eventually, Gabe propped himself on his elbow. He brought his warm lips to mine, his beard a gentle tickle on my face. His hand slipped over the curves of my body.

"You're a genius, Sammy. This was perfect, really, but why don't we go inside and finish the night the right way."

And we did, at least twice before morning broke, as ancient meteors continued to fall outside, leaving trails of fire in the sky.

33

—·—

SECOND NIGHT AT THE CANYON

M y body was hard-coded to Eastern time, and I woke the next morning before everyone else. The whiskey's after-effects were tangible, and I tried to combat them by drinking a tall glass of water while the coffee brewed. A peek in the refrigerator revealed a breakfast casserole and a dish of fruit. I prepped a plate as quietly as I could and carried it outside.

The cool morning air carried summery smells of pollen and earth, and birds chattered faintly from the orchard. Otherwise, a calm hung over the farm. The boondocked RVs rested like slumbering giants on a large grassy area bordered by an aging barn and empty farmhouse, where a rusty swing set moved gently in the breeze. Past the shorn clearing, rows of willowy, dwarf cherry trees stretched to the distant road and the low mountains behind us.

Settling into one of the camping chairs, I took advantage of the quiet and caught up on life for a moment. I called Mom first. She updated me on her day but then dug in a complaint. Oscar had taken up vigil on a lawn chair outside her cottage and was following her everywhere she went. "It's a little much, Sammy. Can you convince him to give me some space?"

I assured her Oscar was only trying to do his job, but I could hear the irritation in her voice, even from three thousand miles away. "Hang in there, Mom. I know this is inconvenient." She told me to quit fretting over her and headed out to her day.

I hung up the phone and thought about Tina. *How could I have forgotten her birthday was this week?* I had been a lousy friend lately. She was going through a likely divorce, and I'd been so occupied that I'd failed to call her constantly, bring her chocolate, and do whatever else I could to make it better. Now this. *What's wrong with me?*

Guilt wouldn't improve the situation though, and I decided a nice present would help. I ordered an online gift certificate from the local spa in Chestnut Hill. A day's worth of care would do her good. A call would be important, too—a text message wasn't going to cut it.

She picked up after a few rings, sounding strained. "Sammy?"

"Happy birthday, Tina!"

"Ah, well, thanks." She did not seem enthused.

"You don't sound birthday-level happy."

"Well, it's a normal crazy day. Trying to get a week's worth of work done, and Nathan has karate."

"Nothing special planned?"

"Well, since Andrew is checked out, I was presuming I might be having dinner with my best friend this weekend? Karate sort of makes tonight moot."

"I would love that." However, with the way my life had been going, I felt like I could only plan twenty-four hours at a time. "There's sort of a lot going on though. Can I get back to you on it?" As soon as the words left my mouth, I cringed.

"You're too busy for a birthday dinner with me?"

The RV door squeaked open, and Gabe came down the steps in a scrubby t-shirt, scratching his beard and blowing on a mug of coffee.

"It's not that I'm too busy. It's just that we had to step out of town again."

Gabe sat down facing me, rubbing his eyes to wake up.

"You're traveling again? Sammy, that's terrific! But also weird. Why don't I know about this? Where are you?"

"I. . . honestly, I can't say."

"*You can't say?* Sammy, what's going on with you?" Tina didn't give me a chance to respond. "And actually, I've been meaning to call. A strange man has been camped out on your porch this week, and I swear he's following your mom around, too. Should I call the police?"

"No. He's okay. Look, I know I've got a lot of explaining to do."

"And yet you're not explaining."

"I'm sorry. I've been a crappy friend lately, too. Listen, I promise I'll call as soon as we're back. I really do want to see you and get an update about everything."

"Okay. Sounds like maybe I need an update, too."

"Oh, I almost forgot. I got you a day at Chestnut Spa. Any three treatments you want. I can watch the boys while you get pampered, okay?"

"Thanks, that's very sweet," she said flatly.

Her boys were shouting in the background, and I realized that, with Andrew gone, no one would be making her day special.

"Listen, I have to run," she said. "But, let me know what's going on soon. I'm starting to worry about you."

"I will. And please treat yourself as well as you can today, all right? We'll celebrate as soon as I get back to town. I promise. . . Love you."

"Love you, too." She sounded miffed. "Bye, Sammy."

We hung up, and I rubbed my forehead. I hated lying to her and not telling her what was happening with my life. It felt all wrong.

"Is that the birthday girl you were mentioning?" Gabe asked.

"Yes."

"Didn't really sound like a festive call."

"She's a little ticked off, I think. I've been a rotten friend. Her husband filed for divorce, and I've scarcely been checking in. On top of that, I'm practically lying to her about my life. It's not great."

Gabe squinted at me. "You haven't told her about the blackmail?"

"I haven't told her *anything*. You sort of asked me not to. I mean, Ian knows about the pictures, but otherwise, I'm sneaking around behind the backs of my friends right now." I didn't look at him. I kept my eyes closed and massaged my temples, disappointed with myself.

"You know, I didn't mean you couldn't share things with close friends. I was just hoping to avoid a broadcast."

"I know this wasn't your design." I tried to remember how everything unfolded, how I got myself in this situation. "Maybe I should have told Tina a while ago. I think I would have filled her in on the way to the concert, but the moment wasn't right. Then after that, it was sort of a secret. Then the blackmail started, and it just seemed too complicated. Now it's all screwed up."

"She came to the concert with you?"

"Yes."

He scratched his cheek, took a sip of coffee, and scrunched his brow while he seemed to work something over in his mind. "I know we're trying to lay low, but do you trust her to keep a confidence?"

"I've known Tina since grade school, and she's never failed me. I trust her completely."

"Well, do you want to call her back?"

"Ugh. I think until I can be with her face-to-face, it might be better to wait. She's kind of angry. I should explain everything in person."

"Well. . . I mean, do you want to call her back together? Maybe we could wish her a happy birthday?"

Tina would pass out. She might even forgive me. "I don't want to make you uncomfortable."

"If she can truly keep it to herself, I'm not uncomfortable." He shrugged. "Maybe it's an idiotic idea, but I'm just sick of myself. I'm so paranoid and uptight that I'm screwing up your friendships. I don't want that. So, I'm thinking. . . baby steps. Let's just say hi."

"Okay. I'm sure she'd love that."

I clicked her contact again and waited while the phone rang repeatedly. I imagined her glaring at my number, trying to decide if she wanted to put up with me twice on her birthday.

She finally answered. "Sammy, what is it?" Here words sounded clipped.

"Tina, listen, I feel like crap keeping things from you. I want to explain what's going on. At least a little bit. I just need your word you'll keep it to yourself, because we really are having some security issues."

"*Security* issues?"

"Yes. Long story. But that's an armed guard you've seen at my house."

"*An armed guard?* Sammy, what have you gotten yourself into?"

"Can you FaceTime for a minute?"

"Fine," she snipped.

Her video flashed to life, her hard gaze and pinched lips leaving no doubt about her sentiments. I turned my video on, too, and panned the image wide.

Gabe smiled and raised his coffee mug to her. "Happy birthday, Tina. Thanks for letting me borrow your bestie. Sorry it's turned into a circus."

Shock and then a disbelieving grin replaced Tina's scowl. "Sammy? What. Is. Happening?" An incredulous smile widened across her face.

"I'm sorry. I know I've been cagey. It's just not been my secret to tell—"

Gabe piped in. "Come on. Let's just sing Happy Birthday to her."

We did our best. Gabe's voice was a melody of sonorous, early-morning beauty. Mine was a dumpster fire. We sang with gusto, though, and Tina was in tears by the end.

"Thank you." She wiped her cheeks with the back of her hand. "Gabriel, I just love your music. Thank you so much." She laughed. "And Sammy, for chrissakes, when you start hanging out with Gabriel Walker, you're supposed to tell me!"

"It's Gabe, Tina, and this is all my fault. You simply *must* forgive Sammy. She's been swimming through a sea of my stupid crap these days."

Tina huffed out a laugh. "Okay, *okay!* You're forgiven." She was smiling and shaking her head, still swiping at her wet cheeks. "Here and I thought this was gonna be the worst birthday ever. . . But, *girlie*, you are in *so* much trouble." Her voice was playful, and her grin was so big I could count her teeth.

I laughed with her. "The good kind of trouble, right? The I-can't-wait-to-hear-about-it kind of trouble?"

"*Oh my God*, yes! I'm clearing my calendar now." Something crashed in the background, and one of the boys started bawling. She glanced over her shoulder and sighed. "I better go check on the craziness. Thanks for the best birthday song ever though, and be good to my girl, Gabe."

He grinned diabolically. "Can I be at least a little bit bad?"

"*Oh my God!* Sammy, *holy shit!*" Tina was laughing and crying all at the same time. I'm guessing she had been sorely in need of a little birthday joy, and she was probably on a Gabe-induced cloud now to boot.

"Tina, I promise to fill you in on the whole thing. But right now, there's some bad stuff going down. Meghan's with me. Mom's safe with Oscar—the big guy on our porch. So, we're all right, and I'll probably be back this weekend, but I just don't know for sure."

"Okay, got it."

"Oh, and please don't tell anyone I'm here or hanging out with Gabe. It's actually pretty important."

"Of course. Whatever you need." She sniffed and looked around eagerly. "Can I at least tell Fred?"

I laughed. "You can tell Fred everything."

"Okay, deal. Please, be safe, though, and call me if I can help."

"Will do. And tell those boys Aunt Sammy said to quit wrestling and start giving you birthday hugs."

"Like that'll work." She was in a good enough mood to roll her eyes.

"Love you, Tina."

"Love you, too, Sammy. Bye, Gabe!"

Gabe nodded at her, a warm smile on his face. "Bye, Tina. Happy Birthday."

An enormous weight of tension tumbled from my shoulders as I disconnected the call. I took a deep breath and looked over at Gabe with an embarrassing amount of gratitude. "Thank you. I can't tell you what a relief it is to see her smile like that today."

"It was the right thing to do." Concern and regret crept over his features, though. "But, Sammy, who's Fred? Should I be freaking out?"

I laughed and got up to kiss the worry away from his gorgeous, whiskered face. "Fred's her golden retriever. We're all good."

I went back inside the RV and left Gabe's fate to the whims of a slobbering, yellow dog.

***

The shower in the RV was blessedly hot. I washed the dust out of my hair and off my body, remembering how nice it had been to spend the day and much of the night outside. As I dried off, I thought about what we should try to fit in today—how to squeeze all of the good out of this wonderful place.

On that notion, I slipped on something special before getting dressed. A very tiny something special. Gabe stepping outside his comfort zone to call Tina was a gift, and this might be a fun way to surprise him back.

***

The sun had risen above the fields to the East, and the kids were mobilizing for a boating trip down the river, bustling about in windbreakers and hiking shorts, the palpable energy from the prior day still lingering in their midst. Meghan wasn't keeping up with them, though. In fact, she looked a little green.

"Not feeling awesome?" I asked her after they left.

She looked at me askance. "Not the best."

"Have a little to drink last night?"

"Maybe."

"Well, drink as much water as you can and get some food in your system. Do you need some Tylenol?"

"Please."

I went back to the RV and returned with the medicine and a cold bottle of water.

"Thanks, Mom." She looked me over carefully. "And thank you for not getting mad."

"Well, you'll need to figure this out eventually, kiddo. I'd advise no more than one drink an hour, and maybe even have a glass of water now and again if you want to feel good the next day."

She downed the medicine and closed her eyes.

"It won't hurt to wait a few more years, though. Stay out of trouble with the law and the universities?"

"There's no law or universities here, Mom."

"True story," I said.

I sat down next to her on a camping chair, opened my book, and just kept her company. Hangovers weren't fun, but it would be a good learning experience for her, and it was well past time I let her have some of those.

***

We arrived at the amphitheater in the evening, and I decided to join the kids on their bikes. We pedaled out of the restricted area, following Trevor and Pria into the campgrounds, where thousands of pitched tents and parked campers served as impromptu shelters. Music played and friendly groups tailgated over coolers and hibachis, hunkered down for a week-long party in the sun. The breeze cooled us as we pedaled, and the landscape remained a stunning backdrop to behold.

By the time we rejoined Gabe backstage, the sun dipped low toward the horizon, drenching the canyon and everyone near it in a fiery bouquet of light.

"Gabe, come take a swing." His bassist, TJ, called out. He was huddled with a few of his bandmates, along with their spouses and kids, hitting golf balls off a miniature driving range facing the endless canyon, and we joined them. My swing was a bit out of shape, but it was still a blast to see the golf balls soar above the glowing cliffs.

Gabe sidled up to me while we waited our turn and draped his arm over my shoulder, "Hmm. . ." He idly stroked the ends of my hair. "Sammy, I know your independence and intelligence are more important, but I have to say, when this light hits your hair, it looks like someone set silk on fire. It's pretty damn bewitching."

I couldn't stop a smile. "Oh, yeah?" I turned to face him and wrapped my arms around his shoulders. "You're pretty damn be-witching all the time."

"I'm sure glad you think so." He bent down to kiss me, sending a current of electricity clear to my toes. Then he shook his head. "You know, I can't believe I'm the one asking again, but will you take a selfie with me? It's too pretty not to."

We found a spot along the fence guarding the rim, and I snuggled into his shoulder as he snapped a picture looking back over the blazing spectacle of the gorge, all lit up by golden hour. After taking a few more for good measure, including one of us kissing, he zapped the lot to my phone.

The crowd was starting to fill the amphitheater, stirring the at-mosphere with excitement and anticipation. I was right where I wanted to be, but I almost envied their vantage point. I couldn't imagine a better way to enjoy a concert than with this awe-inspiring view. "What an *incredible* venue."

"Yeah. Should be a good night. Did you get behind the stage yesterday?"

"No. Can we even do that?"

"I think so, but ask Lucy. It's fun to look out over the crowd." He put his hands around my waist and pulled me close. "I really do like having you here, Sammy. I think I'm a lucky guy, today."

Misty beams of radiant, rosy light cast a blush on his skin and sidelit the warm amber of his eyes. I soaked up the splendor of him.

Marveled at the spellbinding haze of sunlight that enveloped the fathomless canyon. Hummed with desire from the simple touch of his heated palms and the pressure of his hips against mine.

The sharp contrast to what this week could have been suddenly struck me with force, and my heart swelled.

He hadn't been obligated to fly us to this cocoon of safety. He could have handed the threatening emails to the police, let me know, then returned his attention to the million moving parts of his life. Instead, he paused everything until he knew we were cared for: me, Meghan, and Mom.

Every one of us was so deeply flawed, but knowing that he tried, that he would go out of his way to do right. . . it meant so much. If things went well, it would be one of a thousand building blocks of trust, but that particular piece felt foundational.

I held his gaze, full of the sun's brilliant reflection. "You're a warm, wonderful, human being, Gabe Walker. Thank you for bringing us here."

"Of course. I got you into this." An easy smile spread over his lips. "I'd better help get you out of it."

"Well, we got into it together I'm pretty sure." I ran a finger over the stubble along his neck. "I know I would have found a way to keep us safe in Philly, but it would have been stressful and scary—especially for Meghan. It *certainly* wouldn't have been magical."

His eyes drank in mine, and he seemed taken with the moment, too. He peeled a strand of wind-whipped hair from my cheek. "See?" He tucked it gently behind my ear. "Otherworldly, right?"

"Otherworldly."

We kissed, and the universe slipped away for a moment. My cells bloomed, vibrating with the sturdy substance of his embrace and the comfort of his inherent goodness. I let myself get lost in the feel of his luscious mouth, of his strong shoulders.

When we paused for oxygen, he lowered his forehead to mine and blew a long breath. He shifted his hands above my hips, idly fingering the lacy strands of the complicated garment I'd snuck beneath my clothes that morning.

Confusion crossed his face, and he stepped back a pace. He lifted the edge of my blouse with his thumbs, revealing the network of green lace and tight straps that crisscrossed my belly and hips. "*Holy shit!* What is *this*?"

Ha! Got him. I grinned. "Something for you to look forward to."

He glanced at the crowd gathering in the amphitheater, then returned his attention to me. His eyes narrowed and focused. "You know, we're not legally required to start playing right away. I bet we can sneak into one of the RVs and get a better look at this—just for a few minutes."

Thousands of eager fans loomed on the hillside. "I'm not gonna be responsible for a riot, Gabe."

"A riot? Them?" He eyed the masses again. "Look how peaceful they are." He leaned closer. "I bet we could see the sunset from inside the RVs." He waggled his eyebrows. "We could make it memorable."

"*Un-uh!*" Ellen's voice carried to us. She hurried over from the driving range, where his bandmates were departing from their loved ones as they headed for the stage. She barged into our space, wagging a finger, pressing a button on her headset. "*No way.* Don't even *think* about it."

"Think about what?" Gabe's hands were still under my shirt.

"Gabe, I have the hearing of a bat. You should know this by now." She leveled a stern gaze at him.

"Eight? Eight-thirty? Is it really so different?"

She pointed the V of her index and middle fingers at her own eyes, then at Gabe's. "I see you. Do *not* test me." She glanced my way. "You're sending him to the stage, right? Can I trust you here?"

"Yes, ma'am." *She looked my age. Why on earth was I ma'am-ing her?*

"Good." She scuttled off, chasing down some poor soul chatting near the catering carts.

I couldn't help but chuckle. "Do you work for *her*, or does she work for *you*?"

"Hard to tell sometimes. We'd be a mess without her though." He dug his fingers beneath the lacy straps of the lingerie. "Promise you'll still be wearing this later?"

"I promise."

"I'll hold you to it." He planted one more searing kiss on my lips, his hands roving more places than they should have with people around. "See you soon, Sammy."

***

The bus ride back to his home lasted until the wee hours, and half the kids were asleep when we arrived.

I could barely keep my eyes open and was toddling back to my room when Gabe caught up to me. "Oh, no way, lady. You're coming with me." He grabbed me by the hips and all but dragged me into his room.

Where he found the energy to do that much was a mystery, and I laughed. "Gabe, you were sleeping on the way home. Your *drool* is on my shirt."

"There's gonna be drool everywhere. Come on. I have to see that thing."

He locked the door, stripped off his clothes, and climbed into bed, turning on a dim bedside lamp. Though his eyes were barely open, his schoolboy grin spread wide.

Shrugging off the fog of sleep, I tried to play along. I stepped out of my shoes, one by one, then unbuttoned my shorts and let them drop to the floor. Slowly, I inched my blouse over my head and tossed it to the ground.

The lingerie wasn't the most comfortable thing I owned, but wearing it always turned me on. Sheer triangles of forest green lace covered my breasts and bikini line, and a tight, cordlike network of straps gripped my curves, making me feel sexy and a little powerful.

I spun around lightly. "Do you approve?"

"Five stars, Sammy. Ten out of ten." He pulled back the covers and yawned wide.

"Well don't do *that*." The infectious gesture had me yawning, too, and we chuckled as I joined him under the comforter.

Despite the late hour, he didn't skip any steps. He tugged my thigh over his hip and took the time to cup my flesh and caress me over the lacey garment.

Our tongues tangled in a kiss, and when his fingers slipped between my legs, the sensation was a shot of espresso, blazing my nerves awake.

When he had me sufficiently panting, he rolled his warmth and weight onto me. I stroked the long, contoured slope of his back, relishing my body's heated response as his cock hardened against my thigh. He lavished kisses down my throat and teased my nipples, before moving his mouth lower, pulling aside the network of straps as he traced kisses down my belly and over the thin fabric covering my most sensitive nerves. The teddy clung tightly, and he struggled against the straps, before finally resting his head on my belly. He looked up at me. "Help?"

I pulled a key strap over my head, releasing the top of the garment. "Just give it a tug."

He dragged it off me, did the condom thing, and was inside me.

We rocked together, aroused from our haze of exhaustion, and I sucked kisses from his mouth as his nipples grazed against mine with each thrust. His cheek brushed my temple as he moved, the heady sound of his pleasured mumblings in my ears. His broad shoulders sheltered me, overtook me.

In every respect, his body seemed custom-built for mine—perfectly snug, aligned just so—and I kept thinking he might ruin me for anyone else's touch.

Did I care? I could forgo any other man for this so easily. So willingly.

I abandoned myself to it.

I spread my arms and legs wide—wrapped them around his chest, the small of his back, his thick thighs—and decided he could simply keep ruining me for as long as he was willing.

34

A WEAPON

THE OPPORTUNIST

Maybe the gun was supposed to feel frightening. . . or danger-ous. . . or evil.

But it didn't feel like any of those things.

It felt like holding power in the palm of your hand. The stur-dy grip, the dark matte barrel, the trigger cool against your finger. The heft of deadly lead, packed like rows of soldiers in the maga-zine—thick, heavy bullets that could finally make things right.

This was the muscle to get what you needed. The power to make things go the way they were supposed to.

It felt good. It felt final. It felt like the last word.

35

BETRAYAL

SAMMY

The house lay under a sleeping spell the next morning as everyone recovered from two supernatural days and nights. While sunlight didn't wake the masses, eventually the scent of freshly baked muffins and hot smoky bacon suffused the bedrooms, and people began to emerge.

I crept out of Gabe's bed, sneaking back to my own room across the quiet hallway. Taking a few minutes to freshen up, I splashed my face with cool water and brushed the windblown tangles from my hair. I'd need to shower soon, but coffee and a quick call to Mom were more pressing.

Mom was in a hurry when I caught her, heading off to the tournament. She said she'd reached a peace with Oscar. He still followed her but was keeping some distance so she could pretend she was alone. She reassured me she was fine and hustled me off the phone.

Feeling more settled, I found my way to the kitchen, poured a tall cup of coffee, and was taking it to the porch when I spotted Meghan on the outdoor sofa, sharing a blanket with the good-looking, blond boy. When she caught sight of me at the sliding glass door, her eyes begged me to leave her alone. It cost me nothing to do so, and the situation seemed mild enough to be harmless. So instead, I nursed my coffee from the living room sofa, enjoying the view of Mt. Adams and making small talk with Gabe's chef, who really was a miracle worker. I didn't know how long Gabe liked to sleep, but after a while, I decided to check on him. I piled a few muffins on a plate, poured a second mug of coffee for him, and carried everything back to his bedroom.

When I nudged the door open, I found he wasn't alone. Gabe had thrown on a t-shirt and jeans and was sitting at his desk, wrapping up a phone call. Lucy stood nearby, her arms crossed, already dressed and ready for the day. I set his coffee on the desk and took a seat opposite, waiting patiently. When he hung up and turned my way, the look on his face was inscrutable.

"Morning," he said.

"Morning." I smiled.

"Thanks for the coffee." He cautiously sampled it, must have found the temperature reasonable, and took a long swill. "That was the police in Creekside. Evidently, they're making some progress, and Lucy just talked with everyone in Philly."

"Good. That's good." I felt awake enough to hear it all. "What have they found?"

Lucy cleared her throat. "Well, the cops in Chestnut Hill think they spotted Claudia near your house a few times."

"Who's Claudia?" I asked.

Gabe looked my way, a pained expression on his face. "Do you remember that woman at the rooftop bar in Philadelphia? The one who caused a ruckus?"

"She was pretty hard to forget." I could see her in my mind's eye, her flaxen hair and perfect features contorted in anger, raving like a lunatic by the rooftop elevators. Alarm jolted my nerves as I finally registered what he was telling me. "Wait. Are you telling me *that* woman was at *my* home?"

"No, we don't actually think so," said Gabe. "Oscar's been watching things like a hawk, and he hasn't spotted her. The police probably just saw a pretty blonde." He took a sip of his coffee. "I trust Oscar. Don't worry."

"Right. We think it's a false alarm." Lucy shifted her stance. "But the police are trying to get in touch with her anyway. Just to talk."

"There's more from Creekside, too." Gabe said. "The police have reviewed footage from the parking lot at La Fermata and from surrounding streets and doorbell cameras. They've logged all the license plates and have managed to interview almost everyone who was at or near the land that day. There are still a couple rental cars and out-of-towners they haven't chased down, but most folks have been cleared."

"Well, I guess that's progress—getting things eliminated."

"Yeah." Gabe paused, giving me a long look again. "But Sammy, one of the neighbors' cameras picked up something pretty curious. Evidently, a car registered to a Philly P.I. drove by La Fermata a couple times that day. Guy's name is Ian Robinson. Any chance that's your Ian? The P.I you've been working with?"

My world stopped. There was just no way. "That's not possible."

He stared at me a long while, waiting for me to say more. Eventually, he ran out of patience. "It's actually much more than possible. It was *his* car and *his* plates. This Ian. . . he's the guy engaged to Marco, right? The one you showed the pictures to?"

I couldn't accept it. I wouldn't. "I'm telling you: Ian's like a brother to me. He'd never do *anything* to hurt me."

He was quiet for another long moment. "Sammy, taking pictures of people from far away is kind of what he does for a living, right? In fact—to be more precise—he takes intimate pictures of people from far away, doesn't he?"

"But these aren't even professional photos, remember? They're smartphone pictures."

"Well, that's what he told you, which would encourage the police to focus on folks on the grounds instead of people on the roads." Gabe paused again, got up, and walked a few paces to the balcony doors. When he turned back to me, his face was world-weary. "Sammy, if there's one thing I've learned—very painfully—over the last couple decades, it's that most people will do almost *anything* for money if enough is at stake."

I still shook my head, still couldn't believe it.

Tears pricked the corners of my eyes. I thought about everything that had happened recently, about Marco's behavior and the cost of their wedding, about all of Ian and Marco's underlying history. It seemed impossible they would do this, but maybe *everything* was related.

If that was the case, we were well past the point of friendly discretion.

"You know, if all this is true, there's something I should tell you." I took a deep breath and let the words trickle out. "Several years ago, Marco developed a drug habit. He was using cocaine, pills. . . any kind of stimulant he could get. He started stealing from the company, scrounging for cash."

Gabe nodded knowingly, thoughts turning behind his eyes.

"He's a good person though. He was just acting like an addict." I got up and paced a little. "We finally did an intervention. I had our lawyer draw up paperwork, and he was going to lose so much: control of the company, his salary. All of his future dividends would have been net of the money he stole and the costs of hiring people to take over his work. He was going to be left with very little."

I walked back over to Gabe and Lucy. "But he went to a program. Did everything he was supposed to. He's been squeaky clean for at least five years."

"Did Marco know you were headed to Creekside?"

"Yes, but I told him it was a scouting trip. He didn't know about you."

"And you're sure he didn't recognize me? Are there cameras around the brewery that could have picked me up without my helmet and sunglasses? Maybe he put two and two together?"

It hadn't occurred to me. We had security throughout the building and cameras on the patio. "Shit. I think that's actually possible." I was such an idiot. The more I considered it, the more foolish I felt. "Marco *did* know about Creekside, and it's always possible he recognized you. Plus, Ian was the one who set up the brewery's security system. If Marco recognized you even vaguely, they could have logged in and taken a closer look at the morning's footage."

"So, Marco could have had him check?"

"I hadn't thought of it before, but it totally could have happened."

Gabe squinted. "But why would Ian enable Marco? Seems like that's the only piece that doesn't track."

I slumped into the chair and put my head in my hands. My voice got quiet. "Ian's in recovery, too. . . and frankly, if he hasn't come to me for help with Marco yet, maybe it's because they've both fallen."

Slowly, it dawned on me, like a cloud of disorganized pixels finally coming into focus, revealing a crisp, full picture. "There's more now that I think about it, too. Marco's been acting strange lately. He's more irritable and ill-tempered than normal, and he's been asking for advances on cash. On top of that, suspicious things have been happening with the expenses at our newest breweries. . . which *he* helped set up. *My God*, I've been so oblivious."

The door was ajar, but someone knocked anyway. Meghan leaned into the room. "Mom, when do we have to go? The kids say there's a cool hike on the property. Some kind of waterfall. Do I have time to see it?"

I glanced at my watch and did the math. "As long as you don't dawdle, it should be okay. Wear good shoes and be careful, though. There's a big drop off. I don't want you near it. Understood?"

"I'll be careful." She looked the three of us over, taking in the somber mood.

I got up and walked to the door. "Meghan, we're having a private conversation, sweetheart. We need a couple more minutes."

"But I heard you talking about the brewery. You don't need to shut me out. In fact, I've been meaning to tell you—I got all those HopNBrew invoices databased."

"Already?"

"Yup. And actually, Mom, I can't figure out why you don't just ask Uncle Marco about them."

"We divide up the work, honey. Marco's got nothing to do with ordering or vendor payments. That's my responsibility."

"But Marco's the one who approved all those invoices. So, I bet if you asked him, he could help you figure it out."

Her words echoed in my head like a death toll.

I managed to keep my face straight another moment. "That's a great find, Meghan." I gripped the door. "Can we review it on the plane, though? I *really* need to talk with Lucy and Gabe."

"Sure." Her brow crinkled in concern. "Are you okay?"

"I'm okay, Meghan."

She hesitated. "All right." Then she stepped back into the hall, retreating toward the floating stairs.

As soon as I closed the door, I buried my face in my hands, hot tears rushing down my cheeks. I walked over and collapsed on the bed, letting the grief and disappointment pour out.

Gabe sat beside me and put an arm around my shoulders. "Sammy, I'm so sorry. My first band fell apart over this, and Trevor's mom disappeared into addiction for a while, too. I know what it does to the people who are left behind, to the ones who feel like they've come in second place to some stupid drug."

I squeezed his hand. "I'm sorry you went through that."

I grabbed a tissue and tried to pull myself together. Tried to think clearly. It was a lot to process—all the implications and next steps—but as I was wiping tears away, something occurred to me. "You know, maybe this is actually a good thing." I sniffed and wiped my eyes. "Marco and Ian may have gotten back into drugs, and maybe they're scrounging for money. But I know for a fact they'd never lay a finger on me. So the death threats are bunk. I'd bet my life on it."

I took a deep breath, glad I hadn't lost all sense of logic. "Plus, at least I know what I need to do now. I can call my attorney and have her get the paperwork ready." I stood up. "If Marco and Ian go so low as to release those pictures, then it is what it is. Meghan and my mom understand our relationship better now. It may not affect them the way I feared. And you can sue Marco and Ian to your heart's content. Maybe it's time for all this drama to just end."

Gabe didn't say anything for a while. "Do you still want me to send Lucy home with you? Do you want Oscar to stay in place?"

"I think we'll be fine. . . I mean, please keep Oscar with Mom until I get home. It makes me feel better anyways. And Lucy, thank you for everything, but you can stand down. I know we'll be safe."

I thanked them both, then headed back to my room to pack up and finally put a stop to all the tears.

When I was ready, I sent an email to Debbie, asked her to dust off the documents we'd drafted years ago when Marco was using, and scheduled a quick meeting for tomorrow.

The last few days had been incredible, but it was time to get back to Philadelphia and clean up some very nasty messes.

36

— · —

THE CONFRONTATION

At Gabe's insistence, Meghan and I flew home in his Gulfstream, enjoying a few more hours of luxurious tranquility before the rhythms of our life set us spinning again. Meghan read books most of the way, and I stared off into space, thinking about Marco and Ian, wishing I had caught the signs in time, before things got out of hand.

I wondered what the tipping point was, when people stopped using drugs for fun, and the drugs started destroying their lives, convincing them that ruining relationships and a lifetime of work was a reasonable price for another high.

We got in late, returned to our cozy home, and slept like the dead.

***

The next day, we were low on groceries, but I scrounged enough food from the pantry to make a 'thank you' brunch for Oscar. I whipped up a batch of apple pecan pancakes, cooked some bacon, and warmed up the good maple syrup before gathering everyone to dig in.

Oscar popped a bite of bacon in his mouth. "So, who's gonna keep an eye on things, now?"

"Oh. Nobody, Oscar." I drenched my pancakes with enough syrup to get through what I knew would be a stressful morning. "I think we're good now."

He quit chewing mid-bite. "You're pulling security entirely?"

"Yup. Did Gabe not fill you in? We have new information, and it looks like the threat isn't valid after all. I can't tell you how much I appreciate you keeping an eye on Mom the last several days, though. You're sort of my hero."

"He really has been amazing," Mom said. "Did I tell you he spent his nights sleeping outside my door, on that decrepit chaise no less? And he followed me all over town. I know I complained, but I was just being stubborn." She shrugged. "The truth is you made me feel safe, Oscar, and I'll never forget seeing your hulking frame on that flimsy chair every morning. I mean, that's some serious dedication." She pointed at me. "Sammy, you tell Gabriel to give him a raise. He deserves it."

Oscar washed his bacon down with coffee. "Um, thanks, Kate." His eyes seemed to crawl over the kitchen uncomfortably, wandering from the old, warped windows to the back door with its measly chain lock. "Cameras should stay up," he declared.

I set my fork down. "Oscar, we've lived here for years. Nothing bad has ever happened."

He stole glances around the table at Meghan, Mom, and me. "You shouldn't leave it to chance. I'll transfer the account to you. You'll get notifications if anything's wrong." Oscar's eyes returned to his pancakes, and he shoveled an oversized bite in his mouth.

Configuring an app to notify me whenever a squirrel crossed the yard was the last thing I wanted to do today. My mind was a million miles away, and my to-do list was hefty. But maybe I owed Oscar at least enough consideration to heed his advice. "Well, I guess if you have time to set me up before you go, it can't hurt." It would only take a few minutes to indulge him.

We continued our feast. Mom chattered about the tennis tournament and her friend's birthday party and how there was absolutely nothing interesting that had happened otherwise. She pinched my cheek. "See? We did just fine."

"Easy for things to be fine when a couple hundred pounds of muscle is sleeping outside your door," I said.

It turned out Oscar was capable of smiling, but the expression was fleeting. His usual grimace returned almost instantly. His brows knit tight.

After breakfast, he made me walk the perimeter of the yard with him to learn about the cameras. He got the apps downloaded to my phone and showed me how to log in and monitor everything. I thanked him again, impressed with his diligence.

"Don't you guys want this on your devices, too?" He called out to Meghan and Mom, who were washing dishes in the kitchen with music blasting away.

"We're fine, Oscar," Mom hollered over the music. "Quit making Sammy worry. She does enough of that."

"Ignore her," I told him. "You're awesome."

His Uber pulled up, and I walked him to the door.

"Bye, Sammy." He jostled the overstuffed backpack on his hulking shoulders, almost reluctantly. "See you around, I guess."

Halfway to the idling car, Oscar paused and glanced back at the house, almost indecisively. Whatever was hanging him up, though, he worked through it quickly. He tossed his backpack into the vehicle, squeezed his bulk into the car's back seat, and left for parts unknown.

With our visitor finally gone, I heaved a sigh of exhaustion and collapsed on the couch, truly grateful everyone was okay.

Our safety was beyond precious, but everything was so bittersweet. Because underneath the homecoming and the pancakes, and the joy of seeing Mom again, something far darker lurked. I was consumed with worry about the meeting I needed to have with Debbie and dumbstruck that the agreement we'd revive would effectively end an entire chapter of our lives. Marco would be shut out from the remarkable business we built together, and I would be left to carry its burden on my own.

The music in the kitchen died. Mom went out the back door to her cottage, and Meghan took the stairs back to her room two at a time—everyone getting on with their lives. Just for a moment, I took in the peace and quiet before trudging up the stairs for a quick shower. I knew I had to go meet Debbie and draw up those horrible documents, but it felt like I was prepping for a funeral.

***

"Mom?" Meghan called from her bedroom when I reached the top of the steps. She got up from her bed and came to the door. "I didn't want to say anything in front of Grandma, but you seem really sad, which is weird because we just got back from four days of, like, magical mystery land. Aren't you floating on a cloud? I mean. . . I am." She looked confused and concerned.

"Meghan, I'm so glad you had a great time." I managed to smile for her. "And I promise you, I did, too. I mean, *really* amazing. You're sweet to ask about me, but I promise I'm fine. I'm floating."

She stared me down, looking unconvinced. "So, you're just not going to tell me?" Meghan was no fool, and I'm sure my worries had been written all over my face since yesterday. "Is it the blackmail thing, Mom? I thought you said we were safe now. I kind of deserve to know if I'm in danger."

"It's not that. We're safe. But the truth is, even though I had a great time, there are other things going on." I leaned against my doorway. "Sometimes being a business owner is fun, but other times, it's just a lot of stress and pain. I'll get through it. I promise. It's nothing you need to worry about." I crossed the hall and planted a kiss on her freckled forehead. "Now go rest up and get unpacked. You've got a scrimmage tonight, and you need to kick butt so the coach doesn't freak out next time you miss a practice or two."

That got a grin back out of her. "Kicking butt's my specialty, Mom. I've got this."

Then she actually gave me a hug.

A real hug.

***

Ninety minutes later, I was showered and seated in Debbie's office, a storefront on Germantown Avenue that she managed to keep both professional and comfortable. Since it was Saturday and I was more of a friend than a client, she wore a simple t-shirt and shorts. She had probably stopped in on her way to go hiking.

"Thanks for meeting me on the weekend."

"No problem, Sammy. I don't think this will take long. I *did* dust off that paperwork. I can have it ready this week. . . if you really want to pursue this."

"I'm trying to figure that out, but I think Marco has gone off the deep end. I think he's using again." I was quiet for a moment. "Actually, maybe you can help with part of the puzzle. Did you learn anything about HopNBrew?"

"Yes, hold on." She clicked a few files open on her laptop, read back through her notes patiently, and started nodding. "Okay, so there's actually *a lot* that's odd about HopNBrew. Someone registered the company within the last six months, and it's an anonymous LLC—which is not normal. They can only be set up in a couple states. So, it was likely an intentional move. Since the company is so new, there are no tax returns to look at yet, but if I had to guess, I'd say it's a corporation without many assets. The website looks like a two-sided platform—a market where vendors can put goods up for sale and buyers can make purchases.

"Now, that's not uncommon," she went on. "Some of the biggest shopping sites known to man work that way, but this is just a tiny one—restaurant and brewery items. So, it's curious, really. A niche website with overpriced goods specific to *your* company's needs springs into existence under a shroud of secrecy at the same time your new breweries open? Seems pretty suspicious to me."

"Do you think HopNBrew could be used to steal money? Marco's name is all over this; it stinks, and he's been chasing after cash. I'm trying to figure out if this is a separate problem, or if it's part of the Marco mess."

Debbie closed her eyes and rocked back and forth in her chair. She turned and looked out the window, her stare focused in the distance.

After a bit, she pivoted back my way. "I'm not sure, but I'm thinking maybe it could." She leaned forward. "In theory, someone could buy goods at a low cost, then sell them back to the business at a higher price using the website as a front. If they timed it right, they'd have a stream of money flowing in larger than the money flowing out. Plus, with the anonymity of the company, it would be hard to trace back to them."

That had to be it. The final piece of the puzzle. "I think it's time I confront Marco and Ian."

"Do you want me to come?"

"You've done enough, and I already owe you for coming in on a weekend. I'll be fine. Thanks, Debbie."

I left her office and went out to my car, fuming.

***

The antique door knocker of Ian and Marco's Society Hill townhome offered a good way to vent some frustration, and I pounded it impatiently. In that moment, I couldn't bring myself to be delicate with their precious Colonial relics. If they hadn't overextended themselves so often, if they had *any* sense of moderation at all, we might not be in this mess.

Ian swung the door open indignantly, but his expression brightened when he saw me. "Oh! Sammy! Great timing." He shooed me inside. "We're sampling appetizers for the reception."

An extravagant great room encompassed their home's first floor, and Ian hustled to the kitchen area for an extra place setting and a glass of water. "You *have* to try this stuff. The ahi tacos will change your life!"

I'm not sure what I expected—disarray perhaps, or maybe drug paraphernalia left in the open. But their early nineteenth-century townhouse was impeccable. Ornate brass mirrors gleamed against the muted sage walls, and plump pillows neatly bookended their Chesterfield sofa. Their antique dining table overflowed with steaming delicacies plated on fine china.

I seemed to be stuck in place, but Ian forged ahead. He plated a few samples and walked them to me. "Earth to Sammy. Come on, girl." He guided me forward with a hand on my back. "Sit. . . Eat. . . You can help us choose."

I followed him, but when I arrived at the table, I just set the plate down.

"Hey, Sammy." Marco garbled his casual greeting around a mouthful of food as Ian took a seat next to him, forking artfully garnished scallops and caviar-laden crostini onto his plate.

Watching them luxuriate over a lavish spread financed with stolen funds—with money they planned to keep pumping into their lives through my pain— was just too much. I welled up. I couldn't believe their recklessness, their callous disregard for everything we shared.

"You followed me to North Carolina," I finally croaked. "How could you?"

They froze. It grew so quiet I could hear their grandfather clock ticking away the seconds.

Marco clinked his fork down on his plate. "Sammy, you do remember what happened the last time you tried to travel on your own, don't you?"

I couldn't believe he was throwing this in my face.

Marco shifted in his chair. "The Columbus E.R. called me at one a.m.—said you were so panicked you might actually give yourself a heart attack. I had to drive all night to get you. So, I just can't have you that far away without anyone to help. Okay? It's too much stress."

What total bullshit.

Marco wasn't done dishing it out, though. "Ian's been low on work lately, so he had time, and we just did it. We were worried about your safety."

"Sure, you guys were *worried* about me," I spat. "Right up until you took those *horrible* photos and cooked up your little blackmail scheme."

Marco looked at me like I'd sprouted a second head. "*What* did you just say?"

Ian cut in. "Sammy, I swear I didn't take those pictures. I did follow you to Creekside, then up to La Fermata that morning, but that was it. I just needed to know where you were going. I didn't linger."

"You went by more than once, Ian. I know you were there."

"Look, I drove by maybe one more time but only because you hadn't come back to the hotel. Your car was nowhere to be seen, though, and I left. . . Anyway," Ian scoffed, "like I told you, those are smartphone pictures at best. I promise you; I'm a better photographer than that when I want to be."

"Right. You told me that. So, we told the police. Convenient, huh?"

Marco's gaze volleyed back and forth between us. "*Seriously*, what the hell are you guys talking about? What photos? And who is talking to the police about *anything*?"

Ian turned to him. "It's nothing, Marco. Sammy asked for my help with something. It's private."

I smacked my hand down on the tabletop. "It's *not* nothing! It's actually a crime, Ian. And Marco, don't act so innocent. You've been stealing from us again, right? From the company we worked so hard to build? I saw all those HopNBrew invoices. I *know* what you've been doing."

"Alright, that's enough." Marco's face changed. He stood up. "I've got no clue what you're ranting about, and you're trashing a perfectly nice day."

"You know *exactly* what I'm talking about. You've been using that stupid HopNBrew website to buy goods on the cheap then sell them back to the company at a handsome profit. I bet that buys a *lotta* drugs."

"The HopNBrew crap? *That's* what triggered this little tirade? God, I don't like it either, but it's the only way Charlotte can get supplies. Bobby called in a tizzy. They need product faster than our vendors can deliver it, and I didn't have time to screw around finding other options. I just pushed the transactions through. I was *trying* to help."

"It was *a lot* of transactions, Marco."

"Well, in case you haven't *noticed*, Sammy, I'm a little stressed out lately. I'm sorry if I don't keep everything as perfectly organized as you do."

"Now wait a second." Ian tossed his napkin on the table and stood up beside Marco. His face, normally kind and gentle, grew stern. "Let me get this right. I drive all the way to North Carolina—a long, uncomfortable trip, by the way—to help *you*. Then, I run to your house at your beck and call—again, to help *you*. I cash in favors, reach out across the community—all to try and hunt down some rogue paparazzo. For *free*. For *you*. And poor Marco, who's running around trying to manage a business and plan a wedding, he takes time out of *his* day to approve some invoices—which last I checked was *your* job. And *this* is what we get for it? *Accusations? Insults?* Who the hell do you think you are, Sammy?" His eyes were cold, blue steel. "More importantly, who do you think *we* are? Blackmailers? Seriously?"

His face reflected the same outrage I'd felt when Gabe had accused me, but that had been wild speculation. This was different. It came directly from the police. Way too many facts aligned.

"I do know who you are, Ian. I know who both of you are, and I love you both a lot, quite frankly." A traitorous tear snuck down my cheek, and I swatted it away, bristling with anger. "But I also know what addiction does to people. I've seen it before, and I'm seeing it again. *Right now*."

Marco walked to the foyer and grabbed his keys.

"Where are *you* going?" I demanded.

"Well, Sammy, I'm gonna blow off my fiancé, waste this lovely catered food, and go take a drug test. Happy?"

"*Really?* A bunch of fancy appetizers is what you're worried about? Not criminal charges? Not the destruction of your career?" I clomped to the door and yanked it open. "If you want any chance of salvaging your life, take the test today, Marco. I don't care if your food gets cold. If the results don't come back clean, I've told Debbie to reinstate the paperwork from a few years ago. This will all be over—the whole damn thing—and I'll be left without a business partner. *Thanks a lot!*"

I stormed out, barely resisting the urge to slam the door behind me.

<h1 style="text-align:center">37</h1>

RECONNECTING

The pasta from Nonna's Bistro was warm and fragrant, the cannolis and Italian confections looked like the perfect birthday treat, and I had a couple bottles of Tina's favorite wine ready to go. Her boys were with their dad for the night, and after the miserable mess with Marco, I couldn't wait to catch up with my friend, finally. It promised to be a sweet end to an otherwise horrible day. Plus, we could both commiserate over the crazy twists and turns of the last month.

Fred nearly tackled me in wriggling ecstasy when I arrived, the smell of both dinner and Aunt Sammy at the same time proving entirely too much for his golden retriever brain. He followed us to the kitchen, his whole body wagging, and jumped all over me the instant I set our food down. I gave him a proper scratch behind the ears and a good all over body rub, my heart lifting with each blond, shaggy ruffle of fur.

"I'll just wait my turn." Tina leaned against the counter, looking almost relaxed. Her shoulders were at ease, and her bob of curly black hair framed a mellow smile. I gave Fred one last nuzzle then wrapped my friend up in a warm hug and kissed the top of her head. "Happy birthday, Tina. The day you were born is definitely worth a celebration."

I squeezed her hard, and Fred joined right in. We cracked up as he climbed into our embrace, clawing his way up our bodies, trying to reach our faces with his pink, lapping tongue. He clearly intended to be part of the pack tonight.

Amidst the joy and laughter though, a pang of regret squeezed my chest. Tina should have felt wrapped up in love for the last month. And where had I left her? Alone with Fred? "Tina, I'm sorry I've been so distracted." I had promised myself the evening would be focused on lifting Tina up, not asking for forgiveness, but the words simply slipped out.

She stepped out of the hug, sending Fred's front paws skittering back to the kitchen floor. "Oh, stop it, Sammy. You've called. You've texted. Heck, you made the boys their favorite cookies." She blew out a breath. "Look, I'm the one who got all self-absorbed. I curled up in a ball to feel sorry for myself, then had the nerve to get angry when it turned out you have your own life. I'm the guilty party here."

"You haven't done anything wrong. You're allowed to feel whatever you feel."

"Thanks, Sammy." She wandered to the counter, sniffed in bliss at the Nonna's bistro bag, and waggled her eyebrows at me. "Well, I think what I *feel* right now is hungry. Can we eat?"

"Oh, *heck* yes."

We dragged all the food out, opened the wine, and settled in at the kitchen table, where Tina had set out cloth napkins and mismatched silverware—my favorite kind. Fred flopped on our feet, ever hopeful for morsels of food or affection.

Over platefuls of linguini, Tina filled me in on the drama with Andrew and how the boys were handling it. They were too young to understand what was happening, which resulted in heartbreaking questions and the odd reality of Tina having to break the news repeatedly that they, as a family, were moving in a new direction. But from what she shared with me, it sounded like she was managing an impressive balancing act of just enough information, in words they could understand. As usual, her approach to challenges was full of sensible strength and kindness.

When she had fully vented, we pronounced a moratorium on any further mention of the miserable cretin named Andrew, who didn't deserve her and certainly shouldn't be allowed to ruin her birthday dinner.

We sipped cabernet and gobbled forkfuls of pasta while I gave Tina the scoop on the soap opera surrounding Ian, Marco, and Forbidden Brews. My impending professional divorce wasn't half as traumatic as her marital one, but it still involved division of property, taking on your former partner's workload, and, in general, trying to figure out how to move on solo. It was surprisingly cathartic to talk through it all—maybe for both of us—because the conversation unfolded with ease despite the painful topic.

We both wondered what would become of Marco and if there was any way to help him and Ian. It had taken a full intervention to bring Marco around last time, and with both him and Ian in trouble now, I wasn't sure how to begin. We would have to figure it out eventually though. No matter how mad I was about the business, Marco and Ian were my adopted family, and we would have to find a way to drag them back from the edge.

Eventually, Tina couldn't stand it any longer, and she demanded a change of topic, claiming that if her birthday dinner didn't include an exhaustive "debriefing" of the entire Gabriel Walker escapade, I was fired as best friend.

After keeping everything pent up for weeks, I was more than happy to oblige. It's practically a pact among women not to let anyone suffer alone or miss out on living vicariously through each other's thrills—and I'd been badly in violation of it.

I recounted meeting him in the forest, our time at the rooftop bar, the trip to Creekside, and the adventure in Oregon. She asked endless questions, digging in for all the juicy details, and I, of course, gave her most of them. I denied her request to set up an official "Gabe Walker" harem, laughed at how moon-eyed she was over the whole thing, and reminded her that it was super-important to Gabe that we keep things quiet. Tina promised to be an information vault, and I think in reality, she preferred that these secrets remained ours—something for the two of us to share. Well, three if we counted Fred, who seemed content to listen for hours as long as we occasionally dropped cannoli crumbs.

By the end of dessert and after the first bottle of wine, we still hadn't solved the world's problems, so we opened another bottle and tried harder, laughing and crying until it was well past bedtime.

My home was only a couple blocks away, and when we were finally sated, I gave Tina the biggest hug ever and stumbled home. I tucked myself into my own bed, thankful for a full belly, a warm heart, and my hall of fame best friend.

I conked out hard and slept deeply.

38

—·—

WILDFIRE

The next day, I woke to blinding streaks of mid-morning sun stabbing a path of pain through my brain—a sure sign of overindulgence. After slogging to the kitchen to start coffee, I came back upstairs to wash my face, drink water, and down some headache meds, trying to resume functionality. Overdoing it gave me no regrets though. Spending time with Tina was a gift from the heavens. I counted my lucky stars that all the secrecy was over, and I'd finally been able to connect with her and spend a night celebrating her birthday properly.

I did, however, need to send Gabe a note to thank him for everything. In the hectic gush of emotions and activity yesterday, I had forgotten. I snatched my phone off the charger, composing a nice message in my mind.

Those words never made it into the universe.

When the screen came to life, notifications popped up, showing I had missed dozens of messages. I took the phone off sleep mode and opened the texts, expecting some sort of group chat gone wild or maybe Meghan on a late-night rant. But instead, it seemed my extended family, my long-lost friends, and many of my former and current employees suddenly decided to reach out.

OMG, when did you meet Gabriel Walker?!

Sammy, you have to introduce me! He is my absolute favorite!

Just saw your news! So exciting!

Something was *very* wrong.

Clicking the first social media icon I saw on my phone revealed hundreds of notifications. The first one took me to a post made by Forbidden Brews. There was a picture of Gabe and me, cheek to cheek, looking very cozy with the sunlit canyon behind us. The caption nearly stopped my heart: *Did you know Gabriel Walker is having our very own Sammy McCallum design the patio at his restaurant, #La Fermata? Come see the beautiful spaces that captured his imagination!* It listed all the Forbidden Brews locations and tagged me, the Walker Smith Revival page, La Fermata, and several fan groups. It had seventy thousand up votes and thousands of comments.

A wave of panic struck me.

I deleted the post and frantically scrubbed through the other social platforms, taking down similar posts made by Forbidden Brews. *How could this have happened? What if it had been reshared?* I searched the hashtags, and it was everywhere. *Shit, shit, shit!*

I prayed against hope that Gabe hadn't seen it yet. It was still reasonably early on the Pacific Coast.

But the cold, sinking fear in my stomach meant I knew much better. I searched related tags, erasing everything I was allowed to delete. I changed passwords on all of our accounts, then sat back and stared at the mess. The words and images were spreading faster than I could tame them, and I knew it. The posts had been reshared, and I couldn't get them back.

The internet was endless. And permanent.

Any kind of progress had value though, so I sorted through the text messages on my phone and erased the ones from people I didn't normally talk to or who weren't close. When I was done, only a handful remained that merited a response. Only two begged for a quick reply.

Tina's message was simply confused:

Sammy, saw your post. Is everything out in the open all of a sudden? So confused. Had so much fun with you. XOXO

I shot her a message back, explaining that things were *not* supposed to be public and that I was trying desperately to obliterate the posts from existence.

Gabe's text was worse. Much worse.

Surprised and disappointed don't begin to cover it. The only thing I ever asked you for was privacy. I kept telling myself I was being paranoid. That I should trust your intentions and ignore the facts that keep pointing back to you and your company and the possibility this is all just a money grab. So, I don't know what to say. But if this is the direction you're going. . . I'm out.

I put my head in my hands and fought back tears of frustration. The threads of trust in our relationship were still so new and fragile—and now apparently broken. Would he listen if I could explain? What could I possibly say, anyway, if I didn't even understand what was happening?

I checked the logins for Forbidden Brews but didn't see anything out of the ordinary. There were precious few people with permission to post to our homepages, and none of them would have had a picture like that. I needed to think, but the fog of sleep and the remnants of last night's festivities still had me in their grip. I grabbed a bathrobe and headed for the hallway.

Another big glass of water followed by a long steam session in the shower finally unclogged my brain, and that's when it occurred to me.

There was really only one explanation.

I dried off, got dressed, and knocked on Meghan's door before pushing it open. She was sitting up in bed, the laptop at her feet, innocence and confusion painted all over her face. "You took them down, Mom?"

I felt speechless a lot these days, and this was no exception. "Meghan, you had *no* right to do that. I thought I laid the ground rules very clearly before we left for Oregon."

"Mom, it's just one little picture. We learned about this in Marketing class. Did you know celebrity endorsement is one of the simplest ways to boost a brand? I know you've been sad about the business, and this will help. Those expenses you keep worrying about won't matter if your revenue goes up, right? I wish you'd let me help you more."

I cradled my head in my hands, beside myself.

Meghan smiled hopefully. "Mom, don't be upset. Did you see your numbers? Your followers went from like four thousand to more than ten thousand overnight. Don't you see what this can do? You really should have left the posts online. You deserve to be happy."

I had to collect my thoughts. She was a good kid—smart, eager to help, loving—and our relationship was just starting to improve. I really needed to be careful, but the anger and loss I felt threatened to overwhelm my cool.

I trod forward with care. "I'm grateful you want to help, and there's no doubt those posts raised the profile of the brand." My voice threatened to break. "But you did this without my consent, and more importantly, without Gabe's. It's a *huge* violation."

"Mom, this is how the world works nowadays. Trust me. Gabe will be cool with it. It was a great post, and it will boost traffic at his restaurant, too! Plus, the Walker Smith Revival posts pictures of him all the time with his fans. Really, he won't care."

"I think he cares quite a lot."

"Well, just apologize then. What's the big deal?"

I rubbed my forehead. "Meghan, there's a good chance that after this. . . he wouldn't even answer my call." I walked back to the doorway—upset, unsure, and without a parental roadmap. I looked her in the eyes. "I need to think about this, but in the meantime, let me be clear. You are *never* to log onto my computer again without consent, and you are grounded. I don't know for how long."

"Are you *serious?* You're actually *punishing* me for this?" Her face turned pink, and she looked like she was working herself up to a good cry. "How can you be so awful? Why don't you trust me to do anything?" She slammed her laptop shut. "I can hardly go anywhere except under lock and key. I mean literally armed guards. All those kids I met out West, they go to school in California, Florida, Massachusetts, nowhere near their families. It's not even a consideration. But I can't do *anything* unless my mommy approves. Maybe being grounded won't be that different from being free as long as I'm stuck living with you."

She stomped to the door, her face red and trembling. When I didn't immediately take the hint, she gripped the door handle. "Can I *at least* be *alone*?"

Her tears were going to spill the instant I left. I backed into the hallway, and she closed the door inches from my face.

My heart slammed in my chest, but I was in no state of mind to push the situation further, and I certainly couldn't help her learn better emotional regulation by blowing my own top.

Back in my room, I took a few deep breaths and tried to ring Gabe. My call went straight to voicemail. I skipped that and texted instead:

The post was Meghan's. I'm so sorry. I've changed the password on all the social accounts, and I'm trying to get everything taken down as best I can. Meghan is punished. I don't know what else to do.

Also, I confronted Marco and Ian. They swear their innocence, say they followed me to NC to look out for my safety, worried I'd have an anxiety attack. They claim they had nothing to do with the photos. I don't know what to believe, but I should have the results from Marco's drug test in a few days. I don't expect a good outcome. It's a mess.

There was no response. No dancing dots to let me know he was typing back. No indication the message had been seen or even delivered. For all I could tell, he might have blocked my number.

Hot shafts of light from the dormer windows meant the air outside would be scorching, but I needed to center my mind. Slipping on the lightest shorts and tank I could find, I laced up my running shoes, and headed out the door.

***

I had always loved the historic charm of Chestnut Hill—the handcrafted homes built of sparkling schist and the giant shade trees that took root generations ago. It was easy to get lost in the familiar landscape with its blend of family life, parks, and small businesses.

My legs and lungs resisted the run for the first mile, but eventually their complaints quieted. My body settled in, and my breathing fell into a steady rhythm as my feet pounded the sidewalks of my hometown.

I tried to review where things stood and just wrap my arms around what happened. *What was important? What mattered most?*

First, I supposed I should focus on the fact we were safe. Given the events of the last week, that alone was invaluable.

I rounded a corner and plowed up a steep sidewalk beneath the outstretched arms of an enormous sycamore tree.

So, what was next? What else was important?

Marco's impending drug test was a dark cloud, and the results would likely have a dramatic effect on both our lives. I didn't expect it to go well, and I knew things might get ugly. Executing the paperwork without causing a scene would be challenging to navigate, and I needed to figure out what to tell the staff. A transition plan for the coming months would be critical as well.

A mushroom cloud of potential Marco-related problems expanded in my mind, but I refused to entertain it. I could only handle one thing at a time.

I focused instead on my footfalls—on the simple process of moving forward. *Okay, what else?*

Ugh. . . the next thing stabbed my heart with loss. The social media post and Gabe's reaction to it were horrible. Painful. I'd deleted as much as I could, but those pictures had been reposted around the world by now. I remembered a friend who worked in public relations—maybe she could help annihilate it from the web. Before I could forget, I texted her a message from my smart watch, asking if I could have some time this evening to pick her brain.

There. That's in motion.

The road turned and tilted downhill, hammering my knees and quads with impact.

What's next? What else needed to be put in order?

Meghan's blotchy red skin and confused, angry tears rested heavy in my mind. What she had done was very wrong, and she certainly needed to learn how to manage her emotions better, but her heart was in the right place. She was right about at least a few things, too. I had been hemming her in too tight and effectively squashing her dreams.

It was bad parenting, and I knew it.

I also knew opportunity when I saw it. The shock and madness of the last few weeks had obviously defibrillated my nervous system somewhat, setting me back closer to normal. Despite death threats, extortion, and cross-country separation, my anxiety had stayed at bay. I needed to capitalize on this and commit to bigger changes before I slid backward.

That was the final tangle to address—and likely the last thing I had any power over.

I turned my attention back to the uneven sidewalk, to the sweat dripping off my brow, and the rhythmic thrum of my heart and bones. Pistorius Park lay not far ahead, an oasis of lush green peace. I cut through its grassy, expansive lawn and beat a well-worn path back home.

***

After washing up and rehearsing some important messages, I found Meghan sulking in her bedroom. I sat down on the edge of the bed. "We should talk."

She cut her eyes at me, glaring.

I knew she would be venting steam for a while, but I dove in, anyway. "Look, sweetheart, you did some things wrong in the last twenty-four hours. You're young and that means you'll make mistakes, but you can't make them with other people's lives. Do you understand?"

She wouldn't even look at me. "You already lectured me. Can't you just go away?" Her cheeks were reddening again.

"No. Not yet." I swallowed my pride. "Because you're right about some things, too. I've been keeping too tight a hold on you, and I'm sorry. I'm gonna start changing that. You deserve more autonomy, and you sure as heck deserve the chance to have your own adventure, just like I did at your age."

I shifted on the bed and touched a finger to her knee. "Listen, you're still in trouble, but I think we should take a road trip. I'm not sure I want to be in town tomorrow, and I need to get down to Charlotte. Why don't you come with me? We can be normal for a couple days. No armed guards. No celebrities. Just you and me. I can show you how we actually *do* solve business problems—by cleaning up operations and dealing with management issues. We have a working business model. That location just needs to be straightened out."

At least, she was looking at me now. That was progress.

I took a deep breath. "And sweetheart, why don't we look at Duke while we're down South. Maybe hit the University of Virginia on the way home." I gathered strength for my next words, knowing in my heart they were right, no matter how hard they were to say. "Applications will be due soon, and I'm thinking you should apply wherever you want. So, we may as well start getting some college visits under our belt."

The anger disappeared from her face instantly. "Honestly?" she croaked. Her face was still red, but a different emotion spilled out of her now. "For real?"

"Yes. Anywhere you can get in, you can go."

She grabbed hold of me and squeezed so hard I thought my stuffing might come out. She shook with relief, her tears dripping onto my shoulders. "Thank you, Mom. I really needed this."

I held her tight for as long as she wanted. I let her cry it out, making sure she knew I loved her, no matter what.

Even if the rest of my life was in disarray, this one small thing, in this one small moment, was completely right. I held her close.

39

THE ROAD TRIP

"No thanks, Sammy." Mom tugged at the weeds that had rudely taken up residence in her flower beds.

"Mom, seriously? Are you just toying with me?"

"I'm not toying with you, sweetheart." She continued wrenching clumps of Pennsylvania smartweed from the earth, not bothering to look in my direction. "I do actually have a life, and you seem to be doing fine."

"You want to spend time with Meghan, though. Plus, don't you want to see where she might go to school? Come on, it'll be fun."

"Sammy, wrap your head around this." She finally stood up from tending her garden, a riot of sunflowers and zinnias surrounding her with color. "I have a date." She smiled with pride and wiped her gardening gloves across her brow.

"You have a date?"

"Yup. Stan Rosen won the tennis tournament and invited me to dinner. He has a great serve and a nice backside, and I said yes."

"You have a date?"

"Sammy, are you stuck on repeat? Yes, I have a date, and I'm kind of excited. For the love of Pete, honey, get out there and start living your life again. It's been three years. Okay? Now, shoo." She brushed me away. "Besides, I might have a guest, and I don't need you cramping my style. It might get *steamy*." She smooched kissy faces at me.

She may not have been needling me before, but she was definitely doing it now. "Are you sure you won't come? I get that you're fine here, but just because we split up a couple times and survived doesn't mean it has to keep happening."

"And what do you think is gonna happen when Meghan leaves for college next fall? Do you think we're going to follow her there together?"

I had no response to that. She was about to be irritatingly logical again—I could tell. "Fine, Mom. If you're just going to make sense, I'll go back to my day."

She buried her face in her flowers again. "Love you, Sammy," she called as I retreated.

I sighed. "Love you, too."

***

The next morning, I still had not heard back from Gabe. My call went to voicemail again, so I gave up and texted:

Still so sorry about everything.

Not planning to be in town when Marco's drug test comes back. Heading to Charlotte with Meghan. Need to check out the brewery there. . . it's a mess. If you happen to be in Creekside, we'll be nearby if you want to talk face-to-face.

Just like yesterday, there were no dancing dots to show he was typing. No delivery notification. *Nothing.* I tucked my phone back in my purse and got on with my day. I couldn't control Gabe's reaction or his choices. Only *he* could decide to warm his cold shoulder.

***

Meghan and I packed up the Subaru, said goodbye to Mom, and headed out. Escaping the worst of Philadelphia's traffic always took a while, but once we were on our way, the driving was easy. I took the first shift while she played DJ and leafed through literature on Duke. Bubbling with excitement, she filled me in on the lore, the business school statistics, and things to do in the Raleigh area. I listened to her prattle on and asked a few questions along the way. As long as she was Googling, I had her search for the best pizza places in Charlotte and make a plan for dinner.

When I asked her about the blond boy at Gabe's house, her face turned soft and dreamy. "Oh my gosh, Mom. He's *so* amazing. I can't even begin to explain."

"Gabe said his name is Connor?"

"Yup. He starts business school at Pepperdine this fall. He's so smart and so beautiful. Really, he's just perfect."

"Well, I'm sure he's not *perfect*, but I'm glad you like him. What did you guys talk about?"

"Everything. School, sports, friends. He's so easy to talk to, and he says Pepperdine is *really* cool. It's right near the mountains and the ocean, and the weather is supposed to be awesome all year long. It sounds amazing, Mom."

"Are you guys staying in touch?"

"A little bit. We're connected on social media, and he's texted a few times. I know he's headed off to school, so he may get busy, but I *do* think he really likes me."

Oh boy. "And you like him?"

"Um, he's smart and gorgeous and interesting. Of course, I like him."

"Well, I'm glad you're in touch then. Sounds sort of thrilling."

I prayed she was being smart. We had shared a million birds-and-bees conversations over the years. I tried to launch another one, but she shut me down quickly.

"Oh my God, Mom. Please stop. You are *beyond* embarrassing."

I gave in and switched topics. Hopefully, everything had sunk in a long time ago.

We arrived before nightfall, ate way too much pizza, and watched movies in our hotel room until we couldn't stay awake any longer.

She still needed to realize just how wrong she'd been to betray my trust—and Gabe's. But I was incredibly grateful for some much-needed bonding time. Nothing was more important than our relationship surviving the teenage years, and today had been a good day.

I checked my messages before bed but still saw no response from Gabe. . . no matter how long I stared at the phone.

***

Morning arrived too quickly, and if it weren't for the promise of gourmet donuts, I might never have coaxed Meghan from her teenage slumber. I could be persistent when I wanted to be, though, and I was determined to get to Forbidden Brews before the cook staff arrived. So we rose with the sun, stuffed ourselves with scrumptious fried dough, and positively vibrated with caffeine and sugar as we unlocked the front doors of Forbidden Brews Charlotte.

40

In the Clear

GABE

Gabe sat on a rich leather sofa, trying out a guitar riff and gazing at the oasis of Central Park through the hotel's floor-to-ceiling windows. From here, the bustling expanse of Manhattan looked almost serene beneath a shifting veil of gray clouds. He had always enjoyed the simplicity of this suite—nothing fought with the art and beauty. The walls and marble floors were white; the views were astounding, and the furnishings and art were museum quality. It should have brought him peace, but today, it just felt empty. . . and lonely as hell.

Someone knocked, and Gabe grudgingly set his guitar on its stand. He crossed the cold tiles to the front door, where he spied Lucy and Oscar through the peephole.

In no mood to talk, he opened the door a crack. "Hey. Need something?"

Oscar piped up. "Got another update. Thought we should stop by."

Gabe didn't budge. "Does it actually change anything?" He rubbed his forehead in weary annoyance.

"Well, maybe," Oscar said.

Gabe huffed a sigh and let them in. He gestured to the suite's elegant dining table. "You guys thirsty or hungry? Room service sent up a small buffet. Don't know who the hell's supposed to eat it."

"No, we're fine, thanks," Lucy said. "But we've heard more from the police. We wanted to get you up to speed."

"All right." Not particularly interested in listening, Gabe returned to his spot on the couch and picked up his guitar again, fiddling with the tuning pegs.

Lucy started first. "We talked with Creekside. They interviewed that P.I. guy, Ian. He claims he was keeping an eye on Sammy because she has panic attacks. Said he was nowhere near La Fermata that afternoon. Turns out, the receipts and traffic cams seem to confirm it. His car passed through town around midday. He paid for parking near Main Street, stopped in a cafe, then spent a few hours buying art and souvenirs on the strip. Bottom line, he wasn't up by the property."

Gabe stopped tuning the guitar and looked at Lucy. "Well, just because the car and credit card were in town, doesn't mean Ian was, right? Maybe Marco dropped him off at La Fermata and drove the car back to town."

"Nope." Lucy was quick to respond. "Marco was in Philadelphia. Witnesses have him at the brewery in the morning and with a caterer in the afternoon. Plus, traffic cams only show Ian in the car."

Gabe's befuddled gaze searched her face.

"They're cleared, Gabe. It's a dead end," she said.

Gabe set his guitar on its stand again, his forehead bunched in confusion. "That can't be right. I mean. . . it *has* to be them. They *followed* her there. I thought this was all locked up tight." He stood up, agitated. "I don't get it."

He walked to the window and looked over the leafy trees crowding the park, racking his brain. The overcast sky shrouded the most distant skyscrapers in a sullen mist. A camera crew filmed on the street below, oblivious to the impending weather.

He swiveled.

"*Oh my God.* Does this mean it's Claudia?" Panic gripped his chest. "And we pulled security? *Shit!* Oscar, how fast can you get back to Sammy's?"

"A couple hours? It's not far."

"Hold on," Lucy interjected.

Oscar talked over her. "Gabe, you'd need two people again. Sammy's text said she was headed to North Carolina with Meghan, remember? So, the only one in Philly's Kate. But why do you care, anyway? You said you were done with Sammy."

Gabe threw his hands in the air, exasperated. "Well, I did, but I was pissed, okay? Obviously, I don't want her hurt."

He paced in irritation. "And actually, if Claudia's behind this, then it's one hundred percent my fault. *Goddamn!*" Gabe's temper rose. "Oscar, go *now*. . . Take someone with you if you need to. Just *figure it out*."

Oscar turned to leave.

"Wait. Please." Lucy grabbed Oscar by the arm. "Both of you. I talked with the Los Angeles police, and they *did* catch up with Claudia. She and her caravan of paparazzi were on a plane to L.A. the day those photos were taken. I'm not saying she's not trouble—because frankly, I think she's a *big* problem. I'm just saying she wasn't in North Carolina that day. It's *not* her."

Gabe felt the tethers of certainty slip away. "Well, do we have anything at all? I mean *someone* took those pictures, and it had to be someone who recognized Sammy. I *really* don't like that we're lost here."

"We're not lost yet," said Lucy. "Remember those rental cars the police were chasing down? They finally have some data back. One was rented in Ohio, but it was only parked at La Fermata for a few minutes. Based on camera footage, it looks like a family stopped by, tried the door, and left. But the remaining rental was parked at La Fermata all morning and was one of the last to leave after the tour."

Lucy had Gabe's full attention now. "So, the driver might have seen us come back on the bikes?"

"That's what we're thinking," she said. "Plus, the car was parked on one of the neighboring roads later that day."

"Well now we're getting somewhere. Who the hell was it?"

"That's the thing. They don't know for sure, but it looks like the car was rented in Charlotte, and the Regional Commerce team sent invitations to only three companies there. One went to a restaurant that's out of business now. Another was sent to a diner run by an elderly couple." She paused. "Now, catch this. The third one went to Forbidden Brews. They've got a brewery near the South End."

Gabe collapsed into a nearby chair. Why did Sammy's business keep coming up all over this thing? It stank to high heaven. He slumped in defeat.

"That's where it gets a little twisted," Lucy continued. "We looked into the staff, and the manager they hired has a record. Ugly stuff, too. Convictions for fraud and assault. I mean, the guy beat his own sister with a crowbar." She cringed. "Plus, there's a rape allegation he never stood trial for. Dismissed on a technicality. In other words, we're talking about a *very* scary dude. I don't know *how* you miss that on a background check."

Panic rose in Gabe's gut again. His mind raced. "Hold on. Oscar, did you say Sammy and Meghan were heading to North Carolina today?"

"Yeah, but I think they made the drive yesterday. Her text said something about the Charlotte location being a mess. She and Meghan were gonna check it out."

Gabe's skin went cold.

If Sammy was lying, then this was all a giant scam, and she was in it deeper than he thought. But why would she take Meghan anywhere near someone like that?

And if she was innocent—and truly had no idea what she was walking into—then dear God. . .

And why the hell would she be lying about everything? What kind of paranoid bullshit is that? Fuck. Fuck!

His hands shook so badly he could barely unlock his phone. He fumbled around but couldn't hit the right buttons. "Come on. Come on!" When her number finally popped up, he connected the call.

The phone trilled unhurriedly.

"Answer, damnit!" Gabe paced frantically as the vacuum of silence stretched on and the phone rang again. "Come on, Sammy, for the love of God, please answer!"

41

THE VISIT

SAMMY

"Hello?"

I pulled the key out of the door and called again.

"Hello?"

Only the subtle hum of the air conditioner responded. I held the heavy door open for Meghan, then let it fall closed and flipped the lock.

A tangle of emotion swelled in my chest as we stepped beneath the vaulted ceiling of the former warehouse. Meghan was an only child, but the breweries were my babies, too, in a way, and I'd never even seen this one in person. I'd been a neglectful parent.

Similar to the Chestnut Hill layout, a locally-harvested, live-edge bar and long rows of beer taps anchored the center of the space, while vintage tables and cushioned booths offered guests a comfy place to land. A showstopping shiplap of reclaimed tobacco pine covered the rear wall, and a dozen handcrafted, wrought-iron lanterns hung from lofty, exposed beams. The construction and design looked sound—rustic, Southern, and elegant. Very well done.

A lantern had been carelessly left on over the bar, however, and as I examined the dining room more critically, the signs of operational neglect revealed themselves. I waited to see if my daughter would spot them. "Okay, sweetheart, we'll go over things more formally today and meet with staff, but for now, let's just do a walk-through. Any first impressions?"

"Well—" Meghan studied the lofty space— "It's different from the one at home. . . but really pretty." She meandered through the seating area. "I can't believe some of the tables aren't bussed, though."

"Me neither." It was only a few coffee cups and place settings, but I couldn't fathom leaving a mess overnight like that. I walked over to join her. "What else do you see?"

Meghan perused a bit further, peering under the chairs. "Well, it looks like no one has swept in a while. There's crud and bits of food everywhere. I'm not super clean or anything, but that's just gross, Mom. . . hope that's not rude."

"In this situation, being honest isn't rude. I have the same reaction. And nightly close tasks should wind up on process checklists. It's such a simple tool, but those are often the best kind. Plus, they drive consistency. Do you notice anything else?"

"Well, this is picky, but the chairs and barstools are sort of askew, like no one tucked them in last night." She slid a couple back into place.

"Yup, that's a good one."

I helped her straighten a few strays, then we moved to the bar. In addition to beer, Forbidden Brews offered cocktails, and someone had left stainless-steel dishes of maraschino cherries and sliced citrus out to wilt and oxidize. Fruit flies swarmed the mess. "Ugh." Meghan wrinkled her nose. "That's disgusting."

"A hundred percent." My blood pressure rose as I chucked it in the trash. "Wait here." I beelined for the taps and sure enough, more of the tiny pests flitted about, alighting on the sticky drain and countertops. "Hold on, Meghan. I can't walk past this. Give me a second." I filled a pitcher with piping hot water, removed the drip tray, and rinsed everything, my annoyance mounting. Fruit flies were so easy to prevent and so hard to get rid of once they set up camp. Failing to wash things down at night was pure laziness. *Damn it.*

I grumbled and set the drain pan back in place, then returned to Meghan. "Well, what do you think overall?"

"I like the design, but it's not very clean. Maybe people aren't coming because it's messy?"

"Sure seems like it." I waited a beat, but Meghan grew quiet. "Here's another perspective. As an owner, I think a couple of un-bussed tables and some fruit left on the bar could be just a lousy closing job, but the buildup of debris on the floor and the presence of bugs tells me maintenance has been poor for a while. So, my read? This isn't any one crew's fault. Would you see it differently?"

She nodded in agreement. "I think that makes sense."

We reached the far side of the dining area and headed for the bathrooms, tucked in a corner. The tobacco pine walls, porcelain tile, and antique bronze fixtures were gorgeous. Most of the surfaces needed a good scrub, though, and one of the stalls lacked toilet paper.

"So again," I said. "Who's keeping tabs on things here? If customers see dirty bathrooms, they wonder what else is filthy. People don't want to eat in a place that isn't kept up. Management needs to be leading the team and setting standards."

My frustration built, but it was mostly self-directed. I'd been so naïve.

Marco made regular trips during construction, but once we opened, we had attempted to train leadership remotely. No one had been on site to make sure the messages got through and processes were followed. It clearly hadn't worked. We invested monumental amounts of cash when we set up a new location and couldn't afford to have slovenly operations and poor communication ruin everything. Immediate changes would have to be made.

Irritated, but satisfied that we'd seen enough of the front, we walked toward a gap in the back wall and followed a short hallway through to the kitchen.

When we rounded the corner, I gasped.

The kitchen lay in an absurd state of disarray. The foul odor of trash wafted from overflowing bins no one had emptied. Crates of clean dishes and glassware had been stacked high on rolling carts then simply left in a jumble by the dishwashing station. I couldn't imagine how anyone functioned back here. Tall piles of sealed cardboard boxes crowded the back door, cluttered the side walls, and even blocked the cooks' access to the expo station.

Completely unacceptable. We might need to shutter the business for a day or two, while we overhauled the mess and got everything organized.

We squeezed past the boxes toward the galley kitchen, noticing the manager's office, which housed the safe, hadn't even been secured for the night.

I reached in to close the door—and found a man slumped over the desk.

He was collapsed between piles of paper and awkwardly stacked plates littered with aging food. He'd grown a scraggly beard and looked more gaunt than I'd last seen him, but with that shag of sandy brown hair, this was unmistakably our manager, Bobby Boone.

"Is he okay?" Meghan whispered.

"I don't know," I breathed.

He was as still as a corpse, and his arms and face looked sickly pale, almost bloodless.

Did he have a heart attack while working late? I knew Bobby had been strained, but I had no idea it would come to this.

Bile stirred in my stomach, and I cringed reflexively. But my responsibilities included everything and everyone in this building. I forced myself to step closer, no matter how morbid the circumstances.

I leaned over the desk, laid my hand across his limp wrist, and fingered his veins gingerly for a pulse.

No heartbeat fluttered beneath my touch.

His skin still felt lukewarm, though. He wasn't in rigor mortis.

Please, please be alive.

I concentrated, squeezing harder against the flesh of his wrist, feeling around for even the faintest quickening of blood.

He leapt back.

His red-rimmed eyes came to life, bulging over purple half-moons of skin in a puffy, unkempt face. Bobby's gaze darted wildly between Meghan and me, his breath coming in quick huffs.

"*We scared you! I'm so sorry.*" The words burst from my mouth. We must have given him a terrible fright. I tried to sound calmer. "It's me, Sammy. . . You're safe. . . It's okay."

As I took in the scene, however, I realized it was not okay at all. A tiny mirror lay where his face had been, and a dusting of white powder speckled the surface of the desk. Alarm bells clanged like mad in my brain.

He stood up, a manic toothy smile quivering at his lips. "Oh. . . I *know* who you are."

Not good. Not good at all.

We needed to get out of there—and quickly. "This is a bad time. We'll be going."

He pounced, trying to yank open a desk drawer, swearing violently when it stuck.

"Meghan, go!" I turned to shove her out the door, but she was already ahead of me, sprinting down the long galley kitchen, straight for a dead end. "Wait, honey, no!"

She didn't seem to hear me. She scrambled full tilt toward the traffic jam of rolling dish racks. She shoved on the stacked crates, and they clattered together futilely. She started to cry and dashed in a blind panic down the prep hallway behind the galley. My heart hammered so hard I thought it would explode, and I ran after her, praying the boxes mounded by the back door weren't actually blocking the exit.

I could hear Bobby swearing irate curses and fumbling around with the desk, before running across the kitchen tiles, his squeaky footsteps disappearing into the dining area.

"Quick, Meghan, help me."

Boxes were stacked four deep around the emergency exit, and they proved impossibly heavy. We strained to shove them away but couldn't clear a path before Bobby's angry footfalls squeaked across the kitchen tiles again.

He was too close.

I motioned for Meghan to crouch down and be quiet, and we tucked ourselves silently behind the boxes and clutter, hoping beyond hope that he was too high to find us.

I looked around frantically for a weapon—a knife, a heavy iron pan, anything. I scanned the counters but only saw mixers, potato dicers, and huge bags of dry goods.

Then it dawned on me. *The pepper spray!*

Footsteps crashed through the kitchen, jostling the crates of glassware and finally rounding the corner toward the prep hall. Desperately digging in my purse, I found the shape of the canister but couldn't get it out. Was it stuck below the lining? I clawed at it, panicked, almost in tears. *Please come free. Please!*

The hollow, sick echo of Bobby's voice rang against the tile walls. "You better pull that hand out of your purse *real* slow, and it better be empty, or I'll blow it right off your wrist."

I froze. The gun pointed at my face looked as big as a cannon. My heart caught in my throat, but my training kicked in, and I managed to speak. "It's okay. It'll be alright. We'll get you what you need."

"Just get your hand out of your fucking purse!" he screamed. *"That's what I need!"* His brown eyes, which had seemed so helpless on our last Zoom call, now blazed with paranoid rage.

I withdrew my hand as carefully as I could, my fingers trembling, and put my hands in the air. I nodded at Meghan to do the same.

"Give me your fucking purse. Nice and slow."

I did as he instructed, trying to focus on keeping him calm. On just one thing at a time.

"Smart watch, too. Same for you, junior. Phone and watch."

Meghan looked over at me, hesitating.

"Now, goddamnit! Don't *fucking* make me wait."

She unclasped her watch and fished her phone from her pocket, then handed them both to Bobby.

"Now get up. We're going back to my office, and we're gonna try this again."

He kept the gun level with my chest and forced us down the prep hall, through the galley kitchen, and into his cluttered office. He motioned for us to sit, then locked the door and sat opposite us at his desk.

His face jerked suddenly to the door, his eyes tracing paths across the ceiling and walls. He clearly heard something we didn't.

When he snapped his attention back to us, a deranged grin spread across his face. "*You*, Sammy McCallum, must be the dumbest cunt alive. I can't *believe* you just strolled in here. I've never seen a fly so desperate to get trapped in the spider's web in my life." He swirled his finger through the powder on his desk and rubbed it on his gums.

"You know, when you tried to shut down my little HopNBrew racket, I panicked. 'Cause let me tell you lady, you sure as shit don't pay me enough to cover my needs." He rubbed his nose impatiently. "But then, I'm at one of those stupid Commerce Tours you make us attend to 'build relationships and get ideas.' And lo and behold. . . you show up all lovey dovey with *Gabriel. Fucking. Walker.* I mean, that gave me so many ideas I didn't know where to begin. But sneaking back on-site to get a few pictures for the tabloids seemed like a good start."

He grinned broadly, his bloodshot eyes focusing on me finally. "But my my, Sammy. . . you little *slut*. You dropped the biggest gift ever in my lap. You fuck him right there in the open, for all the world to see. And I have to tell you, those pictures are *very* special. I've spent many nights with them."

Meghan's panicked eyes darted between Bobby and me, confusion written across her face.

Bobby followed her gaze, and his smile twisted wickedly. "Oh. . . I see. You didn't tell your little girl, huh?" Bobby walked around the desk toward us. "Would you like to *see* what Mommy does while the rest of us are working for a living?" He paused and ogled Meghan, his head tilting, his eyes narrowing sickly. "Or maybe I could just *show* you." He reached out and traced a bony finger along her jawline.

"You're a fresh, pretty, little thing, aren't you? That would be a nice treat."

The air disappeared from the room instantly. My heart galloped in a frenzy. A whoosh of lightheadedness left me gripping the desk for support.

No. No, no, no... This can't happen now.

Meghan needed me. I had to hold it together—had to get us to safety.

What's real, Sammy? Take stock.

I tried to center myself, but when I looked around, all I saw was the gun, the deranged man. . . the cocaine and chaos. He was completely real—and a living nightmare.

His head jerked up again, his eyes searching the room. "Shut the hell up! Both of you!"

He stumbled back behind the desk, his focus scattered. He dug in my purse, held my phone up to my face to unlock it, then set it on the desk. "Okay. Okay." He scratched at his mangy beard. "Listen! You're gonna do what I say, got it?" He tilted the gun in Meghan's direction and looked back at me, his focus returning, his face scrawled with cruelty and exhilaration. "Do I have your attention, *bitch*?"

I nodded frantically. Tried to respond but couldn't get oxygen. Tears burned my eyes, but I fought them like hell. I couldn't afford to crumble. Meghan needed me whole.

"Good. So, here's what's gonna happen. You're going to call your little boyfriend and tell him *exactly* what I say." He put the gun's muzzle closer to Meghan's forehead and waited.

I put my trembling hands on the desk by my phone, trying to breathe, trying to think. I fumbled with the phone. The screen was full of notifications. Missed calls. From Gabe. I touched one and his contact came up. Somehow, I managed to press the call button.

Gabe picked up after one ring. His voice filled the room in a sudden flood of words. "*Oh, thank God, Sammy. Listen to me!* Don't go anywhere near your Charlotte brewery, understand? It's *not* safe." He paused, waiting for a response. "Sammy? *Sammy?*"

"Oh, she's already here," Bobby said coolly. "Thanks for picking up." He pointed the gun at me now. "Alright, Sammy, tell him you're here with me. Go on."

My hands quivered uncontrollably on the desk, and I couldn't form words. My heartbeat jackhammered in my ears. My lungs were collapsing.

As blackout closed in, a streak of motion flashed before my eyes, and Bobby smashed the butt of the gun across my fingers, breaking them cleanly. A scream ripped from my throat as white-hot pain exploded through my hand.

"*Mom!* Oh my God, *Mom!*" Meghan shrieked. "What did you *do*? What did you *do* to her?"

Meghan was screaming and sobbing uncontrollably, and I couldn't stop crying in anguish—it was impossible. The pain was shocking, pulsing up from my hand in sharp, horrible, jolts.

"*Hey! Do you hear me?*" Gabe shouted over the chaos. "*You have me on the phone! I'll get you what you need! Please, dear God, don't hurt anyone! Stop!*"

"Ahhh, he finally gives a shit," Bobby announced over the fray. "At least I know what gets your attention now. But don't worry, she's got at least seven more fingers I can work with if you ignore me, asshole. *So, try to listen,*" he hissed. "The million-dollar price tag for those photos just went up considerably. If you want to see either of these pretty women alive again, bring your jet to an abandoned airstrip called Henderson Pawley. The runway's a little fucked up, but if the drug planes can land there, you can too. When you arrive, I want at least five million bucks on that plane for me, and your pilot's gonna fly me wherever the hell I tell him. Got it? And if I catch so much as a *whiff* of police, I will waste your girlfriend and her precious little daughter. Am I clear?"

"You're clear. We'll do it. Please, *please* don't hurt anyone."

"Good, because I'm pretty pissed you didn't just pay me when I asked." He swirled his finger around on the desk, stuck it by his nostril and sniffed. "You have four hours."

"Wait!" Gabe objected. "I can do everything you asked, but it can't happen in four hours. Just assembling that much cash will take longer."

"Oh, you'll fucking figure out how to get it done!" Bobby walked around the desk and put his finger on Meghan's jaw again. "In fact, I'm sort of thinking for every hour you're late, I'll take a little piece of innocence away from your girlfriend's mini-me, here. You should see her Gabriel. She's luscious. You're definitely riding the outdated model."

"You're not to lay a finger on either one of them! *Got it?* In fact, you're gonna get Sammy medical attention for whatever the hell you did to her, and if there's so much as a blemish on either of them, you get *nothing*!"

Bobby backhanded me across the jaw, jarring my whole body. I screamed out, the pain from my wrecked hand ripping through me like fire.

"*You're not fucking in charge, asshole*! Understand? These girls are *mine*, and unless I get everything I want, in very short order, you're going to find them *in pieces! So, hurry the fuck up!*" He paused and turned his insanity back to Meghan again. "Actually, maybe don't hurry. I think I'd rather enjoy having a taste of this one."

Meghan's crying got louder, and her red face contorted in fear.

Bobby disconnected the line and took a last greedy look at Meghan before opening a desk drawer and pulling out fat zip ties. "Hold still, got it? I don't want to break your pretty faces right yet." He bound Meghan's wrists together first, then pulled her to her feet and shoved her to the wall. He turned to me. "Get up!"

I lifted myself out of the chair carefully, trying to brace my shattered hand.

"Quit being a fucking baby." He grabbed my wrists and yanked me his way, sending blazing shocks of pain up my arm. He bound me up tightly, then ushered us out, at gunpoint, into the August heat. "Get in the car."

We bumbled our way into the back seat, our bound hands making it difficult to move. He shut the doors and slid into the driver's seat before turning to face us. "I don't want to see a single stray movement or sound out of either of you, and I hope you understand by now that I am more than happy to fuck you up if you don't comply."

"Please don't hurt anyone," I managed to blurt out. "We'll do whatever you want."

"Good. But if you need me to drive a point home, just give me the chance. I bet a well-placed shot could draw a lot of blood without killing you. Might be a fun experiment."

He turned back around and put the car in drive, then sped off down the road.

42

THE HANGAR

The tiny, cramped room was hot and airless. Scarcely bigger than a closet, it was bare except for yellowing walls and a hard concrete floor. Its small grimy window was just clear enough to provide a view of the tattered, overgrown runway and to let in hot streaks of sunlight that were slowly turning the room into an oven.

When we first arrived, Meghan and I stood by the window, watching for our rescue while I struggled to keep my hand elevated. As the heat built up, however, and hours seemingly passed without any relief or water, nausea and dizziness forced us to take refuge on the filthy concrete floor. It provided thin respite from the heat but at least a shorter distance to fall if we lost consciousness. No clocks in the room meant no way of knowing how long we'd been held captive or if Bobby's deadline drew near. A yellow jacket pawed at the corner of the window outside, an omen of the uncontrollable.

"How's your hand?" Meghan's voice sounded fatigued and distant.

The pain from my purple, mangled fingers throbbed like a living thing. I had been trying to disembody myself from it. "Better if I don't think about it." My voice sounded as meager as hers. "How are you holding up?"

"Scared. Hot. Thirsty." She started to work herself up. "I feel like I'm gonna puke."

"Put your head between your knees, it should help."

We lolled forward and grew quiet, the heat an unrelenting pressure on our bodies, the zip ties cutting into our swollen skin. I tried to meditate away the pulsing pain in my hand.

After a while, Meghan finally broke the silence, her voice full of emotion. "Mom, I'm sorry I've been so nasty to you." She lifted her face and wiped away tears with her bound hands. "I felt like you were taking my future away, but I was so wrong. I just want any future at all. I'll take anything." She sobbed weakly, burying her head between her knees again.

"You'll have a future, Meghan. Hang in there."

She tilted her face to me. "But, what if Gabe doesn't show up . . . I'm so scared." Her breaths came in erratic stutters.

"He'll come. . . I know it."

I paid for every word with renewed shocks of pain. It took every ounce of effort to ignore it, to not react. Meghan needed distraction, though. "Did you text Connor last night?" My voice was so weak I didn't recognize it.

Meghan huffed a breath of relief. "Yeah. Pepperdine starts this weekend. He's all packed up." She started crying again. "Mom, I just can't talk. I'm so overwhelmed."

"It's okay. Shh."

We sat in the heat, trying to survive, praying for rescue before it was too late.

***

A key clicked and twisted in the locked door, and Bobby wrenched it open.

"Alright, princess, up you go. Loverboy's a no-show."

Meghan looked over at me, mortal fear and panic on her face.

"Please, I'm sure he'll be here any minute," I begged weakly. "We're so hot and sick. We need water. Please, help us."

"I don't give a shit what you need." His voice oozed cruelty. "Now, get the hell up!" He kicked Meghan in the ribs.

She doubled over, breathing hard, and struggled to compose herself. Getting to her feet was almost impossible with her hands tied in front of her, and Bobby grew impatient. He pointed the gun at her head.

"I'm trying, I swear," she sobbed. She squirmed frantically, scooting her feet under her thighs, then finally staggering her way upright.

Bobby grabbed her arm, stabilizing her as she wobbled before flipping her around and shoving her back against the wall. Her eyes went wild with terror.

"Should we let Mommy watch?" He reached a hand out to her hip, and slid it under her t-shirt, wrapping his grip around her waist.

"Please, stop," I pleaded with all the strength I had remaining. "Please, leave her alone. She's just a kid."

I was dying inside, but I didn't know if I should keep begging for mercy or if that would just make it worse. He seemed to truly enjoy inflicting pain.

"Mmmm. . . so soft." His hand rose up her rib cage, and he watched the fear on her face with pleasure. Meghan's tears were falling everywhere.

A sense of hopelessness was descending when the distant buzzing of engines became audible.

"That's him," I called weakly. "I hear a plane. That has to be him. Please, stop."

Bobby froze to listen. He finally took his hands off Meghan. He glanced in the direction of the grimy window, then back at us. "Don't fucking move!" He rushed back into the hangar, locking the door behind him.

Meghan helped me to my feet, tears still streaming down her face. It killed me not to wrap her in a hug, but my bound, wounded hands made it impossible. We both staggered to the window as the whining engines grew louder. A roaring sound shook the glass as Gabe's jet streaked across the broken runway, straining to stay level as it braked hard on the patchwork blacktop.

Bobby tugged the door open again. "Playtime's over. Get out here."

He hustled us out of the hanger through a gargantuan door, granting us our first taste of fresh air in hours. While it was cooler outside than where we'd been trapped, it was still a torrid August day in North Carolina, offering no real relief for our overheated bodies.

The jet taxied in our direction and came to a stop a short distance away. Bobby urged us forward with the butt of the gun. "Move! I want you in front of me, Sammy. You make a nice shield."

The door to the plane yawned open, revealing a built-in staircase that stretched to the tarmac. Gabe emerged and descended the stairs slowly, his hands up. Oscar followed a few paces behind, toting a briefcase in one hand and holding the other over his head.

"You fucking brought the cops? I'll blow her away, you asshole!" Bobby grabbed my hair, yanking my head back. He pointed the gun at my temple.

"He's not a cop!" Gabe shouted. "Put down the gun! Please!"

Bobby continued to shove me forward by my hair, the gun a hard knot against my temple, my mangled hand jostling with every step. "You better explain quick! This is *not* what we agreed to!"

"Everything is arranged," Gabe promised. "Can I open this briefcase and show you something?"

"Slowly. And no weapons, or she's done."

"Oscar has a weapon, but it stays holstered as long as you don't hurt anyone."

"Fine. Open the briefcase, but my finger stays on this trigger."

I tried to keep my breath calm, to focus on the clouds, to think about anything other than the bullet cocked millimeters from my brain.

Gabe took the briefcase from Oscar and opened it, revealing thick stacks of cash.

"I like the look of that money, but that's sure as hell not the millions I demanded. You're running out of time!" Bobby yanked my head back further, moved the gun to my neck, and pressed it into the soft flesh under my jaw. My nausea and lightheadedness grew, and I fought to stay upright.

Gabe's voice remained calm. "It's as much as we could gather without ringing alarm bells at the Treasury Department. It's more than enough to tide you over 'til the digital transaction goes through."

Bobby lashed the barrel of the gun against my broken hand, sending an agonizing flood of pain up my arm, and I cried in anguish. He pressed the gun to my neck again. "Not! Fast! Enough! I need to get fucking paid, and I need to get on that plane!"

Barely controlled fury rippled under Gabe's expression, and he swallowed hard. "I've looked you up, Bobby. Your fraud conviction, your website, those were sophisticated setups, so I'm trusting you'll understand this. We've initiated a blockchain contract. You know what that is, right?"

Bobby stared at him with hard eyes. "I know what it is."

"Good. Then you know it's a guaranteed thing if the conditions are satisfied. Five million dollars arrives in a private account in the Virgin Islands after two events take place. First, Sammy, Meghan, Oscar, and I have to board a flight at the Charlotte airport before midnight, and second, my pilot has to reenter the U.S. and get through customs by tomorrow night. If those things take place, you start a new life and never have to work again. If any of that falls through, you get nothing except the few thousand dollars in this briefcase, and—I'm guessing—a lifetime in prison."

"How do I know any of that's fucking true!" Bobby spat, prodding the gun deeper into my flesh.

"Check your email, Bobby. We sent a copy of the contract a few minutes ago. Same email where we sent the Commerce Tour invite."

Bobby kept the gun drilled into my neck while he pulled his phone from his pocket and scrolled through the screen. "And what if this is bullshit? Maybe there's a contract, but what if there's fucking police on that plane behind you? Where's my insurance!"

"Bobby, the only thing we want is for this to end safely. That's all we care about. There's no one on the plane but my pilot, and he can take you anywhere."

"Well, then you won't mind joining me, Loverboy. Let's go check it out."

"Hey!" Oscar stepped out in front of Gabe. "He's not going anywhere with you!"

Bobby pointed the gun at Oscar's head. "You don't get a fucking say in it. I will *drop* you, you piece of shit!"

Gabe intervened. "Remember, if he's hurt, the contract fails. Please put your weapon down."

Bobby looked back and forth between us. He finally released my hair and walked toward Gabe with his gun still trained on Oscar. "He comes or there's no deal!" He grabbed Gabe's shoulder. "Let's go, asshole. You face your bodyguard, so he's clear who gets hit if he shoots." He held the gun to the nape of Gabe's neck. "Nice and easy, you prick."

They walked backwards, making slow, clumsy progress toward the plane. Gabe kept his free hand in the air, the other tight on the briefcase. As they climbed the jet stairs, Bobby crouched behind Gabe, eliminating any line of sight for Oscar to get a shot off.

But Oscar's hands remained in the air, trying to keep the peace.

At the top of the steps Bobby pivoted, pointing the gun into the plane. He pulled Gabe into the cabin, out of sight.

It felt like a lifetime, but maybe it was only a few seconds before shots clapped out from the plane. Three haltering staccato pops, punctuated by the sound of breaking glass. Fresh red blood splashed the jet windows.

A man in pilot's gear stuck his head out of the doorway, looking around frantically. *"He's down! He's down!"*

Oscar took off at a sprint, headed for the jet stairs.

The breath left my lungs, and I fell hard to my knees on the broken blacktop, sobbing and out of options. Meghan came running to my side, wailing in grief.

Sirens shrieked in the distance, and we huddled in shock as the tarmac became a blue and red cyclone of strobing lights and screaming vehicles. Police and FBI agents descended onto the property, and ambulances pulled up in front of us, lights flashing and motors rumbling. Uniformed men and women swarmed Meghan and me, cutting the zip ties from our wrists, loading us onto stretchers, and taking our vitals.

I tried desperately to look back at the plane, praying for any sign of life, but the scene was bedlam. Uniformed officers mobbed the area, shouting beneath a chaos of flashing lights.

Finally, one of the vehicles moved, and I caught a glimpse of the jet. Gabe walked down the stairs in a daze, wiping blood from his face. He looked around when he reached the tarmac, saw us getting loaded into the transports, and jogged our way. "Wait!" he called, speeding up. "Wait, Sammy!"

They continued to load me into the ambulance, and he ran the last few yards to me, tears streaming down his face. He hopped into the crowded vehicle, already packed with people and equipment. Hugging my legs—the only part of me he could reach—he collapsed forward on the bottom of the stretcher.

"Sir, we have to go. She needs care."

Adrenaline drained from my system. "Thank you, Gabe." It was all I could get out.

Pinpricks of stars bloomed in the darkness.

Then everything was gone.

43

RECONSTRUCTION

A tom by atom, molecule by molecule, in time, the body rebuilds itself. Fluids regenerate. Rough edges and gaps in bone and tissue are repaired. Bridges are built, cell by cell, until a seamless patchwork of skeleton, muscle, and sinew is intact again. Once doctors have worked their magic, the rest is a thoughtless, microscopic effort that demands little more than time and rest.

A few weeks after our ordeal, the process was well underway.

Amidst that restorative time, punctuated by media curiosity, long intimate nights, and the start of Meghan's senior year, the heat of summer finally broke. The first refreshing hints of autumn whispered into Chestnut Hill, and the promise of something new began.

44

───·───

THE MISSING PIECE

THE STALKER

Claudia unlocked the door to her overpriced West Hollywood apartment and clicked her Ludovisa Viancci roller bag over the foyer's cool, white tiles. It had been a long flight back from Boston, where the film crew had dragged her to enough greasy delis and stinking, dockside lobster shacks to convince her that Americans deserved every butter-coated shred of heart disease they got. Her clothes and hair reeked of boiled crustaceans, and she crawled with germs from the cramped plane. "Fall in New England" might pay the bills, but it sure as hell was *not* her vibe.

She badly needed a reset—a sauna, a shower, and maybe a top-shelf cocktail by the rooftop pool. A strong buzz and a dewy-skinned bikini photo against the glittering skyline of Los Angeles would put her back on brand. The mere thought spread relief through her body.

Claudia set her clutch on the foyer credenza and eased the kinks out of her neck as she strolled to the living room and flipped on the lights.

Her heart clamped down in a violent gush of blood.

Oscar sat in her prized San Violette chaise, unmoving, his eyes dark and simmering with rage. He slowly unfolded his mass from the chair, rising to reveal the Glock G32 in his gloved hand.

She had left it in a locked safe.

Adrenaline and anger exploded in Claudia's chest—her instinct was always for fight, not flight. "*You broke into my fucking apartment?*"

Oscar straightened his spine, gaining another inch of height Claudia had never seen. He walked her way without hurry—a looming, inevitable force—and stopped just out of her reach. His rumbling smoker's voice clawed up her spine. "*You. Stole. My. Fucking. Glock.*"

She glared at him defiantly. "So what! Do you have any idea how many creeps follow me around L.A.? I need that gun more than you do!"

Claudia searched the room frantically, rifling through a mental inventory. The kitchen knives were too far away. There was nothing sharp or heavy on the island. She kept a taser in the credenza drawer— not far behind her. She stumbled back a couple steps.

Oscar closed in. "We have a very big problem, Claudia."

"Well, you obviously solved it. So, get the fuck out!*"

"No. You took my Glock. I *really* don't appreciate that." He lifted the gun to chest height, letting the lethal end drift casually in her direction as he sampled the gun's heft. "Funny thing is, it's got your prints all over it, now. Isn't that interesting?"

Claudia groped the air behind her for the credenza drawer. *A few more feet.*

"It's sad though. A young, unstable woman. A gun. You could hurt yourself." His eyes were empty and cold, set on a path. "Such a shame."

"Do you have a point, Oscar?" If he fired the gun at this angle, the bullet would rip through her chest. She crept backwards.

Oscar kept the pistol level. "Gabe had a gun shoved in his spine last month. *That's* my goddamn point. I don't wanna see it again." He stepped closer, backing her toward the wall. "*It's time. For you. To get a new hobby.*"

"You can't tell me what to do."

"Then *you* tell you what to do." He stared her down. "Because this ends tonight."

Claudia finally felt the credenza knob. She yanked the drawer open and scrambled for the weapon.

Oscar watched her impassively. "You don't own a taser anymore, Claudia. In fact, you don't own *any* weapons. Crazy and sexy is fine. Crazy and armed is horseshit."

She spun on him, furious. "What the *hell*, Oscar? You think that's gonna help? Like I can't get another—"

Claudia's face smashed into the drywall, the soft tissue of her nose and cheek crushed against the edge of a mirror. Her shoulder screamed, wrenched behind her back at an impossible angle.

"*You're not hearing me*, Claudia!" Oscar had attacked like a grizzly.

"*Oscar, stop*!" Claudia tried to wriggle free. "*Oscar, you're hurting me! Stop!*"

He leaned his face to her temple, filling her nose with his stale, cindered breath. "I haven't even *begun*."

She struggled, the pain in her shoulder sizzling.

"What you feel right now? I'm being as gentle as a baby bird. But I can turn up the volume as high as I need to." Oscar leaned into the hold, tearing at the delicate tendons in her shoulder. He pressed the steel cage of his ribs into her back, squeezing the air from her lungs. "You hearing me yet?"

Claudia sputtered under the blazing explosion of pain.

Oscar's damp lips pressed against her ear. "Gabe isn't *ever* gonna want the scary chick. Got it? *Not ever*. The more you show up, the more psycho you act, the more he *hates* you."

Claudia stilled like a trapped animal, lost in crashing waves of pain.

Oscar spat his hot breath on her. "So, I don't *ever* want to see you near him, or me, or my fucking weapons ever again!"

He released her arm from the fiery hold and stepped back.

She took frantic breaths but didn't turn around—wouldn't look at him. . . wouldn't give him the satisfaction.

Oscar flipped the lights off, and low, scraping gravel of his voice echoed in the room. "Figure it out, Claudia. Because either *this* is done— or *you* are."

Oscar disappeared into the darkness.

45

THE BIG DAY

SAMMY

"Meghan, can you help with the zipper?"

"Of course, Mom."

I had tried to secure the gown myself, but the bulky splint on my hand was not built for fine motor skill.

Asking for help had never been my strong suit, and I was eager for the injury to fully heal. As the weeks passed, the blackened bruise had faded to violet, then slowly bled out to amber. The latest x-ray showed the bones had begun to straighten and mend as the swelling decreased. The doctors felt optimistic I could use my hand again soon.

When Meghan finished with the zipper, I stepped in front of the tall, antique mirror in the corner of my room. The pale silk gown skimmed my body from head to toe—the most elegant garment to ever touch my skin.

Meghan looked me over wistfully. "You look *sooo* beautiful."

"You do, too, sweetheart."

She grinned and spun dramatically, swishing the airy fabric of her fluttering dress.

When she finally stilled, I pulled her to me and hugged her hard. "I love you so much."

"I love you, too, Mom. Really."

I stepped back, holding her hands gently. Her smile was still warm, if a bit more guarded. Her limbs were healthy—unharmed and uninjured. Physically, she had bounced back with just fluids and Band-Aids. Emotionally, I'm sure there would be scars, but so far, she seemed remarkably steady given what we had endured together. She was tough. Always had been. I gripped her hands in mine, overwhelmed with gratitude for the simple truth of her heart fluttering in her chest, her warm pink skin, the breath flowing in and out of her lungs. She had her life—and that was everything.

I marveled at the irony of it all. Just a few months ago, I had been so sure that if I kept everyone close to me, I could protect them from the world. However, being near me had gotten her kidnapped and nearly much worse.

In some ways, that horrible truth had released some of my heaviest burdens. It was so painfully obvious that I couldn't control the future she faced. I couldn't control sociopaths. I couldn't prevent aneurysms, or viruses, or acts of God. I couldn't stop the cruelty of human beings or random injuries and illness.

But, I could help Meghan grow into a strong, independent, educated, young woman. I could love and support her.

And I would.

Together, we gathered a few finishing touches—delicate earrings, a spritz of perfume—then we walked down the stairs carefully, our hems nearly touching the wooden treads. At the base of the steps, we found our most precious people gathered in the family room. Tina's boys wore tiny tuxedos, her youngest tugging uncomfortably at his bow tie and collar. Mom looked radiant in a green, A-line dress, and Stan Rosen smiled proudly by her side. Tina sat near Gabe on the couch. She still wasn't accustomed to his company, and her smile was as wide as the sky.

Gabe stood when I entered the room and put a hand to his heart. "You look incredible." He crossed the carpet to me and kissed me gently on the lips, sending tingles of heat through my body, just like always. His hands cradled my face, and his fingers were light in my hair.

He leaned forward to touch his forehead to mine, whispering just loud enough for my ears. "You're coming to Europe with me, aren't you?"

"For at least a little bit," I whispered back. "I promise."

Meghan was right on my heels. "Um, I can hear you, you know."

When Gabe shot her a smile, she spun to show off her dress.

"Well, *you*, my dear, look lovely. You'll break hearts wandering around like that."

Meghan grinned with pride, a blush creeping into her freckled cheeks.

"Come on, lovebirds," Mom said. "The church is a few blocks away. You know Marco and Ian won't forgive us if we're late."

She was right, of course. It was their big day, and we had best not mess it up.

The road to reconciliation with the two of them had been short. Their anger at being accused of fraud and extortion vanished when they realized Marco's failure to run a background check on Bobby nearly cost us our lives. The incident convinced Marco to hire an HR director and an operations lead as well. With our expanded scope, he needed to take some things off his plate, so terrible errors didn't happen, and to reduce his stress, for all our sakes. I was hopeful that after today, he might be back to his normal, charming, only mildly cranky self.

As for Bobby, Gabe had explained there was never any plan for him to leave the runway. The jet had been loaded with FBI agents, waiting to place him in custody. When he managed to get a shot off, they had taken him down with bullets to the head and heart. He would never hurt anyone again.

I drank in the scene with gratitude, so thankful for the people in my life, and I wondered how the day could be any better. Mom was flushed with happiness and new romance. Tina was going through a painful transition, but she deserved so much better than she'd had the last several years. I knew if anyone could transform the wreckage of a failed marriage into a bigger, better life, it was her. Meghan had been moving past her angst and was getting ready to apply to colleges. She was eyeing Pepperdine in particular, and I guessed the handsome blond boy she talked to so often had more than a little to do with it.

And Gabe was my dream man—creative, kind, outrageously handsome, and forever my hero.

Truly, there was only one person missing, and I had an idea. "I know we have to go, but can you guys wait a second?"

Mom glanced at her watch. "Make it quick, Sammy."

I lifted the hem of my gown and raced up the stairs.

My father had given me a locket for my sixteenth birthday, and it never left my neck until the week he died. I'd taken it off in a fit of grief, feeling like such a failure, so undeserving of his love. I reached the doorway to my room and took a deep breath.

His death was not my fault.

I had always known, but something had shifted. I felt the acceptance deep in my bones now, and the precious necklace deserved to be worn. Dad would want to be part of this happiness, to know we had eventually landed on our feet.

I sorted through the chains and pendants in my jewelry chest but didn't find the locket. Actually, I didn't see my other favorite piece either, an emerald set on a gold cable chain. *How odd.* I knew Meghan sometimes snooped in my room, but she didn't usually borrow the real stuff without asking.

I tried to recall when I'd touched the locket last, and a memory surfaced. I saw myself crying in bed three years ago, before taking off the necklace and tossing it in my nightstand.

Relieved, I sat on my bed and eased the drawer open. With my good hand, I fumbled through the flotsam of sleepless nights until I found the thin chain. After dusting off a scattering of lint, I held it up to the light. Somehow, it still shimmered despite neglect and mistreatment.

A shiver passed over me, and I held the locket close.

I love you so much, Dad. I miss you.

He had always shown me steadfast love, had instilled compassion and fairness in me. I was so thankful for the confidence and dogged determination he'd taught me.

And I would need it.

Because the truth was, I might never be the same. Maybe I'd never handle crisis as well as I used to. Or perhaps, eventually, I'd come out of this better equipped than most for managing the worst twists of fate. But either way, avoiding my fears wouldn't change the outcomes of our lives—at least not in a predictable way. Not necessarily in a good way.

Meanwhile, the world refused to wait. Marco and Ian *certainly* wouldn't.

A subtle knock echoed behind me.

"Doing okay up here?" Gabe leaned in the room. 'Need a hand?"

"Quite literally." I held up the necklace. The splint would make unclasping it impossible.

Gabe sat beside me on the bed and wrangled the tiny mechanics of the jewelry, until the familiar weight of the locket found its place over my heart.

He gave my shoulders a gentle squeeze. "Ready?"

"Yes." In fact, I felt more ready than I had in a long time. "Let's do this."

We dashed down the stairs into the warm embrace of my people and headed into the world together—to support Ian and Marco, to celebrate and dance on a gorgeous September day, and to forge our way through the lush wilderness of our mysterious, unknowable tomorrows.

Acknowledgements

Kathy Morley, you generously served as an alpha reader, beta reader, ARC reader, sounding board, critique group, and cheering section all in one! Thank you for your optimism, enthusiasm, and insight. You made the book so much better, and I would never have persevered with this story if it weren't for you.

Thanks to Thomas Jenkins and Susan L. Rosenbluth for your exceptional editing skills. You taught me so much and improved the book dramatically. Tom, your tireless effort to read and re-read as I adapted the novel made a critical difference.

My gratitude goes out to Elina Vaysbeyn, whose invaluable marketing insights delivered a greatly improved product. Hiring you was one of my best decisions.

Mary Ann Smith, thank you for your hard work and patience on the cover design. I am so pleased with where we landed.

Thanks to Hannah Jordan for sharing your knowledge and experience with publishing, marketing, and managing the business side of things. Your assistance provided a critical roadmap I was missing, and your straight-shooting beta read allowed me to polish several rough edges off the book.

I owe a debt of gratitude to the South Jersey Writer's Group. The club's leaders and members have been a wonderful resource for companionship, ideas, critique, and connection. Thank you for creating a welcoming environment and being generous with your time. Plus, an extra special thanks is due to the SJWG beta readers whose advice improved the quality of this novel: Thomas Jenkins, Susan L. Rosenbluth, Hannah Jordan, Noelle Gallagher, NJ Ackerman, Gail Priest, David W. Burns, Amy Hollinger, Eden Mabee, Richard Bareford, and Jim Harris.

In addition to the South Jersey Writer's Group, I also want to thank the other beta readers who donated their time and generously shared their feedback. Thanks go to: John Morley, Clint Morley, Debbie George, Mickey Allard, Don Moon, Marsha Linneman, Colleen Reilly, and Stephanie Zinn.

Erin Warman, thank you for cheering me on, reviewing cover art, looping me in with your tribe at critical junctures, and for connecting me with Jeff Parker. And Jeff, thank you for the tour of Sonder Brewing and for the spectacular beers. (Everyone in the Cincinnati area, please sprint to this haven of deliciousness and treat yourself to a Kenosha Kickers or Nanaimo Cookie Bar Barrel-Aged Stout.)

Nicole Naumoff, you are wonderful! Your thoughtful, detailed knowledge about the homes, history, and landmarks of Chestnut Hill brought authenticity to the pages.

Alicia B., thank you for sharing your wisdom on social media marketing. Dave S., your IT expertise was greatly appreciated. Holt, thanks for reviewing the musical composition notes.

Finally, and perhaps most importantly, thanks to my loving husband and wonderful children for putting up with the long hours I've spent glued to my laptop, for listening to me prattle on about this project, and, as always, for being yourselves. You are my whole heart.